LET THE MONSTER OUT

LET THE
MONSTER
OUT

CHAD LUCAS

AMULET BOOKS · NEW YORK

*For the kids who are learning
that other people's eyes
are not mirrors*

PUBLISHER'S NOTE: This is a work of fiction. Names, characters, places, and incidents are either the product of the author's imagination or used fictitiously, and any resemblance to actual persons, living or dead, business establishments, events, or locales is entirely coincidental.

Cataloging-in-Publication Data has been applied for and may be obtained from the Library of Congress.

ISBN 978-1-4197-5126-4

Text © 2022 Chad Lucas
Book design by Chelsea Hunter

Printed and bound in U.S.A.
10 9 8 7 6 5 4 3 2 1

Amulet Books are available at special discounts when purchased in quantity for premiums and promotions as well as fundraising or educational use. Special editions can also be created to specification. For details, contact specialsales@abramsbooks.com or the address below.

Amulet Books® is a registered trademark of Harry N. Abrams, Inc.

ABRAMS The Art of Books
195 Broadway, New York, NY 10007
abramsbooks.com

PROLOGUE
The Crows Laughed

Branches lashed Wade Elliott's face as he hurtled through the forest. Thick clouds hid the moon. He'd already lost his bearings in the dark, but he didn't slow down. He skidded down a bank, scrambled to his feet, and kept moving. He had to get as far as possible from that room. The room he'd helped build.

No. *No.* He was only trying to fix things, to help people. But they'd turned it upside down.

Pain stabbed his side. His throat burned with the metallic taste of blood. He fell at the base of a pine tree, panting.

Gradually, his pulse stopped pounding in his ears. He heard the trickle of a brook, the rustle of wind tickling the treetops. He rested his head against the tree trunk. He could hear, taste, touch. This was the real world.

Exhaustion set in, but when his eyelids drooped, the things he'd seen in that room came back.

No. He had escaped. He had to fight it. He couldn't let—

A crow's caw stirred him. He gathered his bearings: He was outdoors, in a forest, under a misty gray sky at the break of dawn. He shivered. Had he slept? Was this real?

He stood and paced, shaking stiffness from his limbs. He had to know for sure he was here—and that *here* wasn't all in his head. Balling his fist, he punched the trunk of the pine. His knuckles split and pain pulsed through his hand.

It hurt. He felt it. He smiled.

He punched the tree again. Again. Again. He stepped back and stared at his hand. The flesh swelled and reddened. He savored the steady ache. This had to be real. He threw back his head and laughed and laughed.

The crows laughed too.

Wade looked up. A dozen of them sat in the trees, mocking him.

"No!" he shouted at the birds. "You can't do that! Shut up!"

"Ha ha ha," they cackled. "Isn't this fun? Let's all go into town and watch it burn."

"Shut up!" he shrieked.

"Come with us, Wade. It's such a fun game. A murder of crows, a-murdering we go."

They rose from the branches and circled the clearing, above his head. *A murder of crows, a-murdering we go.* Soon there were two dozen, forty, fifty, a hundred. The sky darkened under a vortex of swirling black birds.

Wade wept. It wasn't over. It would never be over. Not for him.

He brought his aching, trembling fingers to the inside pocket of his jacket. Good. His journal was still there. He had to deliver it, show them the proof, before everyone saw the things he'd seen. If that happened, it would be too late.

So he ran.

1.
TRYING

Bones Malone didn't punch Tony Spezio in the face.

Not after he found Tony picking on his little brothers. Not even after he told Tony to knock it off, and Tony responded by saying something unrepeatably gross about his mother.

Sure, he did shove Tony against the basement wall and yell, "Talk about my mom again and I will *end you*." But that was better than throwing fists, right?

He was trying. That counted for something, right?

Not in Eileen Spezio's book. She thumped downstairs just in time to hear the *end you* part and blamed everything on Bones, as usual.

"You will not behave like a thug in my home!" she screeched.

Bones saw red. A white lady calling him a thug was not OK, but he held his tongue. Well, almost.

"Teach your kid some manners, before he gets himself beat," he shot back.

Mrs. Spezio's eyes bulged and spit gathered at the corners of her mouth as she lost her mind. Tony smirked over her shoulder the whole time, while heat built in Bones's chest. He couldn't stop picturing how satisfying it would feel to shove past Mrs. Spezio and knock that smug grin off Tony's extremely punchable face.

But he didn't. Not this time. He was trying, for his mom's sake.

But that didn't count in her book either. She got an earful from Eileen when she picked up the boys after work. Bones could hear every word with his ear to the door of the spare room where Mrs. Spezio had banished all three Malone boys, even though Raury and Dillon hadn't done anything wrong.

"I know you're new in town, and I was happy to open my home to your boys, but that oldest of yours is so *disrespectful*, so *aggressive* . . ."

Bones couldn't hear his mom's reply, but he recognized its tone: weary. It wasn't the first time she'd apologized on his behalf. When she opened the bedroom door, all she said was, "Let's go." The boys hurried to catch up as she marched out of the Spezios' house and down the sidewalk, each step radiating fury.

"Is the car still broken?" Dillon asked.

"Yep." She practically hurled the word to the sidewalk.

"Bones was only—"

"We are *not* discussing this now."

She met Bones's eyes for half a second. "If I have to give that woman a raise to let you stay," she murmured, "you best believe it's coming from your allowance."

Bones waited as long as he could stand it. He made his brothers wash up and set the table before he approached his mother. She didn't lift her eyes from the pot of spaghetti boiling on the stove, but her shoulders rose.

"Not now, Quentin."

Ugh. He hated his real name. She usually reserved it for formal situations, like the first time they met with a lawyer. When she used it at home, it was a warning.

He swallowed all the things he wanted to say: He was only defending Raury, *again*; the Spezios had been awful since day one; he'd be thirteen in September and he was perfectly capable of watching his brothers, so she should stop paying a useless babysitter anyway.

All of it was true, but he held his tongue. Adults weren't always ready for the truth.

"I only want to say sorry," he said instead. "No excuses. But you won't make me stay home tonight, will you?"

She froze. Bones realized she'd forgotten he had a baseball game. He was surprised how much that stung.

"You definitely have a punishment coming," she said. "Maybe if you missed a game, you'd actually get the message."

"Mom, please! It's my night to pitch. Everyone's counting on me. Ground me, take away my phone, make me sleep in the shed if you want. Just let me have baseball."

His mother gasped. "Quentin Malone."

Two Quentins in one conversation was bad news. He forced a fake laugh. "I was joking about the shed."

"Not funny." She turned back toward the stove. "Go to your game. But I want you home straight after. You are *not* off the hook."

"Thank you!" Bones paused. "You're not coming?"

His mother loved baseball. She was the one who taught him how to throw a slider. They watched Blue Jays games together, and she yelled at the TV when Toronto's manager made bad decisions. She'd only missed one of Bones's games last year, when Dillon had to go to the walk-in clinic with a raisin stuck in his nose.

She exhaled. "Not tonight. I'm still waiting for the mechanic to call about the car. And I just don't have the energy."

"Oh. OK." He tried to sound like it was no big deal that she was staying home.

She carried the pot of boiled spaghetti to the sink. "Watch your release point. Remember, you were missing high last weekend because you were letting the ball go too early."

"Right. Thanks."

He lingered in the doorway. She still wouldn't look at him.

Even as he opened his mouth, he knew he should accept the small victory and walk away.

"I didn't even hit him," he muttered.

As she drained the hot water from the pasta into the sink, his mom released the kind of sigh only a mother can make, a sustained breath declaring, *Boy, you don't even know*. From Bones's viewpoint, the cloud of steam rising toward the ceiling appeared to pour directly from his mom's head.

"You shoved him into a wall, Bones. You threatened him."

"Threatened?" Bones scoffed. "I'm half his size." Tony was three years older, a head taller, broad across the chest where

Bones was still, well, bones. He had a sacred rule about never fighting anyone smaller. But he was short for his age, so that left lots of leeway.

His mother sighed again. "Like that has ever stopped you. We've only been here for two months, and I feel like I've apologized to half the parents in town."

That was a *huge* exaggeration. He'd only been in two real fights in Langille—Tony didn't count—and Bones hadn't started either one. He also had a rule about not starting fights. They just found him, the way some people attracted mosquitoes. Or lightning.

His first fight after the move was a matter of establishing order. He was new, he was small, and this big kid cornered him after gym and said, *"I forgot my lunch money. You need to make a donation."* Bones suggested something he could eat instead, and the kid pushed Bones into the lockers. Two quick jabs made it clear Bones Malone was not bully fodder.

The second fight, he was cutting across the soccer field when he saw a group of ninth graders yelling crude stuff at a girl. He told them to grow up and leave her alone, they told him to get lost, and things escalated. OK, he might have thrown the first punch, and he'd wound up with a black eye and a split lip to show for it. But that hardly made him the bad guy, right?

He didn't rehash this with his mother, though. Open that door and she would bring up other fights before the move. Once she started on the brawl with the Volkering brothers, he was doomed.

"It wasn't a fight," he said. "Only one little shove. And Tony's the worst. I should get credit for not punching him already!"

His mom's eyes narrowed. "You think this is funny?"

"Mom—"

"When are you going to learn? I swear, if you don't come to your senses and control that temper, you'll end up—"

She stopped.

"End up like what?" Bones asked, his voice suddenly husky.

"Never mind."

"You were going to say—"

"You don't know what I was going to say." She looked away. "Call your brothers for dinner. You need to get moving if you're going to make your game."

He left the kitchen without another word.

2.
CONTROL ISSUES

Bones wiped sweat from his forehead with the sleeve of his Langille Falcons jersey. The humid air felt thick as Jell-O. He readjusted his cap over his curly hair and toed the pitching rubber.

Bones defied physics when he pitched. No kid so short and slender should have been able to throw so hard. When he reared back and launched, the baseball rocketed from his hand at warp speed. He loved when other teams watched him warm up for the first time, the nervous stares as the ball struck the catcher's glove with a resounding *pop*.

The problem was he couldn't always control where his pitches ended up. That night against the New Glasgow Titans, he walked his first two batters and struck out the third, but not before throwing a wild pitch that allowed the runners to advance. Then a fluky half-swing single brought them both in to score. He escaped the first inning with no further damage and muddled through the second, but here in the third he'd given up two more runs and still had the bases loaded with one out. He glanced at the dugout where his coach, Carlos Robeson, leaned against the wall, calmly chewing gum. Bones was amazed Coach hadn't pulled him yet. He was stinking up the mound.

His eyes drifted to the empty spot in the bleachers where his mom and brothers usually sat. Her words echoed in his head. *When are you going to learn?*

"Hey. Focus, dude."

Bones turned. Albert Chen, the Falcons' catcher, walked toward the mound. Albert pushed up his catcher's mask and frowned. "What's with you today? You're all over the place."

Bones shrugged, biting back a sarcastic *thanks*. Albert was burly and strong, one of the Falcons' best hitters. He was a decent catcher too, but not so great at inspiring pep talks.

Albert glanced toward the dugout. Silently, Bones vibrated with anger. He knew what Albert was thinking: *Come on, Coach. Take him out*. But Coach Robeson only gave them both a tiny nod. Albert sighed and turned back to Bones.

"Look, I know you have control issues, just . . . try to throw strikes, OK?"

Bones thought of at least four reasons why it was a bad idea for him, the rookie new kid, to talk back to Albert. But his mouth did its own thing.

"Wow, I never thought of that. You're a genius."

Albert stared at him. His left nostril twitched as he exhaled hard. Then, slowly, he walked back to home plate, muttering to himself. He squatted behind the plate and flashed Bones one index finger, the sign for a fastball. Still fuming, Bones wound up and hurled.

As the pitch left his hand, he knew it was a meatball. He watched helplessly as the batter smashed it into the outfield. But the Falcons' center fielder, Kyle Specks, made a running leap and snagged the ball in midair, crashing into the Fluxcor billboard on the outfield wall. Bones scrambled to back up home plate as the runner on third raced home and scored.

He cursed under his breath as he collected the ball. He managed to finish the inning with a strikeout and hurried off the field. He wasn't surprised when Coach met him outside the dugout.

"That's all for you tonight, Bones," Coach said. "Way to battle out of a jam. Good job."

Bones glanced up—way up. Carlos Robeson was six feet six, with deep brown skin and a thin beard beginning to show flecks of gray. To Bones's surprise, Coach flashed him a smile.

Bones lowered his eyes. "I stunk, Coach. We'd be down huge if Specks hadn't made that catch."

Coach patted his shoulder. "Everyone has off nights. Shake it off, big guy."

Bones retreated to the end of the bench. He still couldn't believe he got to play for Carlos Robeson—former center fielder for the Detroit Tigers and San Francisco Giants, seven-time All-Star, Gold Glove legend, and World Series MVP.

Bones had been dead set against moving to Langille at first. He knew his family needed a fresh start, but this little town on the Northumberland Strait seemed hopelessly boring.

"We'll probably be the only Black kids in town," he'd grumbled to his mom.

"Give it a chance," his mom insisted. *"It's not that small. This tech company called Fluxcor has taken off there in the last few years. Royden University is there. I've already found a decent piano teacher for Raury. And there's at least one other Black family in town. Look."*

She showed Bones a year-old article from the *Langille Record* on her tablet. The headline read *Robeson, Giraud Mark Opening of New Sports Complex.*

Bones stared at the photo, eyes wide. *"You're serious? Carlos Robeson lives in Langille?"*

His mom nodded. *"He settled there after he retired. And he coaches Peewee AAA baseball."*

Bones scanned the article. Carlos had donated three million dollars to help the town build a new baseball field, skate park, basketball court, tennis court, and outdoor pool. The local head of Fluxcor, Raymond Giraud, matched his donation. The Town Council debated whether to name the complex Fluxcor-Robeson Park or Robeson-Fluxcor Park, but Carlos put an end to that.

"Only egomaniacs and dead people have landmarks named after them, and I'm not dead yet," he joked. They ended up calling it the Langille Common.

Bones's first weeks in Langille were rocky—it only took three days to land in the principal's office—but making the baseball team was the one good part. Coach often slotted him leadoff and started him at shortstop when he wasn't pitching, even though he was one of the youngest players on the team. The game had never been so fun, especially since the Falcons opened the season with a five-game winning streak.

Now they were in danger of their first loss. And it was his fault.

As the rest of the team piled into the dugout, Marcus Robeson, the coach's son, gave Kyle a friendly thump on the back.

"Wicked grab, Specks," he said.

Kyle responded with a tight smile that was close to a grimace. He made his way down the bench and stopped next to Bones.

"Hi, do you mind, um—"

Bones looked up. Kyle's fingers drummed against his thigh.

"It's just, that's where I usually sit," Kyle said.

Bones tilted his head. "Does it matter?"

Kyle's pale skin reddened. "I guess it shouldn't. It's just a habit, and I'm more comfortable there . . ."

He trailed off. Bones glanced down the bench. His teammates were watching. With a shrug, he slid over to make room.

"Thanks," Kyle said softly. He sat beside Bones, fingers still bouncing against his knee.

"Thanks for bailing me out with that catch," Bones answered.

Kyle nodded, but didn't say anything else. Bones settled in and watched his teammates try to climb out of the hole he'd dug. In the fourth inning, with Albert on first base, Marcus belted the ball deep into the sky. Bones watched in awe as it sailed beyond the right-field fence—a home run. Marcus had inherited his dad's height and talent, and Bones couldn't help wondering how good it must have felt to be able to hit a baseball that far. He joined his teammates as they piled out of the dugout to greet Marcus with a barrage of shoulder bumps and high fives.

But in the final inning, the Falcons still trailed 5–4 as Kyle stepped to the plate with two outs and runners on second and third.

Bones winced. Kyle was the team's best outfielder, but the last guy you wanted in the batter's box with the game on the line. He waggled his bat nervously and watched two pitches go by. Bones and his teammates in the dugout leaned forward as Kyle worked the count full.

"You got this, Specks!" Marcus hollered. Bones wished Marcus was at the plate. Kyle probably did too.

The New Glasgow pitcher started his windup. Kyle cocked his bat—and stood still as the ball crossed the plate. The umpire signaled strike three. That was it. Game over. The Falcons let out a collective sigh.

It was their first loss of the season. And it was all Bones's fault.

His frustration bubbled as he trudged through the handshake line. No, it wasn't *all* his fault. Kyle should have swung. With the tying run on third base, the winning run on second, you have to take your cut. Sure, Kyle saved a few runs with his great catch, but losing by one was still losing.

"How could you just stand there?" Bones muttered as he untied his cleats beside Kyle on the bench. "He threw it right down the middle."

Kyle hung his head, letting his shoulder-length brown hair fall across his face. "I know. I was trying to guess whether I'd see a fastball or a curveball, and I froze."

Bones gritted his teeth. "You have to swing, Kyle. Even if you're going down, at least go down swinging."

His voice rose. The other guys in the dugout turned.

"Bones, easy," Marcus said. He offered Kyle a sympathetic shrug. "You'll get 'em next time."

Great. It was bad enough Bones had been shelled on the mound; now his teammates thought he was a jerk too. He packed his things and hurried off the field.

At home, he avoided his mom as long as he could, but she slipped into his room after he crawled into bed.

"How was your game?" she asked.

"I sucked," he grumbled. "And we lost."

"Ah. Life is pointless, barely worth living." She smiled, an attempt at peace, but he wasn't in the mood.

She smoothed his bedspread. "So . . . I know this reporter who maybe got into it with her editor today, and maybe brought home a mood she should have left at the office . . . and maybe she was harder on her kid than he deserved."

"Maybe, huh?"

"Maybe. I mean, the kid *is* stubborn as a goat, and probably needs to be grounded." She couldn't resist smiling as he groaned. "But maybe she said some things that came out wrong."

Bones picked at his thumbnail. "Maybe that kid said some dumb things too. Though he can't help that he got his stubbornness from his mom."

She laughed, a sound like a rainbow piercing the clouds after a thunderstorm. "Oh, you." She ran a hand over his curly hair.

"Why were you fighting with your editor?" he asked.

His mom's expression soured. "He sent me to a press conference where Fluxcor announced they're launching free Wi-Fi across Langille. It sounds great on the surface, but it smells funny to me. Makes me wonder if they cut a deal with the Town Council. Fluxcor's new cell tower by Langille Beach went up awfully quick, even though a lot of people were protesting the construction. When I asked Mayor MacKenzie and Ray Giraud from Fluxcor if the two were connected, they laughed it off without really denying it. I put that in my story, but Don wanted it out."

Bones frowned. "He changed your story?"

"Not exactly. He went on about how Fluxcor employs half the town, and it would reflect badly on the paper if my article criticized the announcement in the news section while he praised it on the editorial page. The whole thing felt so slimy. And patronizing, like he was mansplaining how the news works." His mom sucked her teeth. "I've got two national reporting awards on my desk, and this small-town hack is lecturing me about playing nice with his golf buddies."

Bones grinned. "Tell me how you really feel, Mom."

Her frown deepened. "I should have told *him* how I really feel. But I need this job. So I let him cut two paragraphs." She covered her face. "It goes against everything I believe in, though. It's like I've stopped being a real journalist."

Bones tensed. "Hey, stop that. You're a great reporter. It's hard being new. I get it."

"I just have this feeling that something shady is going on," she said.

"Like a secret club of evil rich white guys running the town?" He nudged her, trying to lighten her mood.

She raised an eyebrow. "A club of rich white guys runs *every* town. It's my job to keep them in check."

"You're like the Black Lois Lane," Bones joked.

"Boy, please. Lois Lane wishes she could carry my notebook."

They both cracked up. His mom held up her fist and he gave it a bump. Then she kissed him on the forehead and bade him goodnight.

His thoughts wandered as he grew sleepy. Things had been rocky since the move to Langille. He'd hoped his family could put their old life behind them in a new town, but starting over wasn't easy. His knack for finding trouble didn't help either. He had to stop causing his mom grief.

At least we ended the night on a good note, he thought. As long as he and his mom could make each other laugh, they were cool.

3.
THE END OF THE STREET

Kyle paced his room in his pajama shorts, squeezing a blue foam ball. He walked a narrow loop from the window to his floor-to-ceiling bookcase, which was nearly overflowing with novels and books on climate science, renewable energy, music—all the things that interested him. But pacing didn't help. He'd already taken a shower, and practiced his cello, and tried to read, and attempted a breathing exercise that his well-meaning aunt had showed him, but nothing had helped. His body hummed with agitation, an electric current radiating to his fingers and toes.

He tried simply willing it to stop, but that had never worked. Not once.

He flopped on his bed and stared at the sheet music for Claude Debussy's Cello Sonata that he'd taped to the ceiling. He couldn't play it yet, but sometimes visualizing the music helped him relax. Tonight, though, that was useless too. He knew he wouldn't fall asleep for hours in this state. So he hopped up, pulled on a T-shirt, and went to the living room, where his parents were drowsily watching something British.

"I need to go for a walk," he announced.

His parents sat up. "Kyle, it's dark," his mom said.

His dad patted the empty couch cushion next to him. "Do you want to talk?"

"No." Kyle balanced on the balls of his feet. "I know it's late, but I'll just walk to the end of the street and back."

His mom turned to his dad. "I have an early shift tomorrow. Peter, can you—"

"I want to go by myself," Kyle interrupted. "It's Langille. I'm thirteen. I'm only going to the end of the street."

His parents did multiple things with their faces: furrowed their brows, pursed their lips, gave slight nods. Kyle often struggled to decipher the secret codes embedded in other people's expressions, but he'd learned to tell when his parents were disagreeing about him.

Finally, his mother sighed. "Just to the end of the street."

"Thank you." Before she could change her mind, he headed for the back door, slipped on his sandals, and stepped into the night.

Even after dark, the air was uncomfortably thick. July had opened with a heat wave, and Kyle tried not to think about climate change, warming oceans, extreme weather—topics that often kept him up at night. He had enough on his mind.

As he started up Maple Street, he replayed the drive home from the baseball field. He'd sat in the backseat, staring out the window, fingers tapping on his knee, while his parents tried to cheer him up in ways that somehow made him feel worse.

Dad: *That was an amazing catch, Kyle!*

Mom: *I know! I couldn't believe you got to that ball. You should be so proud of yourself.*

Kyle: . . .

Dad: *Hey, don't worry about that strikeout, kiddo. Remember, even the best hitters in baseball get out seven times out of ten. It happens to everyone.*

Kyle: . . .

Mom: *Are you upset about that, honey? You seem agitated.*

Kyle: . . .

Mom: *None of the other boys gave you grief, did they? Because they all get out sometimes too. If anyone's picking on you—*

Kyle: *No one's picking on me.*

Mom: *Oh.*

Silence.

Mom: *Are you finding baseball stressful? It's supposed to be about fun, and friendship—*

Dad: *Hannah.*

Mom: *What? I'm just asking.*

Kyle: *I still like baseball, Mom.*

Dad: *That's good, son. Remember, seven out of ten. Baseball's a great teacher of resilience. You'll get 'em next time.*

His dad was right. Even great hitters failed seven times out of ten. And Marcus had said the same thing: *You'll get 'em next time.*

But Bones was right too. He should have swung.

It wasn't even the strikeout that bothered him most. It was the feeling like he and his teammates didn't share the same language.

22

He tried to explain to Bones why he didn't swing, and it went badly. He hadn't even tried to explain the catch. When his teammates slapped him on the back, he was bursting to tell them how he'd plotted the arc of the ball as it soared through the sky and sprinted to where he knew it would come down. How he'd timed his jump perfectly. How the *smack* of the baseball landing in his glove had felt so satisfying that he started to laugh, even as he'd crashed into the fence. But he didn't say any of that, because he didn't want his teammates to stare at him and say, *What the heck are you talking about, Kyle?*

So he just smiled, and said *thanks*, and kept the rest to himself. But he wished he'd tried.

Baseball was a new experiment, and Kyle was as shocked as anyone when he made the AAA team. It turned out he was a natural at chasing down fly balls. But figuring out his teammates was still a work in progress. He hadn't spent this much time around kids his own age since the fifth grade. That was the last year he'd gone to public school, the year that *What the heck are you talking about, Kyle?* became the class's running joke. His parents had made phone calls and arranged meetings, and his teacher and school administrators tried to help. He'd ended up spending most of his time in the learning center or the library, working at his own pace, but by the end of the school year he'd felt more alienated than ever. That summer, his parents had decided that homeschooling might suit him better.

His team seemed nicer than his fifth-grade classmates, but six weeks into the season he was still worried about doing anything too weird. Sometimes it was lonely.

Maybe he needed to try harder. Talk more. Maybe Bones was right about that too. *"Even if you're going down, at least go down swinging."*

Kyle reached the cul-de-sac where kids played street hockey during the day. He eyed the gravel footpath that cut through the woods to the west, toward Oak Street. *The end of the street,* he'd promised. But he didn't feel like turning around yet, and for a moment he debated if the path was technically still part of Maple Street.

A shout from the woods changed his mind. Older kids, like Tony Spezio, hung out back there at night. Kyle's mom was a police officer, and when his dad asked about how an overnight shift went, she often said, *"Oh, you know, the usual calls about teenagers doing teenager things."* She rarely described what she meant by *teenager things,* but she'd cautioned Kyle to stay away from Tony and his crew. Not that Kyle needed the warning. One of his own encounters with Tony was still burned in his mind.

"Hey look, it's the hermit kid! Your parents let you out of the house? I thought you were too weird to be allowed out in public."

Kyle was turning toward home when another shout from the path startled him.

"Wade? Wade!"

Kyle froze. The voice sounded upset. Desperate. Should he check it out? Before he could decide, a man emerged from the path. He cupped his hands to his mouth and hollered again.

"WAAAAADE!"

Kyle jumped. The man noticed him and headed toward him. Suddenly he was too close, shoving his phone under Kyle's nose. Kyle took a step back.

"Have you seen this man? My husband. His name is Wade Elliott. He didn't come home last night, and I called his office and I called the police but no one's taking it seriously. I mean, he's a workaholic, he's *always* at the lab, but this is different—"

Kyle went rigid. The man was too close, too emotional, throwing too much at him. He couldn't form a response or even focus on the phone enough to tell if the face on the screen looked familiar. He took another step back.

The man sighed. "I'm sorry. You're just a kid. I didn't mean to—" His voice hitched. "If you see him, please call the police, OK?"

Kyle nodded stiffly. The man cast a glance down Maple Street. With another sigh, he turned and headed back into the woods, calling Wade's name as he went.

Kyle stood still, waiting for his heart to slow, trying to understand what had just happened.

How on earth did anyone go missing in Langille?

4.
SON OF A GUN

As he ate breakfast, Bones's eyes drifted from the clock to the hallway. His mom would storm in at any moment, annoyed at her own lateness. She'd unleash a string of commands, and the kitchen would fill with noise and chaos and exasperation, but the four Malones would tumble out the door just five minutes behind schedule, as always.

He clung to this thought, but his brothers grew quieter as a suspicion that something wasn't right settled over them. Raury, the ten-year-old worrier of the family, squirmed in his chair.

"You have to do something," he told Bones. "We're going to be late."

Reluctantly, Bones padded down the hall. His mom would be so upset when she realized the time. Maybe she'd snap at him for not waking her earlier. He dreaded the scene about to unfold.

He tapped on her door. "Mom? You up?"

Nothing. After a moment, he pushed the door open.

She sat on the bed, fully dressed, facing the window. He sat beside her.

"Mom? It's almost eight. Time to take on some shady white dudes," he joked.

She blinked but didn't turn her head.

He touched her arm. "Mom?"

It felt like an eternity before she let out a slow breath. "Take the boys to Eileen's, OK? I need a few minutes."

Take his brothers to the Spezios' by himself? She'd never asked him to do that before. But he swallowed. "OK." When she didn't say anything else, he went on. "You're going to work, right?"

Silence.

"Mom?"

She pinched the bridge of her nose. "Of course. I said I just need a minute. It's fine. I'm fine."

He nodded and made his way toward the door, watching her as he backed out. She remained motionless.

His brothers peppered him with questions as he ushered them out the door, but he fended them off. He had no idea what to tell them. He'd seen his mother upset, but he'd never seen her so deflated. She was not fine.

Tony was still sleeping when Bones left the Spezios' house for baseball practice. He felt bad leaving his brothers behind, but he was happy to get away. Normally he'd have been even happier to be heading to the field. But between rehashing his terrible performance the previous night and worrying about his mom, he took to the field feeling heavy. He wasn't the only one, it seemed. Jokes and laughter flowed less freely than usual as the Falcons put on their cleats. After a few minutes, Coach called everyone into a huddle by the dugout.

"Congratulations," he said. "We lost a game. Well done."

The boys looked at each other. Kyle slowly raised his hand.

"Are you being sarcastic, Coach?"

Coach smiled. "Not at all, Kyle. Honestly, you guys were making me nervous with all that winning. But now, this is when the real fun starts."

More puzzled silence. They looked at Coach, waiting. His grin widened.

"Know how many games I lost in my career? Hundreds. That's how baseball goes. But ultimately, how you handle the losses says more about you than the wins. Losing helps you figure out what kind of team you really are." He looked at each player. "Now we get to find out who we are."

"We're the Falcons!" Marcus whooped, and the team cheered. Kyle still seemed perplexed by Coach's speech, but everyone else raced out to the field. Everyone except Bones.

He bent to tighten his laces. As he straightened up, a large hand landed on his shoulder.

"I'm pretty sure by now you'd leave a puddle of blood on the field if you thought it would help win a game," Coach said.

Bones shrugged. "I try, Coach."

Carlos laughed, a deep, gentle sound. "*Try* is an understatement. You're one tough son of a gun, Bones Malone. It's a joy to watch you play." He bent so he was at Bones's eye level. "But even if you've got the ball in your hand, baseball's a team game. Nobody wins or loses alone. Get what I'm saying?"

Bones nodded. Coach was telling him to stop sweating his lousy night. Coach liked to make his point with a nudge instead of a lecture.

"Good." Coach squeezed his shoulder. "Now go have some fun out there."

As Bones jogged onto the field, Marcus called him over. "Come warm up with me?"

They spaced out in the outfield and casually tossed a ball back and forth. For a moment, Bones wondered if Coach had put Marcus up to this, as another way to shake him out of his funk. But then he figured it was probably just Marcus being Marcus.

He hadn't known what to expect from Marcus at first. It turned out Bones was right that Langille hardly had any other Black kids, so he'd hoped Marcus might be friend material, even though he was a year older. But on his first day at his new school, Bones had spotted Marcus surrounded by other kids in the cafeteria and instantly realized that *everybody* wanted to be his friend. Marcus was clearly the Cool Kid—popular and rich, a gifted athlete with a famous dad. Maybe he'd also turn out to be the most big-headed kid in town.

But after the first baseball tryout a few days later, Marcus had ambled over and playfully squeezed Bones's right bicep.

"Yo, that arm is a cannon," he'd said. *"I'm glad we'll be on the same team so I don't have to face your fastball."*

His smile caught Bones by surprise. *"You think I'll make the team?"*

Marcus laughed. *"Are you kidding? Dad nearly choked on his gum the first time he saw you throw."* He held up his hand for a fist bump. *"Glad you moved here, man."*

Now Marcus cracked jokes and loosened up his teammates as they moved into stretches and ran a lap around the field. Last night's game faded from Bones's mind, but his thoughts returned to his mom. He couldn't forget the vacant look in her eyes, like she'd woken up with a piece of herself missing. What was going on? Maybe work was stressing her out more than she was admitting? And it probably didn't help that he was causing grief with the Spezios. *No more fights*, he chided himself. He'd just have to put up with Tony, even if the thought left a sour taste in his mouth.

His teammates' chatter washed over him as he unlaced his cleats after practice. As the dugout emptied, he realized Kyle was still sitting next to him. Kyle's fingers drummed on his knee. Bones had the feeling he was sucking up the nerve to say something. Maybe he was peeved about Bones calling him out the previous night.

"Something on your mind?" Bones said gruffly.

Kyle went stiff. He stared straight ahead. "I was wondering if you're all right. You're not very chirpy today."

Bones tilted his head. "Chirpy?"

"You usually talk a lot. And you move so quickly, it reminds me of a hummingbird. Although hummingbirds don't chirp. But that's the word I picture when I think of you. Chirpy. Well, I also think about skeletons. Because of your nickname, obviously."

Bones stared. This was the most Kyle had ever said to him at once. Now his white skin reddened under Bones's glare. His fingers tapped on his thigh.

"That came out wrong. I'm not good at . . ." He sighed. "I only meant you don't seem like yourself. So many people are acting unusually lately. Ms. Vanderpol wasn't herself today either."

Bones rubbed his forehead. "Who's Ms. Vanderpol?"

"My neighbor. She's always in her garden in the morning, unless it's raining, and I say hello, and she waves and says hello back. But today, it was like she didn't even see me. I said hello a second time, and she still didn't respond. She always waves. She knows I—" Kyle's words tumbled out faster and faster until he stopped, fingers bouncing. "Anyway. I just wondered if you're feeling all right."

Bones was touched Kyle noticed something was up, even if Kyle thought his usual state was "chirpy." Then it struck him what Kyle was saying.

"Wait. Your neighbor was zoned out like a zombie? And you've never seen her do that before?"

Kyle shook his head. "She's always friendly to me. She didn't seem like herself at all."

Bones hesitated. He barely knew Kyle. And maybe this neighbor was just having a bad day. Like Bones's mom. It was a coincidence, right?

It didn't feel that way in his gut.

He checked to ensure they were alone. "My mom's like that too. I'm distracted because she was acting so weird this morning."

He told Kyle about his mom's behavior and their conversation the night before.

Kyle leaned forward. "I read your mom's story this morning."

"You did?" It dawned on Bones he hadn't even done that.

"I always read the *Record*. And I think free Wi-Fi across Langille is a good idea. But the announcement was held at the library, which means your mother was at the library yesterday."

Bones scratched his head. "So?"

"Oh, I forgot, you don't know Ms. Vanderpol." Kyle dropped his eyes. "Tell me if my thinking ever seems hard to follow."

Bones shifted impatiently. "It's hard right now. What does the library have to do with anything?"

Kyle closed his eyes, gathering his thoughts. "Ms. Vanderpol is the head librarian. Your mother was at the library for the announcement. Today they're both acting strangely, in what sounds like a similar way. That seems—"

Bones jumped up. "We should go to the library."

Kyle's eyes flew open in surprise. "I was going to suggest that, but I worried you might think I was overreacting. Being weird."

Kyle drummed on his knee again. Bones wondered if Kyle got called weird a lot. He felt a flash of guilt as he remembered chewing him out the night before.

"It's not weird," Bones said. "It makes sense. Let's go to the library."

5.
THE RIVER

Bones slung his bag over his shoulder and followed Kyle downtown to the Langille Library, a brick building next to Town Hall on the main street running parallel to the Langille River's north bank. Inside, Kyle approached the checkout desk, where a woman organized books on a cart behind the counter.

"Hello, Mrs. Whittle," he said. "I'd like to speak to Ms. Vanderpol, please."

The woman didn't look up from her sorting. "She's not here. Called in sick."

Kyle blinked. "But she's always here."

"Not today she's not."

"But—" Kyle's fingertips tapped against his thigh. "We have questions about yesterday's announcement with Fluxcor and—"

Mrs. Whittle sighed. "Listen, all I know is it was a big hullabaloo and now we're behind on reshelving. If you'll excuse me, it's very busy today and I have work to do."

Bones could only see three other people in the library: an elderly man on a computer and two teenagers browsing the DVDs. "It's not busy at all," he said. "We need to know who was here yesterday. What happened at the announcement? Where did they hold it?"

The librarian glared at Bones. "Young man. I will not be spoken to in that tone. Unless you have actual library business, good day to you both."

She returned to her cart, making it clear the conversation was over. Bones glowered at the back of her head before stomping outside. Kyle followed close behind.

"Well, *that* was helpful," Bones grumbled.

Kyle scratched his head. "You think so?"

It was Bones's turn to be puzzled. "It wasn't helpful at all, Kyle. I was being sarcastic."

"Oh." Kyle looked away. "At least we confirmed something isn't right at the library."

"We did?"

"Yes. Mrs. Whittle is behaving oddly too. She's not usually that grumpy."

Bones kicked a pebble toward the brick building. "So what now?"

"I'm not sure." Kyle paused. "There's something else I should tell you. Last night, I went for a walk, and I met a man who was looking for his missing husband. He was very upset." His fingers drummed on his thigh. "Maybe none of this is related, but it's all so strange."

A missing person? A librarian who didn't show up for work? Bones shivered. He remembered that he'd left his mom sitting on her bed, and he had a sudden urge to call her.

She didn't pick up until the fourth ring. "Bones?" she answered briskly. "What's going on?"

"Uh . . . nothing. Just wanted to see how you're doing."

"Fine. A little busy."

"You're at work?"

Bones could feel her annoyance escalate in the pause before she answered. "Of course. Where are you?"

"I'm, uh, out. With Kyle. From baseball."

"Does Eileen know where you are? Where are your brothers?"

Whoa. How did this turn into an interrogation? He'd called to check on *her.*

"They're at the Spezios'. They're fine."

"Keep an eye on them. And behave yourself. You *cannot* have any more incidents with Eileen."

"OK, but—"

"I have to go. See you tonight."

She hung up. Bones frowned at his phone.

"Was that your mother?" Kyle asked. "Is she doing better?"

"She's at work, anyway." She sounded more like herself, but something still felt off. Bones shook his head. "I need to get back to the Spezios' and check on my brothers."

Kyle winced. "You stay at Tony's house?"

"You know him?"

"We live on the same street." Kyle tucked his hands in his pockets. "But I try to stay away from him and his friends."

"I wish I could stay away from him," Bones muttered. "But I guess we're headed in the same direction."

They made their way back past the Common and over the bridge that spanned the river, connecting the town. The houses on the south side of the river, where Bones and Kyle lived, were smaller than those looking down on the northern bank from the hill behind the university. As they came off the bridge, Kyle veered toward the park at the foot of the bridge.

"Let's take the river path," he said. "It's quieter. We won't have to see all the Fluxcor advertising."

Bones glanced at a billboard across the street, towering over the gas station. A smiling woman in a virtual reality headset flashed a thumbs-up beneath the words FLUXCOR: LIVE THE FUTURE™.

"You're not a fan?" he said. "I thought everyone loved Fluxcor around here. Like didn't they save the town with all their jobs or something?"

Kyle shrugged. "They have done a lot for Langille, I guess. But their slogan is irritating. How can anyone *live the future*? You can only live in the present. It's a paradoxical statement."

Bones grinned. "You're not supposed to think so hard about it. It's only marketing."

"It's also hypocritical," Kyle argued. "If Fluxcor cares about the future, they should invest more in green energy and sustainable technology. Their carbon footprint is enormous."

Bones stared at him. "You just, like, know this?"

"I think about clean energy a lot."

They fell into an awkward silence as they tromped along, gravel crunching under their sneakers. Normally the path was busy with joggers, moms pushing strollers, kids on bikes, but Bones and Kyle met few travelers in the early afternoon heat. Bones wiped his brow. Sweat pooled in the middle of his back where his gear bag pressed against his T-shirt.

"I don't remember seeing you around school," he said, for the sake of saying something. "You're a grade older than me, right? Like Marcus?"

Kyle kept his eyes on the path. "I'm homeschooled."

"Oh." Bones pondered this. "I think I'd get bored if I was home all day."

"I like learning what I want. And I don't stay home all day. Sometimes I work at the library, or I sit in on some of my dad's classes."

"He's a teacher?"

"He teaches environmental science at Royden."

Bones scratched his sweaty neck. "The *university*? No wonder you don't go to middle school. So you're a science genius who's going to save the planet?"

"Not exactly." Kyle dodged a root sticking out of the path. "You're new in Langille, right? Why did you move here?"

Two months in, Bones still hated that question. "My mom got a job at the *Record*."

"What about your dad?"

Bones gave Kyle a side-eye. That question was worse. Bones caught the looks when the Malones went out for dinner or groceries. The new Black family in a mostly white town, a mom and three boys . . . People talked. He knew they did. But hardly anyone blurted it out like that.

"He's not around. He's the worst. End of story."

"Oh." Kyle waited a beat. "Do you visit him sometimes, or—"

"You know what *end of story* means, right?" It came out sharper than Bones intended.

Kyle recoiled. "Sorry. I only thought . . . Never mind. Sorry."

Cicadas buzzed in the trees. The Langille River churned past in a steady swish. Bones's stomach rumbled, reminding him it was past lunchtime. How much farther was it again?

"My dad's white," he blurted. He was never sure why he offered this. He didn't owe anyone an explanation, but sometimes he did it anyway.

Kyle started tapping his thigh again. "I didn't mean to be nosy. Sometimes I accidentally ask rude questions. I try not to."

Bones snorted. "You try, huh?"

Kyle hung his head, as if he thought Bones was mocking him. Bones gave him a light punch in the shoulder. Kyle studied Bones's face. Slowly, he smiled.

A splash in the river caught Bones's attention. He stopped. Something was out there. An arm split the surface, then a bearded face.

"Hel—" the man called. His head dipped below the water.

"Whoa. Did you see that?" Bones pointed to the river. "That guy is drowning!"

The man surfaced again. Kyle gasped. "We need to call 911. Do you have a phone?"

"Yeah, but he needs help *now*." Bones handed his phone to Kyle. "You call." He dropped his gear bag and pulled off his shirt.

"What are you doing?" Kyle asked in alarm. "The river has a strong current."

"We can't let him drown!"

Without waiting for a reply, Bones rushed into the water and sliced toward the flailing figure with brisk, strong strokes. He grabbed the man by one wrist and turned back toward the shore. The man thrashed and flailed, whacking Bones in the head. Bones slipped underwater and came up coughing. He pulled with all his might, paddling with his free arm and kicking as hard as he could, but the current and the man's waterlogged weight dragged against him with every stroke. He could barely keep his face above the surface.

His lungs burned. The shore was still too far away. He wasn't going to make it.

"Help," he croaked to Kyle.

He should let the man go, save himself. He knew it was the sensible option. But he kept fighting. One more stroke, one more kick. Until he couldn't do it anymore.

He was sinking.

As he slipped underwater, he grasped for the surface. His hand grazed something rough and solid—a tree branch. He managed to grab hold and hang on as Kyle reeled him in. His feet found the rocky river bottom and he pushed to the surface with a gasp. Kyle waded into the river to grab him, and then they both dragged the man to shore.

Bones collapsed, gagging and spewing water. The man lay still, eyes closed. His waterlogged flesh had a ghostly green tinge.

"Come *on*," Bones wheezed. "You're not allowed to die, you jerk. Not after all that."

He pounded the man's chest. Once, twice. The man gasped and his eyes flew open. He coughed.

"Is it too late?" he cried. "We have to stop them, before it's too late!"

The man frantically patted at his jacket. He reached inside and withdrew a Moleskine journal. He thrust it into Bones's hands. "Take this. Keep it safe." He spat a mouthful of river. "Don't let them have it. Especially not—"

Coughs wracked the man's body. Kyle tried to guide him onto his side so he didn't choke. Bones heard the urgent wail of sirens drawing nearer. Acting on instinct, he tucked the notebook into Kyle's backpack, lying an arm's length away on the shore.

Keep it safe. Don't let them have it. Bones shivered. The day kept growing stranger. And he doubted it was a coincidence.

6.
PURE HAVOC

Kyle leaned against an oak tree, trying to ignore the gross squelchy feeling in his soaked clothes and sneakers as he tapped his fingers against his thigh. Thumb to pinkie and back again, a habit he'd adapted as an outlet for when his anxiety swelled. Tapping his fingers felt good and didn't draw too much attention in public. He hung back, away from the buzz of activity near the river, where the emergency responders' radios crackled and two paramedics carted the nearly drowned man to a waiting ambulance. It was all too much.

"I said I'm *fine*. Jeez."

At a picnic table, Bones squirmed as another paramedic pressed a stethoscope to his back.

Kyle still couldn't believe Bones had jumped in the river without even considering the water temperature, the velocity of the current, the mass of the drowning man. The situation was impossibly dangerous—nearly *fatal*—yet Bones dove in anyway. Every time Kyle pictured Bones disappearing under the surface, his heart started thumping all over again. He tapped harder against his thigh.

When the paramedic attending to Bones relented, Kyle edged to the picnic table. He tried not to stare at the scar on Bones's back, a thin pink line running across the top of his shoulder blade and then veering along the inner edge, like an inverted L. He handed Bones his T-shirt, and Bones slipped it over his head. Bones scanned the park to make sure no one was listening.

"I stuck the journal in your bag," he whispered. "Don't let anyone know about it."

The journal. Questions raced through Kyle's mind. He strongly suspected the man they'd pulled from the river was Wade Elliott, the missing man whose husband he'd encountered last night. If he was, where had he been? How did he end up in the river? And what was he guarding in that book? As Kyle pondered, he tried not to picture the soggy notebook sitting on his baseball cleats, soaking them too. He'd have to air out both pairs of shoes later.

"Kyle! Oh my goodness!"

He barely had time to turn before his mother embraced him. He stiffened. He didn't mind her hugging him, but this was an unusual setting with no warning, and he was already on edge. She must have sensed his discomfort because she quickly let go.

"Are you all right?" She took in his soaked clothes. "When I heard the call from dispatch, I didn't know it was *you*."

Kyle pulled at his wet shirt clinging to his chest. "I only helped a little. Bones was the one who swam him to shore."

His mother turned to Bones. "Well. You're quite the pitcher, and I guess you're quite the swimmer too." She held out her hand. "I'm Constable Hannah Specks. Kyle's mom."

She shifted into police mode as she questioned Bones. He didn't mention the journal, which made Kyle antsy. It was probably evidence. Maybe they were breaking the law if they didn't hand it over.

His mother slipped away to talk with the other officials on-site. When she returned, she eased back into mom mode.

"The paramedic says you're clear. But are you sure you're all right?" she asked Bones. "That must have been frightening. Is your mom coming to pick you up?"

Bones's eyes widened. "No. Don't bother her. She's on deadline. I'm fine. I just need to get back to my brothers. They're at the Spezios' house."

"You stay with Eileen?" Kyle's mom paused. "Do you have dry clothes there?"

Bones shook his head.

"We live down the street. Come over and Kyle can lend you something to wear."

Bones grinned. "That is an excellent idea."

Kyle froze. "Are you sure? Don't you need to check on your brothers?"

His mother frowned. "Kyle. He's soaked."

"Yeah, Kyle. I'm soaked." Bones did strange things with his face: squinting, raising his eyebrows, jerking his head to the left. He was trying to communicate something, but Kyle couldn't tell what.

"Have you boys eaten?" his mother asked.

"No," Bones said before Kyle could respond. "And I'm *starving* after saving a man's life."

"It's settled, then. You're coming with us."

They walked to Kyle's mother's cruiser. "This is perfect," Bones murmured. "Now we can check out that journal."

"We should tell Mom," Kyle whispered. "It's evidence."

"No way," Bones shot back. "That guy gave it to me. You heard what he said."

"But Mom is—"

His mom turned. "Hmm?"

Bones pinched Kyle's arm. Hard.

"Ow!" Kyle rubbed his arm. "Why did you do that?"

"You had a tick on you." Bones waited until Kyle's mother opened the driver's door before he shot Kyle a glare. Kyle could read his lips well enough: *Shut. Up.*

Kyle was quiet on the short ride home. He filed the journal away for the moment. He had a more pressing concern: Bones was about to enter his house.

When his mother pulled into the driveway, he immediately bounded out, pausing only to strip off his wet socks and shoes on the front step.

"Take yours off too," he commanded Bones.

His mother sighed. "Kyle—"

He didn't wait for an answer. He hurried to his room and closed the door. Bones knocked twenty seconds later.

"Kyle? Can I—?"

"I'm changing! Just wait. I'll get you some clothes."

He sorted through his shorts, calculating what might best fit the smaller boy. Should he offer Bones dry underwear? Would that be weird? Would it be weirder if he didn't? What if he only gave Bones shorts and he wore them with no underwear underneath?

"Kyle?"

"Just wait!"

He settled on shorts and underwear and decided he would never ask Bones to return either. He opened the door a crack and thrust them out.

"Here. You can change in the bathroom across the hall."

As soon as Bones took the clothes, he pulled the door shut again and surveyed his room.

Kyle didn't spend much time in other boys' rooms, but he knew they didn't look like his. The sheet music on the ceiling was unusual enough, but he suspected the whiteboards on the wall above his desk would make him seem like a weirdo.

He kept lists. For everything. Projects he was working on, with self-imposed timelines. Upcoming baseball practices and games. His mother's shift schedule. An inventory of books and music on loan from the library, sorted first by due date and then alphabetically. Time was a slippery concept, and Kyle felt less anxious if he could map his life in a way that made sense to him.

He'd started with one whiteboard, but he had to cram too many things onto it, and sometimes the details got smudged. So now he had two boards.

As he changed, he considered taking the boards down and sliding them under his bed before he allowed Bones in his room. But something might smudge. That would be worse.

Kyle tensed. Bones was in the bathroom. There was a list there too, taped beneath the mirror.

MORNING ROUTINE
Towel and clean underwear
Shower: Use facewash every day, shampoo hair
Tuesday & Friday or if very sweaty
(e.g., after baseball)
Hang up towel, put dirty clothes in hamper
Brush teeth
Brush hair
Deodorant

Bones would notice for sure. *Great.*

Kyle left his room, closing the door, and found Bones in the kitchen. He'd already begun constructing an enormous sandwich out of the ingredients Kyle's mother had set on the counter: Kaiser buns, slices of deli roast beef, cheddar and Swiss cheese, lettuce, tomato slices, pickles, mustard, and mayonnaise. Bones piled on a bit of everything until he could barely close his hands around the bun.

"This is great," he said. "Thanks, Mrs.—uh, Constable—"

Kyle's mom laughed. "I'm off the clock, Bones. Mrs. Specks is fine."

"Oh. Well, thanks. Do you have any hot sauce?"

"I don't think so, but you're welcome to check the fridge."

Kyle assembled his own sandwich quietly. His mom made small talk with Bones as they ate, and she kept glancing at Kyle in a way that meant *Jump in anytime; try to be social.* But too many bizarre things had already happened, and he had to focus on reorganizing the world in a sensible manner again.

Eventually his mom left to go back to work.

"Sorry if that was too much," Kyle said when she'd gone. "I don't have people over a lot."

"No biggie. Your mom's nice," Bones replied. "Moms always get all mom-like when you have someone over for the first time. But that sandwich was *great*." He burped. "Let's check out dude's journal. You think it's the missing guy you heard about last night too, right? What's his name again?"

"Wade Elliott. And yes, I do." Kyle spread a dish towel on the table before he retrieved the soggy journal from his backpack, making a mental note to set his cleats on the porch to dry. At the table, he gingerly opened the cover.

The book was a mess of smeared blue ink, pages plastered together in sodden clumps. Kyle could barely make out anything, other than a few runny letters at the top of the first page.

He squinted. "Does that say . . . 'reget key'?"

"Reget key?" Bones repeated. "Maybe he was trying to get back a key he lost. But a key to what?"

"I'm not sure. *Reget* isn't a real word. And why didn't he write retrieve, or recover?"

"Maybe he's bad at spelling," Bones offered.

"Or maybe it's an acronym? Although acronyms are usually based on real words." Kyle leaned closer to the page. "Maybe we're reading it wrong. It's hard to tell."

"Is it all that bad?" Bones tried to turn the first page. A wet fragment came away in his hand.

"Easy," Kyle cautioned. "We should probably dry it out before we try to look through it."

"Good idea. You have a hair dryer?"

Kyle frowned. He couldn't stand the sound of hair dryers, and they were an enormous waste of energy. "That might damage it more. We should research how to restore a book."

Bones wrinkled his nose at the word *research*. "Fine. Where's your computer?"

"In my room." Kyle stiffened. "It's a laptop. I'll go get it."

Bones folded his arms. "Are you a serial killer, Kyle?"

Kyle froze. "I . . . what?" he choked out.

"You won't let me in your room. You got bodies under the bed or something?"

Bones was joking, right? He looked like he was holding back a smile.

Kyle's heart raced. As nervous as he felt about letting Bones in his room, maybe it would be worse if he didn't. Reality was less awful than Bones imagining he was hoarding corpses. What if Bones spread rumors about him? He wanted to believe Bones was better than that, but other kids had made up stories about him before.

With a sigh, he led Bones to his room. He squeezed the door handle to steady himself before he pushed the door open.

"Whoa." Bones studied the wall and whistled. "Are you a detective? The only people I've ever seen with boards like that are serial killers and people who chase serial killers." He wandered around the room, offering a running commentary as Kyle braced himself, barely breathing.

"You're really into lists, huh? I saw the one in the bathroom. You must be super organized. This is the neatest room I've ever seen. It's like a museum in here. Hey, cool ceiling. I take it you like music. You'd like my brother. He pretty much lives on the piano, when he's not reading. But you like that too, obviously. This is the most books I've ever seen besides a library. And are they in alphabetical order?" Bones turned to him. "Do you have OCD?"

Kyle ran a hand through his hair and struggled to find his voice. "I'm not obsessive-compulsive. But I'm . . . I don't think I'm neurotypical. My brain works differently."

Bones hesitated. "Like autism?"

"Maybe. I don't have an official diagnosis." Kyle drummed on his thigh. He hated this conversation. *Exactly how are you abnormal?* People wanted an explanation. A formula. Even his parents argued about it. They didn't disagree about much, but they disagreed about him.

"Don't you think it would help him, Peter? Don't you think it would help us?"

"I think the last thing he needs in this little town is a label, Hannah. He's thoughtful, passionate, and creative. He sees the world differently. Why is that a problem to be solved?"

"You know that's not what I think . . ."

Bones scratched his head. "So you don't know for sure? I mean, the way you talk and think is obviously different, but—" He winced. "Sorry. That came out wrong. I didn't mean—"

Kyle's face went hot. "I know enough, all right? I've done my research. I know I can barely do some things other people find easy, and I'm the only person on our team who doesn't understand all the jokes in the dugout. And most of the time, people talk to me like they're trying to figure out what's wrong with me. When you're weirder than everyone else, you get the message eventually."

He looked away. He hadn't meant to erupt, but on a day when so many unexpected things kept ambushing him, it was no surprise that he'd lose control. Maybe it was better this way. Now Bones knew why he usually sat by himself on the bench. Bones could make an excuse to take the journal and leave. They could go back to barely talking at the baseball field, and Kyle could snuff the glimmer of excitement that had steadily been building under everything else. If he was going to wind up disappointed, better to get it over with now.

Bones blinked. But he didn't leave. "Is that why you don't go to school?"

"I didn't fit. I'm not the right kind of smart for school. It was too noisy, and I got upset a lot, and people didn't . . ." Kyle trailed off. He'd said enough.

"I get that." Bones sat on the corner of Kyle's bed. "Sometimes people are the worst."

A dozen questions immediately sprang to Kyle's mind. They all bordered on intrusive and possibly rude, but he had waded through his most hated conversation, so Bones owed him now, right?

Before he could speak, Bones hopped up, suddenly animated. "This is perfect. You're exactly who I need."

Kyle fell still. No one had ever said anything like that to him before. "I . . . am?"

"Totally." Bones waved toward the whiteboard. "You notice stuff. You like research and lists. You have a whiteboard. Two of them!" He laughed, but it wasn't a mocking sound. It was so joyful it almost made Kyle laugh too, even if he wasn't following yet.

"Think about how bananas today has been," Bones continued. "My mom's acting like a different person. The librarians have gone haywire. We saved a missing dude from drowning, and then he warned us to keep his top secret notes away from some mysterious bad guys. It all has to be connected, right?"

Kyle nodded. He couldn't help grinning, if only because the delightfully unusual phrase *the librarians have gone haywire* kept running through his mind. He whispered it under his breath to himself and had to fight back a laugh.

"We've stumbled into something big." Bones stretched his arms to make his point. "Like a stealth alien invasion, or a spooky cult, or a government conspiracy. Maybe all three! And someone's always the first to notice when things get freaky." He slugged Kyle's shoulder. "We are *those guys*, Kyle. Like, I'm Will Smith and you're the brainy science guy who figures out the aliens' weakness, and together we blow stuff up!"

Kyle blinked. "What?"

"Will Smith fighting aliens was a whole thing in the '90s. My mom loves those movies. Anyway, the point is we might have to save Langille!"

Whatever was happening, Kyle suspected there was a more logical explanation than a secret government-backed alien cult. But he couldn't help being swept up in Bones's enthusiasm.

"Let's figure out how to dry that notebook," he said.

He opened his computer and started searching. Bones peered over his shoulder. The results were disappointing: According to multiple websites, the key ingredient for drying a book without wrecking it was time. That would take days.

"Ugh," Bones groaned. He glanced at the time on Kyle's computer. "Wait, it's three o'clock? I seriously need to go."

"I'll start drying the notebook," Kyle said.

"Great. Start a list too. Everything we know so far." Bones gestured at his borrowed shorts, which hung below his knees. "And I'll make sure to bring these back tomorrow."

"You can keep them."

Suddenly Bones went solemn. He poked Kyle's shoulder. "You basically saved my life today. That guy and I probably would have drowned without your help. So . . . thanks."

Kyle didn't know what to say, other than the obvious. "You're welcome."

Bones backed toward the door. "Let's walk to practice together tomorrow. But give me your cell number, in case anything urgent comes up."

"I don't have one."

"What? *Kyle*. Even if you're homeschooled, you should have a phone. Tell your mom it's important. She's a cop—play the safety card. You need it for emergencies. How would you have called 911 today if I hadn't been there?"

"Hmm." Kyle rubbed his chin. "That's a valid argument."

"Of course it is. We need to be connected if we're going to unlock the mystery of the Alien Zombie Librarians!" He slapped Kyle's doorframe, and with that, he was out.

Kyle scratched his head. Then he burst out laughing.

He had secretly admired the smaller boy's reckless confidence on the baseball field, but now he understood clearly: Bones Malone was pure havoc. He'd barged into Kyle's house, borrowed his clothes, built a hideous sandwich in his kitchen, and thrust himself into his world the same way he'd jumped into the river: with no regard whatsoever for logic, boundaries, or basic safety. The potential for disaster was high.

But he was fascinating. And he wanted Kyle's help.

You're exactly who I need.

Kyle was going to need another whiteboard.

7.
AN IMPOSSIBLE SITUATION

Leaving Kyle's house, Bones was in his best mood all day. The feeling evaporated as he spotted his brothers on the Spezios' steps. Dillon stood when he saw Bones approaching.

The seven-year-old folded his arms. "Where were you?"

"Stuff came up. I didn't mean to be gone so long." Bones looked at Raury. His brother hunched with his arms around his knees, head down. "What happened? Are you guys OK?" Bones asked.

Dillon kicked a rock in the driveway. "Tony's been a jerk all day. And Mrs. Spezio's grumpy. We hate it here. It's worse when you're gone."

The door opened behind them. Mrs. Spezio glowered at Bones, hands on her hips. "There you are. Where on earth have you been?"

She obviously didn't care to know, because she launched into a lecture before Bones could say a word. He bit back the torrent he wanted to unleash in response. How could she leave his brothers sitting on the step in the hot sun? She was the worst babysitter ever. They were a paycheck to her, nothing more. But he kept quiet, remembering his promise to his mom.

When Mrs. Spezio ran out of steam and retreated inside, Bones dug out his phone. He had amends to make.

"What do you want for dinner?" he asked his brothers. "Let's get takeout. My treat."

Dillon brightened. "Can we order Chinese?"

"Sure." Bones thought wistfully of the money in his sock drawer he'd been saving for new batting gloves, but his family needed this. His mom could stand a night without cooking.

He was pleasantly surprised when his phone connected to the Internet. Mrs. Spezio was as stingy with her Wi-Fi password as with everything else. Maybe he was picking up a neighbor's signal.

He nudged Raury. "What do you say? Some General Tso?" He struck a kung fu pose. Raury tried to resist, but a smile cracked his lips.

***

Just minutes after they arrived home, Bones's mom called him to the kitchen. He'd barely rounded the corner before she started in.

"I gave you simple instructions. Behave yourself. No trouble. How hard is that?"

His shoulders tightened. "Mom, I didn't even do anything."

"No? Then why did I get a call from Constable Specks? You were in the *river*?"

Bones sighed. Of course Kyle's mom called his mom. Moms couldn't let a little thing like a near drowning slide. Moms had a mom code.

"The guy was going to die if I didn't do something, Mom." He tried to keep his voice even. "You're not seriously mad at me for saving someone's life, are you?"

Her jaw twitched. "Look, can you please just avoid any more drama? I managed to keep your name out of the news, but it won't stop people from talking. This town's so small."

The doorbell rang. "Hold that thought," Bones said. He dashed to his room, grabbed his cash, and raced to the door. He returned with two steaming bags of delicious-smelling goodness. "Surprise! Dinner's on me."

He thought she'd be happy. Instead, her frown deepened.

"You ordered takeout? How did you pay for this?"

"I had some money I was saving."

"And you spent it on dinner? You shouldn't have done that, Bones. I was going to throw a lasagna in the oven."

He fumbled, trying to understand why this was going south. "We had pasta last night. It's been a weird day, and you weren't yourself this morning. I thought if you didn't have to make dinner . . . I'm trying to help."

His mother blinked. The house went quiet. Then she burst into tears.

Bones's brothers came running. They hovered in the doorway, unsure what to do.

"Mom?" Bones moved toward her. "What's wrong?"

She waved him off. She tried to speak. Finally, she covered her face and hurried to her room.

Bones followed. *"Mom."*

But she closed her door without another word.

He leaned against the wall. He felt dizzy, like gravity had gone wonky on him. Nothing made sense. Even when he thought he was doing right, he ended up being wrong.

Whatever was going on with her, maybe it was getting worse.

When Bones finally made his way back to the kitchen, his brothers were still standing there, shell-shocked.

"We might as well eat," Bones said.

"But what about Mom?" Dillon asked. "What's wrong with her?"

"She's just tired. It's nothing. Everything's fine."

"You don't know that." Raury's voice was softer than usual. "She's not fine. She's acting weird."

Bones sighed. "I know things seem messed-up. But Mom will feel better tomorrow. Now let's eat."

They sat. Raury and Dillon picked at their food, barely eating a thing. Bones felt the tide rising in his chest. Everything was so screwed-up. He was *trying*, but—

Dillon pushed away from the table, leaving a half-full plate behind.

"Sit down," Bones snapped. "Finish your dinner."

Dillon stuck out his lip. "I don't want to."

"Dillon. Eat."

He knew it wasn't Dillon's fault and that this argument was pointless, but the heat in his chest kept building. He clenched and unclenched his fists.

"I'm full."

"You are not."

"Yes I—"

"Sit down and EAT!" Bones pounded the table. Their plates bounced. Raury jumped and dropped his fork.

Silence. His brothers stared at him. Wide-eyed. Afraid.

They were only worried about their mom. He was making it worse.

He hung his head. "Guys, I'm sorry. You can go."

Without a word, Raury and Dillon fled.

Bones carried their plates to the sink and put the ample leftovers in the fridge. As he cleared his mother's untouched place, he hurled her fork across the room. It bonked against the wall with enough force to leave a chip in the paint and clattered to the floor. He left it there.

In the dark, a mournful melody wafted from a piano. Notes melted into one another like a chalk drawing dissolving in the rain. As Bones's eyes adjusted, he found himself standing in the middle of a cavernous concert hall. Raury sat onstage beneath a dim spotlight. He looked tiny behind the nine-foot grand piano on a stage large enough for an orchestra. The rest of the hall was a shadowed sea of empty seats. Raury's song grew murkier, more ominous, until a low growl cut through the music.

Raury stopped. Even from a distance, Bones saw the fear in his eyes.

The growl crescendoed to a thundering roar. From the back corner of the hall, an enormous polar bear charged the stage, teeth bared, white fur rippling along its flank. Its front paws sent seats flying with every stride.

Bones sprinted in the same direction as the bear. "Raury! Run!"

Raury sat frozen in fear. Bones kicked into another gear, but the bear was faster. It leaped onto the stage and reared on its hind legs, towering over the piano.

"Raury!" Bones bellowed.

His brother scrambled away just as the bear crashed upon the piano. The instrument exploded in a dissonant *GONG* of keys and strings and splintering wood.

Raury stumbled down the stairs at the edge of the stage. Bones reached him and pushed him toward a side exit. The bear leaped off the stage and landed a few feet behind them. There wasn't time for words. Bones shoved Raury through the door as the bear charged. The animal slammed into the doorframe, sending a shudder through the wall. Bones felt a rush of air as the bear swiped at him, barely missing.

The boys darted through the depths of the building with the bear in pursuit, snarling as it skidded around corners and thunked into walls. Bones scanned for a way out. The building was hopelessly confusing, a maze of hallways doubling back on one another in an infinite loop. As the bear briefly slipped out of sight, Bones dragged Raury into a side room and pulled the door shut. The pulse of Raury's pounding heart felt loud enough to fill the tiny storage closet.

"It's going to be all right," Bones whispered. "I'll protect you. I promise."

Raury whimpered. "Don't do it, Bones. Don't go out there."

"Raury, what? I'm not—"

"Bones?" a tiny voice said from beyond the closet door.

Dillon. Why is he out there?

"Dillon!" Bones whisper-shouted. He opened the door a crack. Raury's hand clamped on his arm.

"Bones, don't." Raury grew frantic. "It'll hurt you."

"I'm not leaving Dillon," Bones said firmly.

"You don't understand," Raury cried. "It's not after Dillon. It's you."

Dillon screamed. The bear roared. Bones grabbed a broomstick from the back of the closet and burst out. The whole situation struck him as impossible even as he charged down the hall, thrusting himself between Dillon and the bear.

"Get into the closet!" he hollered to Dillon, then turned to face the animal. He was a boy against a thousand-pound polar bear, but he had to try to protect his brothers. Adrenaline coursed through his blood. The bear swung an enormous paw, snapping the broomstick and sending Bones crashing into the wall. He didn't have time to catch his breath before the bear was on him, one paw pressing its enormous weight into his chest, sharp teeth closing in—

"No no no!"

Bones couldn't tell if the shout or the elbow to his cheek woke him, but he knew which hurt more.

"Ow!" He rubbed his face. Raury lurched forward, shaking. Bones touched his shoulders.

"Hey, it's all right. I'm here."

Slowly, Raury eased back into the bed. Bones checked his clock. One in the morning. He had a vague, sleepy memory of Raury crawling into his bed around eleven.

"Nightmare?" he asked, once Raury's breathing had steadied.

Raury sniffled. "It felt so real." He wiped his cheeks. "It was about to eat you."

Bones went cold. "What was?"

"The polar bear."

"Were you playing piano? And then—?"

Raury's eyes widened. "How did you know?"

Bones paused, for it seemed almost too incredible to say out loud. "I had the same dream."

They stared at each other. *How is that possible?*

Raury's lip trembled. "Is something wrong with us? With our family?"

"It's not us, Raury. It's this weird town. With its Alien Zombie Librarians," Bones muttered.

"What?" Raury giggled in surprise. Encouraged, Bones sat up.

"What, you don't know about the ancient meteor buried beneath the Langille Library? And how, every five hundred years, tiny alien spores awake from hibernation and take over the librarians' brains?" Bones shook his head. "I can't believe you didn't learn this in school. The spores must have gotten your teacher too."

As Raury laughed, Bones threw in some details about how the possessed librarians were amassing a polar bear army, until he was sure Raury was over his nightmare. Eventually Raury yawned and settled against Bones's side. Bones draped an arm around him.

"You know I got you, right? Nothing's going to eat you tonight."

"I know," Raury murmured, drifting away. "You always protect me. The monsters don't come for me. They're always after you."

"Am I always in your dreams?" But Raury didn't answer. He was out.

Bones, on the other hand, was wide-awake. And he had to pee.

He padded to the bathroom. The moonlight cut a pale beam across his light brown belly as he stood in front of the toilet. Out of the corner of his eye, he thought he glimpsed a shadowy movement in the mirror.

He froze. Slowly, he looked again.

Nothing. Of course there was nothing. He shook his head, peeved at his own skittishness. It was late, and maybe this town made people loopy, but he was *not* about to start jumping at shadows.

"I'm not afraid of anything," he told his reflection in the mirror.

Falling asleep wasn't an option yet. Raury's dream dredged up things he'd rather forget, and he needed a distraction. He crept to the living room and settled in to watch the final innings of a West Coast baseball game with the TV muted.

A pang flashed in his chest. He wished he could call Kyle right now. Maybe he'd have some scientific explanation for how two brothers could have the same dream. Maybe he'd listen to Bones vent about how his mother's behavior was getting worse.

Bones didn't want to deal with this on his own.

He rubbed his face. This was no time to go soft. He'd figure it out. Once the drowning man's journal was dry—

Another notebook caught his eye, poking from his mother's purse on the coffee table. With a twinge of guilt and a peek down the hall, he reached for the coil-bound pad. She would freak if she caught him rooting through her stuff. But maybe her notes held some useful information.

He studied them by the light of his phone. But it didn't work; the notebook was practically in another language. He was amazed his mom could read her nest of squiggles scrawled on the fly as she conducted interviews. Even when letters were legible, they rarely formed whole words. She had a shorthand code Bones didn't have the brainpower to decipher at one thirty in the morning.

Still, he picked up a few things. Next to some passage from the day of the library announcement, she had scrawled a note: *???—chk vs 6/18 X stry-invu w/BK.*

She marked that note with a star, so it was clearly important. The numbers maybe referred to a date: June 18, three weeks earlier. He flipped back to see who his mom had interviewed that day, but he couldn't make out anything useful. After cursing her lousy handwriting (*Can't believe she gives* me *grief for my schoolwork*), he searched the *Record* website on his phone. She didn't have an article dated June 18, and her story from June 19 was a breezy piece about preparations for the Langille Jamboree. This year marked the hundredth anniversary of the town's annual mid-July celebration, which would start next weekend. Decorations had sprung up on lampposts and in storefronts downtown. Jamboree chairwoman Brenda Klassen gushed about how this year was bound to be a doozy.

Wait: Brenda Klassen. *BK*. Bones skimmed the story again, but it was so fluffy it made his eyes glaze. Not his mom's best work.

But maybe it wasn't the story she wanted to write. He remembered her editor had chopped two paragraphs from her Wi-Fi story. The "X" in her notes might refer to something that was cut from this piece.

Maybe she'd saved her original version if she mentioned it in her notes. She probably kept all sorts of information that hadn't made it to print. He knew she often poked at a story for weeks, even months, filing away tidbits until she was ready to break something big. In her previous job at the *Express*, she'd won awards for uncovering a federal official's ties to an offshore drilling company and how he was secretly trying to strike it rich in protected waters off Nova Scotia's coast. The project folded and the official resigned, all because of his mom's hard work.

Rachel Malone was smart, tough, and relentless. It didn't make sense she was holing up in her room. There had to be a reason why.

Bones carefully returned her notebook. He crept back to bed with a questionable idea brewing in his head.

8.

AZL'D

In the morning, Bones tried to slip away from the Spezios' quietly, but his brothers weren't having it.

"You can't leave us all day again," Dillon insisted. Raury nodded, quiet but determined.

"I have practice," Bones said. "And I need to talk to Kyle. It's important."

Dillon didn't budge. "Take us with you."

"I won't be able to concentrate if you're there."

"We'll be good. I'll play on the playground. Raury will read. *Please.*" Dillon's defiance gave way to desperation. "We hate it here."

Bones hated leaving them, and he couldn't resist when they both looked at him with puppy dog eyes. "Fine," he sighed. "Don't make me regret it."

He steeled himself as he headed over to convince Mrs. Spezio to let him take his brothers to the Common. He found her sitting on the couch and made a strong case to her: They'd be out of her hair, he'd be responsible for them, and wouldn't she like a few quiet hours to herself? He even promised that he wouldn't tell his mom. He laid on the charm so thick he nearly made himself gag.

She sat, staring unblinkingly at a morning talk show.

Bones waited, but when she didn't respond, he tried again. "Mrs. Spezio?"

She mumbled a "yes," her eyes never leaving the TV.

Bones hesitated in surprise. He'd expected some pushback, because she always acted so horribly inconvenienced if the Malones asked for anything, ever. But he'd take a break for once.

"Thank you. We'll be back around lunchtime."

She grunted. Bones backed away.

The encounter was strange, even for her. By the time he and his brothers got to Kyle's house, he decided it was more than strange.

"I think Mrs. Spezio has been AZL'd," he whispered as they started toward the Common.

Kyle's eyebrows furrowed. "What?"

"You know. Alien Zombie Librarian-ed. AZL'd." He pronounced it like "hazeled" without the h.

"That's what we're calling it? AZL'd?"

"Yes." Bones hadn't really considered it until that minute, but it seemed right. "Any luck with the journal?"

Kyle shook his head. "It'll take a few days. But I did visit Ms. Vanderpol last night."

"Did she tell you anything useful?"

"No. It was like she wasn't really listening to me. Out of nowhere, she told me a boat captain proposed to her when she was young. She loved him, but he wanted her to travel with him, and she was afraid to leave Langille. He left, and she never saw him again." Kyle drummed on his thigh. "She urged me to risk everything for love. Then she started crying. It was strange, and mildly inappropriate. Maybe the AZL Effect is getting worse."

Bones thought about his mom bursting into tears the previous night. He didn't want to dwell on the memory, or the thought that she might get worse.

"We can't wait for the journal. I have another idea. I'll explain later." He nodded at his brothers ahead of them, indicating the need for secrecy.

"I've been thinking too," Kyle said. "We should tell my mom—"

"No way!"

"But she's—"

"A cop. I know." Bones tugged the straps on his backpack. "She called my mom about the river. Mom made a big deal about it."

"It *was* a big deal. You risked your life to rescue someone, and he gave you his secret journal. It's the most unusual thing I've ever seen."

"And he told us to protect his secret," Bones argued. "Trust me, all right? We can't talk about this before we figure some things out. What if your mom got involved and the wrong people found out? That could put her in danger."

Kyle pondered this. "But *we're* involved. By that logic, we're already in danger."

"Not if we keep it tight. We're safe if it stays between us. Got it?"

Kyle wrestled, fingertips tapping his thigh. "I suppose. For now."

"Good." Bones poked his arm. "I'm counting on you, Specks. We're in this together."

Coach ran two official workouts a week, but most mornings he offered to run the batting cage if anyone wanted extra practice.

"He's retired, and he lives in Langille," Marcus once joked to Bones. "It's not like he has much else to do."

Most players showed up for the optional sessions, because there wasn't much else for them to do in Langille either. Bones hadn't missed one yet. More baseball and less time with the Spezios was a double victory.

He felt sheepish bringing his brothers, but it didn't seem to bother anyone. "It's a Malone trio!" Coach called out, making Dillon giggle. And within minutes, Marcus found Dillon an extra glove and started a game of catch with him. Bones watched them as he waited for his turn in the batting cage.

"You're up, slugger," Coach called. Bones eagerly took his spot in the cage, grabbed his favorite bat, and dug into the batter's box.

Sometimes a guy just needs to hit a baseball. For five minutes, Bones shut out everything else and just swung. Coach usually paused between pitches to offer tips—*straighten your front foot, try not to dip your elbow*—but that morning he didn't say anything. He fed ball after ball into the pitching machine, and Bones sent each one screaming back toward the protective screen with a sharp *ping* and a tremor of satisfaction shivering through his forearms.

"I'd better check you didn't bust any stitches on those balls," Coach teased after Bones wrapped up. "You're in the zone today. Needed to blow off some steam, huh?" His smile stayed wide as ever, but the wrinkles at the corners of his eyes said he wasn't entirely kidding.

"Sort of," Bones said.

Coach's voice went softer. "Everything all right, big guy?"

Bones glanced up before returning his gaze to his worn cleats. Coach Robeson was the most patient, good-natured man he'd ever met. Bones almost said something, but if he got started, then he might blurt out everything.

"I'm good, Coach." He tried to sound like he meant it.

Coach waited a moment. "Well, great work. You were bringing your hands through the zone perfectly on every swing. Keep it up."

Bones left the cage and leaned against the fence as Coach worked with Kyle. After Kyle's first three wild swings produced two whiffs and a dribbler that rolled back to the pitching machine, Coach stopped and guided him in a calm, low voice. Kyle's shoulders relaxed, and on his next cut, he sent a line drive through the middle of the cage.

"Your swing's looking good," Bones told him when he finished.

"It's easier in the cage, with Coach reminding me what to do," Kyle said. "I have a harder time in games. The noise makes it hard to focus."

"Maybe you should wear earplugs when you're batting," Bones suggested.

Kyle frowned. "That wouldn't be weird?"

Bones laughed. "You're not a real baseball player until you have a weird hang-up, Kyle. Last year, I struck out twelve guys the day I wore new socks, so I didn't let my mom wash them for the rest of the season."

Kyle gagged. "That's beyond disgusting."

"Yup. By September, they reeked so bad that Mom made me keep them in a paper bag in the shed. Wearing earplugs is no biggie compared to that, right?"

"I guess not." Kyle's shoulders loosened. "Thanks for the suggestion."

They lingered, tossing a baseball and watching every-one else take their turn in the cage. Bones had things to tell Kyle in private, but he was in no hurry to leave. His brothers were happy, and nowhere made him feel more content than the baseball field. After a while, he and his teammates leaned against the fence along the third-base line, watching a crew of workers on scaffolding who were building a catwalk beyond the outfield fence.

"What's that all about?" Bones asked. "Are they putting up a billboard or something?"

"I think it's a new scoreboard," Gavin Caraway said.

"Not just any scoreboard," a man's voice called behind them. "It's a state-of-the-art FluxBoard."

The boys turned. A few of them gasped. "Ray Giraud," Albert Chen breathed.

Bones almost asked, "Who?" until he remembered from the article his mom showed him that Giraud was the head of Fluxcor in Langille. The man standing just on the other side of the fence was short, in his mid-thirties, Bones guessed, with stiff blond hair and eyes hidden behind designer sunglasses. Everything about him looked expensive, from his flawless whitened smile to the Rolex on his wrist glinting in the sunlight.

"Morning, guys," he said. "I hear you've got quite the team this year."

Albert's face lit up. "You've heard about us?"

"Of course." Giraud smiled. "I always keep tabs on the team. I played too, back in the day. Shortstop."

Like me, Bones thought.

"Langille's come a long way since then. Our field was rougher than the moon. I had to guess how ground balls would bounce when they hit the crater behind the pitcher's mound." Giraud chuckled. "But this place—*wow*. And now you'll have the Flux-Board to match. It's fully digital, the whole works. We're going to officially unveil it at the Jamboree Game next week."

"That sounds expensive," Kyle said. "How much power does it use?"

Albert groaned. "Seriously, Kyle?"

Giraud grinned. "Great question. It's a low-energy LED display, and the board will mostly run on solar power. We're working hard to move to renewable energy at Fluxcor. I mean, if we're about the future, we have to think about the environment, right?"

Kyle blinked. "Oh. That's good. Have you thought about wind energy as well? The hills north of town near the coast would make a great spot for a wind farm."

Giraud lowered his sunglasses. "You really know your stuff. What's your name, son?"

"Kyle Specks."

"Specks?" Giraud stepped closer to the fence. "You're one of the boys who rescued Wade Elliott from the river yesterday."

The other players stared at Kyle.

"Specks?" Gavin gaped. "That was you?"

Kyle's fingers tapped his thigh. "Bones jumped in the river. He's the real hero."

All eyes turned to Bones.

"*Dude*," Gavin said in awe.

Bones's chest puffed up as his teammates studied him like they were just seeing him—not the new kid with a wild arm and a big mouth, but a lifesaving hero. Then he heard his mother in his head, urging him to keep a low profile. *This town is so small.*

Oops. Too late for that.

"So you're the famous Quentin Malone," Giraud said. "You must be pretty strong for your size."

"Sure am. And the name's Bones. How do you know Wade Elliott, anyway?"

Giraud straightened the watch on his wrist. "Wade's part of the Fluxcor team. Brilliant man. We're all deeply saddened by what he's going through. Listen, I'd love to show my gratitude to you two. Maybe we can arrange—"

"Ray! What a pleasure. Good to see you, as always." Coach Robeson approached from the batting cage and held out his hand. Ray Giraud took it slowly.

"Good morning. I was just telling the boys about the new FluxBoard. It'll be up and running by the big Jamboree Game."

"That's great, Ray. Thanks for your generosity."

"It's nothing, really. My pleasure."

The two men were smiling, but they still clasped each other's hand, as if waiting to see who would let go first. Finally, Giraud pulled away.

"Well, I won't hold up practice. Big game coming up and all. Can't wait to see you all in action." He pointed toward Bones and Kyle. "Thanks again, you two. I won't forget what you did for Wade."

With that, Giraud headed toward the workers beyond the outfield fence. Bones turned and caught Coach giving him a look he couldn't quite read.

"Gavin, you're up next," Coach said, heading back to the batting cage.

Bones turned to Kyle. "So that's the Fluxcor guy? What's Fluxcor all about, anyway?"

"You don't know?" Albert butted in. "They're world leaders in virtual reality. Have you played *StarClash* online?"

Bones shook his head. "I've heard of it, though." Albert's *how could you not know this*? tone stung more than he wanted to admit. *Some of us aren't rich enough for that stuff*, he considered shooting back, but he thought better of it.

"I haven't played it either," Kyle said.

"It's the coolest game ever. Fluxcor built the VR headset you use to play it and also helped design the software." Albert dropped his voice. "And that's only the stuff people know about. My dad works in finance there, and he has no idea about most of what happens on the development side. He's not even allowed to know. I've heard they make super-realistic training simulators for the military. But it's all top secret. Like Willy Wonka's chocolate factory, except with superintelligent robot assassins."

"That seems unlikely, and unethical," Kyle said. "We can't just give weapons to sentient machines."

Albert scowled. "I didn't mean it literally, supergenius." He wandered off to get in line for the batting cage.

Kyle hung his head. Bones's body reacted even before his brain reached an obvious conclusion. He and Kyle were a team now, and that meant Bones would stand up for him like he did for his brothers. It didn't matter that Kyle was older and bigger; he found it hard to fit in, so he needed an ally. Bones wouldn't let anyone mess with him again.

He thought about hollering something at Albert, but making a scene wouldn't do him or Kyle any favors.

"You ready to get out of here?" he asked Kyle. "I need your help anyway."

Kyle nodded. Bones called to his brothers. Raury closed his book and hopped down from the bleachers, but Dillon put up a stink.

"I want to go to the playground," he insisted.

"We can stop on the way back," Bones said.

Dillon sighed like no one in the world had ever been treated so badly. Bones glowered at him. This is what he got for taking Dillon out?

Marcus watched the scene unfold with a grin. "Some of us are going to hang around and play ball." He nodded toward the basketball court next to the playground. "If you won't be too long, you can leave your brothers here if you want. I'll keep an eye on them."

Bones blinked. "Are you sure?"

"Yeah. No problem." He held out a hand and Dillon gave him a low five. The little boy flashed Bones a defiant grin.

"Fine. You can keep him," Bones muttered. He gave Marcus his cell number and warned Dillon to behave himself. Then he and Kyle set out for downtown.

"Where are we going?" Kyle asked.

"To see Brenda Klassen, chairwoman of the Langille Jamboree." Bones grinned. "I did some research of my own."

9.
THE ENDLESS MARCH OF PROGRESS

Bones led Kyle toward Town Hall. He'd learned from a web search that the Jamboree Committee had an office there. As they walked, he filled Kyle in on his mother's notes. He didn't mention the nightmare he'd shared with Raury, though. In the light of day, it felt silly. Maybe it was just a bizarre coincidence.

Kyle stared toward the river as they walked, and Bones couldn't tell if he was paying attention.

"Hey, don't sweat what Albert said," he told Kyle. "He seems like a know-it-all."

Kyle turned. "Hmm? I wasn't thinking of that." He flexed his fingers. "Well, maybe I was, a little. But I was mostly trying to figure out how Ray Giraud knows we rescued Wade Elliott. The article in the *Record* only said he was found by two boys. It didn't give our names."

"It didn't?" Bones remembered his mom saying she would keep their names out of the story, but he hadn't actually checked. He really needed to start reading the *Record*. "He must have found out from someone else, right? Mom says everyone here gossips. Maybe someone told him since the half-drowned dude works at

Fluxcor. Speaking of, that seems important, right? Like maybe it's connected?"

"Fluxcor is one of the biggest employers in the county, along with the university. I don't think we can assume it's connected, without further evidence." Kyle frowned.

"But . . ." Bones prompted.

Kyle gave him a quizzical look. "But what?"

"You have this look like you're about to say, 'But something smells fishy.'"

Kyle laughed. "Why would I say that? I don't smell fish at all. Do you?"

"That's not what I . . . never mind. Let's find the Jamboree office."

They entered the old stone building and tracked down the Jamboree's headquarters in the basement, marked by a sheet of paper stuck to a half-open door. Bones knocked and stepped inside.

The office had clearly been bustling once. Papers and flyers littered the four desks in the room, and a heavily marked calendar occupied the middle of the far wall, flanked on either side by whiteboards laden with color-coded notes—like a busier, messier version of Kyle's room. But now it was silent. A lone gray-haired man sat facing them, beneath the calendar. The nameplate on his desk read *Walter Boone*. He stared into space, unblinking behind his wire-frame glasses. Bones said his name twice before the man's mouth curled into a frown.

"Can I help you?" His monotone implied he would rather do anything but.

"We need to speak with Brenda Klassen," Bones said. "It's important."

Walter looked at the boys. "How old are you?'

"I'm thirteen," Kyle volunteered. "How old are you?"

Walter's frown deepened. "How rude! Is that how you speak to your elders?"

"But . . . you asked us that exact question. I was only . . ." Kyle stared at the floor.

Bones's blood boiled. He wanted to chew the man out, but instead he plastered on an apologetic smile. "We just need to speak with Ms. Klassen for a minute."

Walter's eyes glazed again. After an uncomfortable silence, Bones coughed. The man jumped.

"Brenda's gone," he said curtly. "She quit. On Monday."

"Quit?" Bones repeated. "Isn't the Jamboree next week? Why would she—"

"How am *I* supposed to know?" Walter's voice rose, making Kyle flinch. "Why should I know anything around here? Brenda was barely out the door before some young punk from Fluxcor swept in and said he was in charge now. Kid was barely older than *you*."

Walter stepped out from behind his desk. He jabbed an accusing finger at the boys, as if they'd plotted this coup themselves.

"Thirty-eight years!" he bellowed, turning redder with each word. "Thirty-eight years I've worked for this town. Not a single living soul knows Langille's history like I do. But does that matter? No! Not when some rich young thing rolls in with his gadgets and fancy buzzwords. It's the endless march of progress, boys. The wheels are always churning, churning, churning. Get on board, or the future will chew you up and spit you out."

Walter drew closer and closer until he was nearly poking Kyle in the chest. Kyle shrank against the wall.

Bones thrust himself between Kyle and Walter. "Hey, back off!"

Startled, Walter jumped. He glanced around, as if he'd forgotten where he was. Without a word, he returned to his desk and collapsed in his chair with a violent sigh, like an air mattress deflating.

"Let's go," Bones whispered to Kyle.

He had to hustle to keep pace with Kyle's long strides as they left Town Hall. Neither spoke until Kyle turned toward the bridge.

"I have to go back for my brothers," Bones reminded him.

"Oh, OK, see you later," Kyle mumbled. He kept walking. Bones hurried to catch up and grabbed his arm. Kyle flinched and jerked away.

"Whoa." Bones stood in Kyle's path. "What's wrong?"

Kyle stared at the ground, hair hanging in front of his face. His fingers beat a rhythm on his thigh. He didn't speak for a while. Bones waited.

"I'm trying." Kyle's voice trembled. "But I always say the wrong thing."

"What?"

"I shouldn't have asked his age. I was only trying to make small talk. But I always get it wrong."

"Hey." Bones reached for Kyle again, more cautiously this time. "It is OK if I, uh . . ."

Kyle nodded. Bones set a hand on his shoulder. "Listen. None of that was your fault. Walter Boone was AZL'd. Did you notice how spacey his eyes were? And I bet he was a kid-hating old crank to start with. He had no business getting in our faces like that. You didn't do anything wrong, Kyle."

Slowly, Kyle lifted his head. Bones stuck close to his side as they headed back to the Common and picked up Raury and Dillon. When they reached Maple Street, Bones sent his brothers ahead to the Spezios' and continued up the street with Kyle. Neither of them said anything about it, but Kyle didn't object either.

When they reached the Specks' house, the front door stood wide open.

10.
CHAOS

Dread twisted in Kyle's stomach. There weren't any cars in the driveway. His parents weren't home. Why was the door open?

He ran, clearing the front steps in one leap. He didn't slow down until he skidded into the living room and came to a halt. The room was a disaster. Drawers opened, cushions stripped from the sofa, books strewn across the floor.

Bones caught up to him and swore in surprise. "Someone robbed your house!" He dropped his voice. "They might still be here. Stay put, OK? I'll check it out."

Bones crept down the hall. Kyle didn't move. He could barely think. The mess was too much to process, an assault on his senses.

After a moment, Bones returned. "All clear. But the rest of the house looks like this too. And your room—"

My room.

Kyle raced past Bones down the hall, barely registering the disaster in the kitchen, the contents of cupboards and drawers spilled everywhere. He stepped into his room and let out a strangled cry.

Both whiteboards were on the floor, along with all his books, his blankets, and the parts from his electronics bin. The bin had been tossed aside, knocking his cello to the floor. His closet door was half yanked from its hinges, and clothes had been flung everywhere.

Nothing was where it belonged. Everything was utter, incomprehensible chaos.

Kyle leaned against the wall, pulling at his hair. He didn't know where to start, what to do. He could barely breathe.

"Dude, I'm so sorry." Bones set a hand on his shoulder. "I'm going to call your mom, all right? Is she working today?"

Kyle couldn't form words. He flexed and unflexed his fingers; his skin itched and his whole body hummed. Tears sprang to his eyes. He felt like screaming, or crying, or both, but he didn't want to do either with Bones watching, so he did the one thing he could manage. He picked his weighted blanket off the floor, crawled into the back corner of his closet, and draped it over his head.

He heard Bones leave the room. Of course Bones would go—what else was he supposed to do? Retreating to the closet with a blanket over your head practically shouted *Leave me alone*. Still, the helpless, out-of-control swirl in his chest grew stronger. He had messed up with Albert and messed up with Walter Boone and someone had destroyed his house and now Bones didn't know what to do with him—

"Hey. Can I come in?" Bones said.

Kyle lifted a corner of the blanket. Bones squatted in front of the closet, at Kyle's eye level. He had come back.

Kyle let the blanket slip down to his shoulders. Bones sat beside him and handed him a glass of water. Kyle gulped it down.

Bones shifted, lifting a corner of the blanket from underneath him. "What's up with your blanket? It feels heavy."

Kyle raised his arm. Bones scooched closer, and they sat shoulder to shoulder, huddled under the blanket.

"Huh," Bones said. "That feels neat. Kind of soothing."

Kyle nodded.

"I called your mom," Bones said. "I found her number on the fridge. Well, I found it on a card that used to be on the fridge. She's on her way."

Kyle nodded.

"Maybe I'd get in less trouble if I had one of these blankets," Bones said. "Sometimes I just want to smash something, you know? Or sometimes I curse when I'm *really* mad. If you want to curse, I won't tell your mom."

Kyle laughed. He didn't mean to, but Bones's suggestion was so unexpected that he couldn't help it. Then Bones snorted, and Kyle laughed harder, and they both lost it. The situation was the opposite of funny—the whole day had been terrible, and now his room was a disaster. But the more Kyle considered how strange it was that he was laughing, the harder it was to stop.

He and Bones had just caught their breath when his mom rushed into the room. She put a hand to her mouth as she took in the mess.

"Oh, Kyle," she said.

That's when he burst into tears.

Kyle could hear his parents in the living room, talking with Constable Whaley, one of his mom's colleagues. He could also hear Bones pacing in his bedroom. When his dad had burst in the front door, followed quickly by the police officer, Kyle's chest started to buzz again and he retreated to the bathroom to be alone. He knew the others were waiting for him, and that only made the buzzing worse. Finally, he washed his face, took a deep breath, and emerged from the bathroom. Bones met him in the hall.

"You good?" Bones asked.

Kyle managed a small nod, and they joined the others in the living room. Constable Whaley explained that they'd already arrested a suspect, a young man who'd been caught breaking into another house four doors down.

"He was barefoot and confused. Didn't even know where he was, really," Constable Whaley said. "He's at the station now, and we're going to try to get him some help." He offered Kyle a reassuring smile. "There's nothing to worry about now. It's over."

Constable Whaley left, but Bones was still there. When Kyle was ready, the two boys went back into the turmoil of Kyle's room and started returning clothes to hangers and drawers. This curiosity helped distract Kyle from the anxious thrum in his chest as they tackled the mess. Bones could be abrasive and reckless, but he'd treated Kyle with such kindness after the Walter Boone fiasco and the break-in. After an exhausting day, Bones made him feel safer. Less alone.

No other kid had ever made him feel that way.

He watched Bones pick up books. The situation made the younger boy seem older somehow: assured yet weary, as if he had experience dealing with catastrophic messes. This, too, was curious.

Suddenly Bones gasped. "*Kyle*. Where's the journal?"

Kyle straightened up. In all the confusion, he'd forgotten about it. He gestured for Bones to follow and hurried from his room, calling to his parents that he needed some air and he'd be right back. They headed to the shed in the backyard. Kyle relaxed when he saw the shed's combination lock still in place, and he breathed even easier when they entered and found the journal exactly where he'd left it that morning: standing upright on a towel on the workbench, next to the shed's small window.

"You left it by an open window?" Bones said. "Anyone could have seen it!"

"This was the best spot I could find for drying. But the shed gets hot in the summer." Even as he said it, Kyle wiped sweat beginning to bead on his forehead. "I opened the window because air circulation helps with drying. And no one comes into our backyard. I was planning to put it away before anyone else got home."

Bones stared at the book. "What if this was about the journal? What if someone was trying to steal it?"

Kyle frowned. "But it's still here. And you heard what Constable Whaley said—"

"I know, but . . ." Bones paced the small shed. "I know this sounds bananas. But we've seen a lot of people acting weird this week, right? What if that person trashed your place and broke into the neighbor's house as a cover, to make it look like a regular robbery, but really, they were looking for the journal? Maybe they AZL'd the poor guy who got arrested and left him to get caught on purpose. The cop said he barely even knew where he was. And maybe he just missed the book because they didn't think to check out here."

Kyle paused. "It sounds unlikely, but I guess it's not impossible," he admitted. "But that would mean someone knows I have the journal. Which means we should tell Mom."

"*No.*" Bones dropped to a whisper. "It means they *thought* you had it, and now they probably think you don't. We still need to be careful who we trust. I trust your mom, of course," he added, to head off Kyle's protest. "But there's shady stuff happening around here, and we need to do more digging."

"What do you have in mind?" Kyle asked.

Bones grinned. "How do you feel about a sleepover?"

11.
SERENITY

Bones braced as his mom stuck her key in the lock on the front door. If his theory was right and the break-in at Kyle's was a cover for someone who wanted the notebook, he half expected to find his house ransacked too. But when his mom opened the door, everything seemed fine. The house was no messier than the usual state of their three-boy bungalow, anyway. Still, he combed his room to make sure nothing was out of place. He was inspecting the corners of his underwear drawer when he sensed a presence behind him.

"Bones?" Raury said. "What are you doing?"

What *was* he doing? Checking if his room had been bugged? He almost laughed. Clearly, he'd seen too many spy movies. He had to stop letting this town mess with his head.

"Nothing," he said. "Let's go see if Mom needs help with dinner."

He peeled carrots and watched his mom closely while she seasoned the pork chops and slid them in the oven. She sighed a lot, and she didn't say much beyond a distracted "That's nice, honey" as Dillon told her about playing catch with Marcus. Bones kept sneaking glances at her eyes, to see if she looked as altered as Walter Boone had that afternoon.

He hated feeling like he had to tiptoe around her. He wasn't sure he could bear it if she burst into tears again. Or worse. He caught himself imagining her throwing a tantrum like Walter had done: yelling, towering over the boys, teetering on the edge of violence.

It was too familiar.

No. *No.* This was different. His mom wasn't Walter Boone, and she was nothing like his dad. It was just the AZL Effect. And he was going to fix it.

Bones waited until they sat down to eat before he asked, "Can Kyle spend the night? I know it's a weeknight, but Kyle lives on the same street as Mrs. Spezio. He can leave with us in the morning. He's pretty quiet, and we won't be loud or stay up too late."

He held his breath in her silence. Finally, she set down her fork.

"Maybe tomorrow. Let me talk to Kyle's mother first."

Bones bit back his disappointment. He hated to waste time when they had important things to discuss, but it wasn't a total loss. She didn't say no. Or cry. Or get mad.

"OK," he conceded.

The evening passed quietly. Raury practiced piano on their secondhand keyboard. Bones helped Dillon build a Lego spaceship. Their mom hunched over her work laptop at the kitchen table, a mug of tea growing cold next to her.

"Working late?" Bones asked.

"Research," she answered without looking up. "I'm trying to . . ."

He waited, but she never finished her sentence. She was both there and not there.

After the boys were in bed and their mom announced she was going to take a hot bath, Bones eyed her laptop. Maybe she'd found something while researching. He tiptoed down the hall and made sure he could hear her in the tub. Then, carefully, he opened the hall closet and rummaged through the doohickey box, where his mom had dumped all the odds and ends that she couldn't be bothered to sort when they were packing. Since the move, if the boys needed spare batteries or a charging cable, their mom always answered, "Check the doohickey box."

Success! Bones emerged with an old flash drive and returned to his mom's computer.

It was password protected, but he guessed correctly that she'd written her password on the inside cover of her notebook, which he found sticking out of her purse. His mother was great at lots of things, but remembering passwords was not one of them.

Bones logged on and searched his mom's documents. After two months at the *Record*, she already had dozens of lists and folders of background and interview notes on dry topics like the municipal snow-clearing budget. Bones wondered once again how she didn't grow bored here, writing about Jamborees and small-town politics when her byline used to grace the front page of the biggest newspaper east of Montreal. But he knew the answer. She didn't do it for her career. She did it for them.

Which was why he had to do this for her.

"Why are you on Mom's computer?"

Bones leaped out of his seat. Raury stood next to the table, as if he'd silently teleported from his room.

"I just needed it for a minute," Bones whispered. "For . . . checking something. Don't tell Mom, OK?"

Raury frowned. Before he could ask why, Bones went on the offensive. "What are you doing out of bed? You should be asleep by now."

Raury dropped his eyes.

"Another nightmare?" Bones asked.

Raury shook his head, his loose curls bouncing. "Couldn't sleep."

"Oh. Well, go back to bed and I'll come check on you in a couple minutes."

Raury didn't move. He slouched, arms wrapped around himself. Bones sighed. He quickly selected every file he could and saved a copy onto the flash drive. Then he ejected the drive and closed the laptop. He could look through them later with Kyle.

"Come on," he said, then led Raury back to bed.

Arranging a sleepover with Kyle turned out to be more complicated than Bones had expected. First, there was a long mom-to-mom conversation in the morning, where Bones's mom mostly said "mm-hmm" on repeat while shooting him a narrow-eyed look that said *I thought you promised this was going to be low-key.* Finally, she handed the phone to Bones.

"Kyle wants to talk to you. Make it snappy. We need to leave soon."

Bones took the phone. "Hey."

Long silence.

"Kyle? You there?"

"I think you should sleep over at my house instead," Kyle blurted.

"What?" Bones made sure his brothers weren't in earshot. "We talked about this, remember? Raury needs me home."

Raury had lain awake for what felt like hours last night before his breath finally settled into a rhythm that told Bones he was asleep. They didn't share another nightmare, at least. But still, Bones was reluctant to leave him for a night.

"I know, but . . ." Kyle faded into another awkward silence.

Bones's mom poked her head into the kitchen and tapped an imaginary watch on her wrist while ushering his brothers toward the door.

"But what, Kyle? I have to go to Tony's."

"I've never gone on a sleepover before."

"Oh." Bones paused, then cringed as his mom hollered, *"Let's move!"* from the front door. "Look, it'll be fine. Mom said she'll order pizza. Bring your heavy blanket if that helps. And your computer and the journal. Is that cool?"

"I guess," Kyle conceded.

"Great. I have to go. See you later." Bones hung up and dashed out before his mom could get mad and change her mind.

Dinner was awkward. Kyle fidgeted. Raury looked ready to fall asleep, and so did his mother. Bones tried small talk, but Kyle was too nervous to offer more than a word at a time. Dillon complained that the pizza's sauce was weird and they should have ordered from the good place instead. Bones wolfed down two slices, anxious to get the meal over with.

He was on edge too. The truth was, he hadn't hosted a sleepover in ages. He'd only had one close friend back in Bedford, and they'd always hung out at Noah's place, never his. He invented excuses whenever Noah asked why, until the day Noah walked past Bones's house while Bones sat in the car with his father, bearing the tail end of a heated lecture that started on the ride home and continued in the driveway. Noah looked away when Bones noticed him, so Bones knew he'd heard. His dad was yelling so loud, half the street probably heard.

They never talked about it, but after that, Noah's house was home base without any more questions.

Now, for the first time in months, Bones felt a particular twinge. Not homesickness, really, because he missed little about his old life, but he found himself thinking about Noah. He didn't have to explain so much to Noah. It was different with Kyle.

"Want to watch a movie?" he asked.

"I have to practice first," Raury interrupted. He sat at the keyboard and launched into his scales.

Bones rolled his eyes. "Fine. We can play catch in the backyard. Kyle?"

Kyle stood, listening to Raury play. He took a step closer.

"You're very good," he said when Raury paused. "Do you have a favorite composer? Mine's Debussy. I play the cello."

"I really like 'Claire de Lune,'" Raury said. "I can play a little bit of it."

He started to play, and that was it— Raury and Kyle disappeared into a music bubble. Bones shrugged and settled in to play Uno with Dillon instead. Eventually Kyle and Raury joined in, while their mom stretched out on the couch with a romance novel. She didn't turn the pages very often, Bones noticed, and whenever he looked up he caught her staring into space. But she was there, and things were mostly OK.

Still, Bones was glad when his brothers went to bed and he and Kyle could get down to business. He led Kyle to his room and closed the door.

"How's the journal?" he asked. "Can we check it out yet?"

Kyle didn't answer right away. His eyes drifted around the room, and suddenly Bones was aware of the dresser drawers he hadn't fully closed that morning, and the bed he'd only half made, and the pile of shorts that was peeking out of his tiny closet.

"OK, so I'm not as organized as you." He yanked up the covers on his bed and sat down. "Focus, Kyle. The journal."

Kyle pulled it out of his bag and carefully opened the cover. "It's drying out slowly. It still needs more time, and I don't want to risk pulling too many pages apart. But there's a section near the front I can actually read now. Sort of."

He sat beside Bones and turned to a page he'd bookmarked with a sheet of paper towel. Bones hunched closer. The ink was smudged in places, but most of the page was legible.

Two successful tests today!

Subject A: moderate phobia of spiders

Serenity exposure: 15 min

Result: Subject experienced normal vitals with visual exposure to Cross Orbweaver. Subject was even able to make physical contact. Vitals remained stable, no outward reaction

Subject B: moderate to severe phobia of snakes

Serenity exposure: 15 min

Result: Subject experienced normal vitals with visual exposure to Northern Ribbon Snake. Physical contact produced slightly elevated pulse and mild discomfort, yet well within normal emotional range and vastly muted response from control study.

Excellent results. Serenity is proving consistently effective. Ready to proceed to phase 2 tests for exposure length vs. duration of inhibited response. If all goes well, we

Bones reached to turn the page, but Kyle stopped him. The next pages were still stuck together.

"Does this make sense to you?" Bones asked. "What does 'Serenity exposure' mean?"

"It sounds like Dr. Elliott was doing an experiment to help people with their fears," Kyle said.

"So Serenity's a pill? You take it and you're not scared of spiders anymore?"

"I don't think it's a pill," Kyle said. "*Exposure* sounds like something on the outside, not something you swallow. Like being exposed to sunlight, or a chemical in the air."

"Maybe Serenity's a fancy tanning bed," Bones joked. "But what does it have to do with the AZL Effect? Honestly, Serenity sounds like it would be a good thing, not a bad thing."

Kyle shook his head. "We don't know enough yet. I think we have to wait until we can read more."

"We can do some other research while we wait." Bones pulled the flash drive out of his pocket. "Did you bring your laptop?"

Kyle took his computer out of his backpack. "What did you find?"

"Don't know yet." Bones lowered his voice with a glance at his door. "It's more like, what did my mom find?"

Kyle flinched. "You took your mom's files?"

"I didn't *take* them, I just copied them. What if she found out something important? Or what if someone went after her on purpose because of something she's working on? We need to know."

Kyle went quiet.

Bones huffed. "I know it's not great, Kyle. But wouldn't you do it if it was your mom, and you thought you could help her?"

Kyle's fingers tapped against his thigh. "Yes," he finally said. "I would."

He inserted the drive into his computer. A window popped up, and Bones cringed. He hadn't looked closely at the drive's contents before copying and pasting. Now he noticed the folder named *Divorce*.

"Everything's in the unnamed folder," he said quickly, hoping Kyle would open it and move on without mentioning anything else on the drive. Fortunately, he did.

"Wow, your mom keeps a lot of notes," Kyle observed. "Where should we start?"

"How about the day of the library announcement," Bones said. "That's when we first noticed weird stuff happening, right? If we need to, we can go back and look at older notes later."

Kyle opened the file. Bones started reading and groaned. His mom's typed notes were more legible than her notebook, but they weren't much easier to decipher. In between blocks of transcribed quotes, she had a mix of half sentences and shorthand that seemed like code. They did pick out some of the same questions that Bones had already found in her notebook—*Cell tower permit? Related?* But they didn't learn anything new.

"Let's try a different file." Bones scanned the list. "How about that one?"

Kyle opened a document called *Water*. Rachel Malone had pages of research on the security of small-town water supplies, and a running list of questions about Langille.

Annual reports missing/incomplete? Inspections overdue?

Bones leaned forward. "Mom could be onto something here, right? Maybe the AZL Effect is in the water? We did pull Wade Elliott out of the river!"

"The river doesn't feed the town water supply," Kyle said. "And if it has something to do with the water, wouldn't the effect be more widespread?"

"Dude, how many people do you actually see in a day?" Bones pointed out. "Maybe more people are AZL'd and we just haven't noticed yet."

Kyle thought for a moment. "That's true. And some people have their own wells, so maybe they would be less affected. I guess it's not impossible."

"Add it to our list of possibilities, then!"

"We have a list?"

"We do now. You're the official list keeper, by the way."

A knock made Bones jump. He gestured frantically for Kyle to shut his laptop, then dove across the bed and shoved the journal under his pillow just as his mom opened the door.

Bones struck a casual pose, sprawled across his pillow. "Hey, Mom! We were just . . . looking up baseball stats. We're getting pretty tired, though. Going to turn in soon." He let out an exaggerated yawn.

His mom gave him a funny look. "Yes, it's bedtime. Do you need anything, Kyle?"

"No, thank you, Ms. Malone," Kyle said.

"You're so polite." She nodded toward Bones. "Maybe you could help him with that."

"Mom," Bones groaned.

She said goodnight and pulled the door closed.

"We should probably shut it down for tonight," Bones whispered. "We can look at more later."

He cleared a spot on his floor for Kyle to set up his sleeping bag and pillow. Once they were both settled, Bones flicked out the light.

"Bones?" Kyle said in the dark.

"Yeah?"

"Thanks for inviting me. I'm glad I came."

"I'm glad too," Bones said. Gradually, they drifted off to sleep.

12.
EVERYTHING ALL AT ONCE

Kyle stood on a deserted road in the dead of night. The grim sky was starless, yet shadows of trees stretched across the potholed asphalt. *Strange*, he thought. *How could the trees have shadows with no source of light?* Their silhouettes stretched in impossible dimensions, throwing off his sense of proportion. He took a tentative step to test if the laws of physics still held.

Smoke rose from a ditch. As Kyle approached, his skin prickled. The smoke poured from the crumpled hood of an upside-down police cruiser, a shell of battered metal and broken glass.

His mother was in there. He knew it with a dreadful certainty that gripped his entire body. He wanted to go to her, but he couldn't move.

"Help!" he cried. "Somebody help!"

The night was eerily still—and then it was not. Day broke and the street flooded with people and noise, dogs barking and car horns honking and children crying and mothers shushing and men talking on cell phones. They jostled past Kyle as if he were invisible. He hopped anxiously, swimming against the crowd all moving in the opposite direction, being pulled farther and farther away from his mom. Each bump from a stranger was an electric jolt. He stood in the middle of a city, surrounded by skyscrapers and sounds of construction and taxicabs swerving through the streets, yet somehow he knew his mother's cruiser was still on the other side of the intersection, if only he could reach her.

"Please!" he cried to the crowd. "Let me through. Please."

They didn't hear, didn't understand. He couldn't make out their blurry faces, couldn't look any of them in the eye. A torrent of details overwhelmed him—a man's bright red tie, the click-clack of high-heeled shoes, light glinting from the face of a watch. Nothing would settle into a solid image he could grasp to ground himself. The mass of humanity hummed like a swarm of locusts. Kyle's cells vibrated from sensory overload. He wanted to cover his ears and hide away, but his mother needed him.

She was hurt. She was dying.

"Please," he repeated.

"Kyle?"

He squinted. One recognizable face emerged from the chaos: Bones, standing at his elbow. Kyle called his name in relief, and Bones winced, as if he had a headache.

"This is wild," Bones said. "Where are we?"

Kyle blinked. It was as if he was seeing a reflection, Kyle realized, like he was looking into a mirror and Bones stood behind him. The glass slowly splintered. Bones's face twisted in pain as the cracks grew. Something glistened along the fault lines. *Is that blood?*

Then the mirror shattered. They were falling.

They landed on a crowded pier on a city waterfront. Voices buzzed in languages Kyle couldn't understand. Warnings flashed on a billboard. Kyle could tell the message was urgent, but he couldn't read it. The letters didn't make sense. He struggled to catch his breath in the smog-choked air. Rain began to fall and the wind picked up, quickly gathering strength until it whipped debris along the pier and Kyle had to lean into it to stay upright.

We need to get out of here, he thought, but he couldn't move, couldn't form the words.

The ocean churned. Suddenly, an enormous wave crashed over the end of the pier, snatching a dozen people into the sea. The remaining crowd panicked, fleeing for their lives. Waves crashed, water surged over the pier alarmingly fast, and there was nothing to do but run. Kyle reached desperately for Bones as they were swept in the screaming crush of people, elbows lurching against him on every side. They fled but the rain and wind pelted them and the waters kept rising and there was nowhere to go. The city was drowning, entire buildings sinking into the sea, and his mother was still trapped in her car. She was dying and she needed him—

He woke with arms flailing. For a terrible moment, he had no idea why he was lying on an unfamiliar floor, and his heart thumped even harder. Then he remembered he was in Bones's room, and sheepishness set in. How horrible that he'd have a nightmare the first time he stayed at a friend's house. He hoped Bones was still asleep and hadn't noticed.

He lay still, pondering the dream. It often took him ages to quiet his thoughts enough to sleep, and he'd lain awake thinking about everything they'd learned from the journal and Ms. Malone's files long after Bones had started snoring. But his dreams were rarely so—

"That was freaky, right?" Bones peeked over the edge of the bed. "Are your dreams always that intense? Whole cities falling into the ocean?"

Kyle sat up. "Wait, you were *there*? You appeared in my dream, but . . ." He rubbed his forehead as Bones nodded. "How is that possible?"

"I was hoping you could tell me. The other night, I had the same dream as Raury."

"What? Why didn't you mention that?"

"Because it seemed impossible. I wasn't sure you'd believe me. I'm not worried about that now."

Kyle brushed his sleep-tossed hair to one side. He tried to sort things out. His dream. Bones in his dream. Waking up in Bones's room, which was smaller and warmer and smelled different from his own (not bad, just different). Kyle wasn't used to starting his day in a new setting and jumping straight into a conversation.

"So somehow, you can enter people's dreams?" he asked. "Has this happened a lot?"

"I don't think it's me. I think it's part of the AZL Effect."

"But . . . we're not zombies." Kyle paused. "Are we?"

"I don't think so, but maybe nightmares are the first symptom." Bones rubbed the sleep from his eyes. "Your dream was wilder than Raury's. That's one of the weirdest experiences I've ever had. I felt like my head was going to explode. It's like my senses went into overdrive and I could see and feel and hear everything all at once."

Kyle closed his eyes. "That's . . . kind of how it is for me."

"All the time?"

Kyle didn't know if he wanted to see Bones's expression. *One of the weirdest experiences,* Bones had said. Should he even bother trying to explain that he often felt stuck in a slightly tamer version of his dream—an overwhelming foreign city where he was the only one who didn't speak the language and didn't have a map? Was there any point?

"That must be hard," Bones said.

Kyle winced. As he much as he hated being teased, pity was worse. *Poor Kyle.* Sometimes when people realized he was different, they talked extra slow or offered to do the simplest things for him, like he was a toddler. He despised that.

"It's just how it is," he said gruffly. "It's all I know, so I deal with it. End of story."

To his surprise, Bones grinned. "That's hard-core. If you can deal with all that and still be an excellent center fielder and investigation partner, that means you're super tough."

Tough? Kyle had never considered himself that way before. He'd certainly never heard anyone else describe him like that. Bones's words made him feel so warm and giddy that he almost laughed, but he didn't know if that would seem strange.

"I suppose you're right," he said instead.

Bones stretched and hopped out of bed. A flash came back to Kyle, the moment that stood out as a different kind of strange than the rest of his dream.

"What happened with the mirror? I think that was you, not me."

Bones scratched his shoulder. "Huh?"

"When you appeared in my dream, I was looking at you in a mirror, until the mirror broke. And it was *bleeding*." A connection formed in Kyle's head. "The scar on your back. Does it have anything—"

"Don't." Bones stood perfectly still, but the air around him was alive, electric, *angry*.

Kyle pulled his knees to his chest. "I'm sorry," he offered. "I shouldn't have—"

"It's fine. It's just . . . never mind. We need to move. Mom hates being late." Bones made his bed and started for the door, avoiding Kyle's eyes.

They barely talked as Bones and his brothers wolfed down breakfast. Kyle politely declined offers of cereal and toast; his stomach felt too twitchy to eat. When it was time to leave, Bones offered him the passenger seat and slid in the back with his brothers. A sinking desperation filled Kyle's chest as the drive to Maple Street passed in silence. He'd said the wrong thing, and now Bones was mad at him.

They reached his house, and he gathered his things from the trunk. When he closed the lid, Bones was standing next to the car.

"Um, hey." Bones pressed the flash drive into Kyle's hand. "See if you find anything else on here, OK? We'll catch up later. But thanks for last night." He stuck his hands in his pockets. "It was fun."

"Yeah," Kyle said. "It was fun."

Kyle heard his mom arrive home from her night shift just as he was turning on the shower. He stayed under the hot water a long time, pondering the past few days. He tried to focus on how much he'd enjoyed spending time with Bones, but his mind kept turning to Bones's sudden shift when he asked the wrong question. Then came flashes from his nightmare, Albert's scowl at practice, and Walter Boone's empty eyes and finger jabbing in his chest.

Trying to figure out other people all the time was exhausting. He wanted so badly to do better, especially with Bones, who was the first person to invite him for a sleepover in years. He'd been nervous about spending the night in an unknown environment, but Bones had been so kind and comforting yesterday that Kyle had thought *maybe*.

Maybe Bones saw past the things that made him different and still wanted to be friends.

He hoped Bones would give him another chance. He'd be more careful from now on.

After he emerged from the shower and dressed, his wet hair slicked back and hanging loosely against his neck, both his parents were in the kitchen. They said good morning and went back to chatting as his father made apple-cinnamon pancakes. They were doing the thing where they pretended not to be intensely curious about his social encounters and waited for him to volunteer information instead. He'd decoded some of their techniques.

Finally, his mom couldn't wait any longer. "You and Bones had a good time?"

"Mm-hmm," Kyle said.

"Did you sleep OK? You felt comfortable there?"

"Mm-hmm."

"Maybe you could have Bones sleep over here next time." His mother opened the fridge, closed it, opened it again. "I imagine the Malones are still settling in. It might be nice to have the whole family over for dinner some time."

"That's an excellent idea," Kyle's father said.

"I want to find out for sure if I'm autistic," Kyle said. He pushed his damp hair from his forehead. "Or something else."

He hadn't planned to announce it so abruptly. Yet as he said it, he realized he had been considering it for a while, and he was certain it was what he wanted.

The refrigerator hummed. The scent of cinnamon wafted through the air. His parents looked at him and each other. After a few false starts, his father found his voice.

"Kyle, did Bones say something? Or one of the other boys on the team?"

Kyle shook his head. "No one said anything. I want to know, for me. Examine the evidence and eliminate any unknowns that I can. That's good science. Right, Dad?"

His mother pressed the back of her hand to her lips. His father cleared his throat.

"I suppose I can't argue with that." He swallowed. "As long as you understand that whatever the doctor tells you, whatever *anyone* tells you, you are who you are and that's perfectly OK."

"I know, Dad. Also, your pancakes are burning."

"Right." His father turned to the stove. He wiped at his eye. Kyle's mother smiled, but her eyes were watery.

He didn't like making his parents sad.

"I also need a cell phone. For practical reasons. It would have come in handy when we found that man in the river. Or Wednesday when someone broke into our house."

His parents glanced at each other again.

"A phone seems reasonable," his father conceded.

"With some rules," his mother added.

"Of course." Kyle waited a beat. "How is Mr. Elliott, anyway? Is he still in the hospital?"

His mom hesitated. He tensed, fighting the urge to drum his fingers. He needed to seem casual and unsuspicious.

"I haven't been able to interview him," his mother said. "He's in and out of consciousness, and when he's awake he doesn't make much sense. He's being transferred to the Halifax Infirmary this morning."

Halifax? Kyle suppressed a frown. There went any hope of speaking with him directly.

"Did you know Wade taught at Royden for a while?" Kyle's father said. "In neuroscience. I remember hearing he went to Fluxcor last year. Who knows what they'd need a neuroscientist for." He sighed. "They've poached a lot of good people lately. Hard to turn down a corporate paycheck, I guess."

"What about the person who broke into our house?" Kyle asked. "Did you figure out why he did it?"

His mother exhaled. "He's a student, doing a summer internship at Fluxcor. Constable Whaley's on the case, but it seems like the young man may have partied too hard and taken something he shouldn't have. He was pretty disoriented, probably didn't know what he was doing."

"They *both* work at Fluxcor? And they both have Royden connections?"

Kyle instantly regretted his tone. His parents exchanged another look.

"Half the town is connected to Fluxcor or Royden," his father said. "Or both."

"I know you've had to deal with some strange and scary situations this week." His mother frowned. "*Very* strange, come to think of it." She quickly smoothed her voice. "But they were random events, Kyle. You don't need to worry. If you want to talk about anything—"

"I'm all right, Mom."

He was beginning to suspect that Bones's wild theory might have some merit. But he didn't say anything. He knew his parents well enough to tell that between the strange events and his sudden request for a diagnosis, they were worried about him. Now was not the time to mention conspiracy theories about the journal. Or Alien Zombie Librarians.

He ate two pancakes and bade his mom a good morning's rest before she headed to bed. She hugged him for longer than usual. His father squeezed his shoulder and offered to take him shopping for a phone on Sunday. Kyle tried to gauge if his father was upset that he wanted a diagnosis. He'd surprised everyone with the request, including himself.

"That would be fun, Dad," he said. "I'll do some research."

"Good man." His father ruffled his hair. "Always wise to arm yourself with knowledge."

Once his father had left for Royden and his mother was sleeping, he dug out the journal. He'd left it spread open under Bones's bed overnight—not the best conditions for drying, but it had done enough that he was able to carefully unstick two pages somewhere near the middle. He strained to read the ink-smudged text.

It's astonishing what Fluxcor is able to accomplish. Money really does talk; I don't even want to know what they're spending, but the results are impressive. Room 2B is the perfect simulated environment to advance Serenity testing to the final phase, though I must confess the possibilities are both astounding and frightening. I'm trying to schedule a meeting with Ray to raise my concerns that we must proceed cautiously. This is a critical juncture and

The rest was illegible. Kyle drummed on his desk in frustration. He reread the fragment, and one reference jumped out at him: Room 2B. What was Room 2B?

The journal wasn't in good enough condition to read more, so he returned to the contents of the flash drive. He still felt a twinge scanning Ms. Malone's notes, but Bones was right: Ultimately, they were doing this to help her—and maybe the whole town.

He ran a search for "Room 2B," but nothing came up. He did find a file of background information on Fluxcor, though. Kyle already knew a version of the story: Fluxcor began as a gaming company in California that branched out into augmented and virtual reality training programs for everything from flight schools to fire departments. Ray Giraud had risen through the ranks and led construction of Fluxcor's research and development facility in his hometown of Langille, Nova Scotia—the last place anyone expected a cutting-edge tech firm to set up shop. Fluxcor bought and repurposed an old railcar plant on Langille's outskirts, replacing a dying industry and breathing fresh life into the region's struggling economy.

It was usually told as a good news story, but Ms. Malone had questions about the company's relationship with the town, Kyle learned. Whatever Fluxcor wanted, Langille delivered. Property tax breaks? Sure. Fast-tracked building permits? No problem. Quietly rezoning and selling public land for a cell tower? Hey, a company as advanced as Fluxcor needed good coverage! They were creating jobs, drawing new residents, boosting the economy. They could have gone anywhere, but they chose Langille.

From Ms. Malone's notes, Kyle gathered that town officials didn't always appreciate her questions. She even seemed to be at odds with her own newspaper on how to cover Fluxcor. He found a note that read *Record accepting free Fluxcor Internet—conflict of interest???*

But there were so many things unanswered by her notes. He went back to the *Water* file and learned that Mayor MacKenzie had refused an interview about the town's water supply and accused Bones's mom of "fearmongering."

Was he hiding something? Could the water really be causing the AZL Effect? And what did Serenity have to do with anything?

Two questions bugged him most of all: If his shared nightmare with Bones was a symptom of the AZL Effect, where had they been exposed? And what would happen to them next?

Kyle pushed at his hair in frustration. None of the pieces came together into anything coherent. He closed his computer and fanned out the journal again to help it dry. Maybe soon it would reveal more answers.

13.
A TRIP TO WRIGLEY FIELD

On Saturday morning, the Langille Falcons faced off against the Cumberland Vikings. Bones trotted onto the field and took his place at shortstop. He tried not to look over his shoulder, where Kyle stood in center field. They hadn't talked since they'd said goodbye in Kyle's driveway the previous morning. Bones had avoided him during the pregame warmup, trying not to make it too obvious. He knew they had things to discuss, and he was curious about what Kyle might have found on the flash drive, but he was worried Kyle would bring up the one thing he didn't want to talk about: his scar.

He also tried not to glance at the stands, where his mom's usual spot was empty again. She'd had a long week and said she needed a low-key morning. She was sorry to miss another game, but she'd be there next time.

She'd never missed two games in a row. Bones pounded his fist into his glove. Nothing made sense with her anymore. It seemed like she was doing a little better when Kyle slept over, but now she couldn't get it together enough to come to the field.

A nagging thought kept creeping into his mind. *Maybe there is no AZL Effect. Maybe she's just falling apart.*

He shook it off as Marcus took the mound. The tall lefty didn't throw quite as hard as Bones, but he had great control and mixed his fastball with a looping curve that kept hitters off-balance. He struck out the side in the first inning, and the Falcons jogged off the field for their turn at bat.

Bones was hitting leadoff, and he dug into the batter's box. He swung at the first pitch and drilled it over the left fielder's head. He sprinted, rounding second base at full speed, and dove headfirst into third ahead of the relay from the outfield—a lead-off triple. Cheers rained from the bleachers, and his teammates roared as he brushed dirt from his jersey, beaming.

When Albert poked a single into right field, Bones scored easily, and the Falcons didn't let up for the rest of the game. Bones added two more hits and scored twice more as Langille cruised to a 9–1 victory.

Winning again felt good—and this was the first thing that had gone completely right all week. He felt even better when Marcus approached him afterward and said, "You busy tonight? Albert's spending the night. You should come too."

Bones was about to say yes when Kyle rushed over.

"We should talk," Kyle said. "Can you come over tonight?"

Bones paused. "Marcus just invited me over."

"Oh." Kyle glanced at Marcus. "This is important," he said in a low voice, still loud enough for Marcus to hear.

Bones cringed. Of course he knew it was important. But he'd played a terrific game, he felt great, and suddenly he wanted nothing more than to hang out with Marcus. He wasn't sure about Albert yet, but he had to be decent if Marcus considered him a friend, right? Bones was ready for a break from mysterious journals and Alien Zombie Librarians and his own mother holed up at home. Couldn't he have one night doing normal things?

Marcus spared him from choosing. "You can come too, Kyle. Let's make it a party."

Kyle froze. "I don't . . . but . . . are you sure? You haven't asked your parents."

Marcus turned. "Dad! Bones and Kyle are coming too, 'K?"

A few feet away, Coach waved without pausing his conversation with Albert's father.

"See?" Marcus said. "All good. We have a pool, so bring swim trunks."

Kyle drummed on his thigh. "Uh . . ."

Bones almost wanted Kyle to say *no thanks*. He'd be able to relax more if he didn't have to worry about Kyle accidentally blurting something off-limits to Marcus and Albert. Immediately, he felt terrible. Kyle was his partner now, and Bones knew he was just trying to help. He couldn't keep blowing him off.

Swallowing a sigh, he turned to Marcus. "Give us a minute." He pulled Kyle aside. "What's wrong?"

Kyle looked at his shoes. "It's going to sound silly."

"Kyle. I saw your nightmare. I think we're past that point."

Kyle exhaled. "I know I slept over at your house, but I had time to plan. I don't know what Marcus's house is like, or what they eat, and I don't know Albert very well . . ." His voice dropped even quieter. "When I don't know what to expect . . . it's hard."

Bones thought. "You trust Coach, right? He's really nice. And so is Marcus."

"Yeah."

"I bet they'll make you feel at home. I'll be there too. And if you don't want to stay, I bet your parents would come get you."

"That's true," Kyle admitted.

"So chances are it'll be OK, right?"

Slowly, Kyle shrugged. "I guess I could try it."

"Heads up!" Bones shouted. He took a running leap off the diving board and flipped in midair before plunging into the pool. As he surfaced, Marcus's sister Shayla applauded teasingly. He took a half-submerged bow.

He'd felt another tug of guilt when he dropped his brothers at home and slipped back out with a quick explanation to his mother, but he pushed it from his mind. He and Raury hadn't shared any more nightmares. They'd be fine without him for a night. He deserved a break.

The night was perfect. Everyone swam while Coach grilled burgers. When their stomachs settled after eating, they took to the Robesons' backyard for a game of touch football that was somehow both competitive and hilarious. Marcus was the youngest of five siblings, and all together the Robesons were a whirlwind of jokes and laughter. Bones grinned as Marcus took heat from his sisters, Shayla and Jayden. They were triplets, but the girls were a few minutes older so they called Marcus *little bro* even though he stood a head taller than either of them. Bones had wondered how a guy as talented as Marcus could be so humble, and now he saw it: His family kept him in line.

The Robesons jumped on Bones too, ribbing him about how much he ate for his size, and his flashy moves in the football game.

"We need to hook you up with the one guy in town who knows how to cut Black hair. You're looking ragged, kid," Marcus's oldest brother, Joel, said, ruffling Bones's unruly curls.

Bones grinned. The family teased him like they'd known him forever. Like he belonged.

As stars dotted the darkening sky, Coach lit a fire in the firepit and told stories about his MLB days while the boys roasted marshmallows. Even Kyle relaxed under the spell of Coach's deep voice and the fire's dancing flames at the end of a satisfying night. Bones felt pleased with himself for convincing Kyle to come. The Robesons welcomed him like they welcomed Bones, and he seemed happy.

As the fire dwindled and they shuffled toward the house, Coach pulled Bones aside.

"I've missed seeing your mom our last couple of games," he said. "Is everything OK with her?"

"She's just busy, Coach."

The surface response came automatically, but something deeper tugged at him. Coach noticed his mom was missing, and he cared. He was opening a door, and Bones felt sleepy and raw and tired of trying to hold up the world on his own.

He scratched his arm. "I think she's still adjusting to the move, maybe. She hasn't been herself lately."

"I was the man of the house at your age too," Coach said. "Not easy, huh."

"No," Bones said softly.

Coach looked off into the distance. "Parents are complicated. Took me a long time before I understood mine just weren't good together and that it had nothing to do with me."

Bones's hands curled into fists. "My dad wasn't good for us at all. We're *way* better off without him."

The words tore out of him before he could stop them. Coach's soft brown eyes searched his face, and somehow Bones knew he understood.

"You're a good kid, Bones Malone." He gently tapped Bones's chest. "If you ever need anything, anything at all, I'm on your side. Got it?"

Bones wanted to tell Coach how much those words meant, how much this night meant, how being around the Robesons was the happiest he'd felt in ages, but it all snagged on the lump in his throat. All that came out was, "Thanks, Coach."

Before he could see anything, Bones heard the overwhelming jumble of hundreds of different conversations. When the world finally took shape, he stood on the second step of a baseball dugout—a real one—staring at a pristine diamond with crisp green grass cut in alternating stripes. Thousands of people packed the bleachers above the ivy-covered outfield wall. Men in blue-and-white Chicago Cubs uniforms tossed a baseball around the infield while the pitcher warmed up.

Wrigley Field. He was at Wrigley Field.

"Whoa," he breathed.

"Uh, Bones?"

He turned. Marcus, Kyle, and Albert stood behind him. They all looked paler than usual—and Bones could see almost every bit of them, because they weren't wearing any clothes. They held baseball gloves in front of themselves to try to cover up.

Bones laughed. "You guys, why—oh!" A sudden breeze alerted him that he was naked too. He scanned the dugout steps and scooped up a batting helmet for cover.

"What's going on?" Marcus asked.

"This is a nightmare," Albert moaned.

"You're exactly right," Kyle said. "I'm guessing it's your nightmare, Albert." He looked around in awe. "It's vivid and lifelike, but it's not the way I usually see things. Is this what it's always like for you? So plain and simple?"

"Nothing about this is plain and simple!" Albert protested.

"NOW BATTING FOR THE ST. LOUIS CARDINALS," the announcer's voice boomed, "THE CATCHER, NUMBER 37, ALBERT CHEN."

Kyle nodded. "Definitely Albert's dream. Fascinating."

Boos rained down from the bleachers, and Albert turned a ghastly shade of green. Bones could practically see his heart thumping beneath his skin.

"What do I do?" Albert looked around, wild-eyed. "I can't go out there like this!"

"AL-bert, AL-bert," forty thousand people chanted in mocking unison. Among the masses, Bones spotted a group of kids he recognized from school. They pointed at Albert and doubled over with laughter.

Albert rocked on his heels. "Oh man oh man oh man."

"Well, we have to do *something*," Bones said.

"Like what?" Marcus asked. He didn't look so hot either.

The Cubs fans grew louder. "ALBERT SUCKS!" They stomped the bleachers with each syllable. The booms reverberated through the dugout. "ALBERT SUCKS!"

"I think I'm going to pass out," Albert whispered.

Bones rolled his eyes. "You guys take care of Albert. I'll pinch-hit for him."

Marcus's eyes widened. "What?"

Bones grinned. He popped the batting helmet on his head, grabbed a bat, and climbed the dugout steps. Dream or not, naked or not, this was *Wrigley Field*. He wasn't going to miss the chance to play here.

The crowd fell silent in shock at the sight of a boy striding toward home plate in nothing but a batting helmet. Then the stadium erupted: cheers, boos, laughter. Bones waved. The Cubs' catcher rose from his crouch and stared.

The umpire scowled. "You can't be out here like that! Security!"

Two large guards hopped over the wall behind home plate and jogged toward him.

"Aw, man. I really wanted to hit." Bones turned to the dugout. "Guys, I think we need to go."

"Go?" Marcus looked up in alarm. "Go where?"

"I don't know! Away from them." He jerked his thumb toward the growing horde on his tail. Marcus and Kyle dragged Albert out of the dugout and onto the field, barely three steps ahead of security. Bones raced into the outfield. Everything felt so real: the soft grass under his feet, the sun on his back, the sound of an entire stadium roaring. Maybe it was a nightmare to Albert, but Bones couldn't stop grinning.

Kyle caught up with him. "This is so strange. I always wondered what the world felt like to a typical person."

Bones laughed. "This is not typical. We're streaking at Wrigley Field!"

They darted across right field, zigging and zagging to avoid the mob behind them.

"If this is a dream," Marcus panted, "how do we wake up?"

Bones pointed across the field. "If we can get to the tunnel in the Cubs' dugout, maybe we can escape."

He veered toward the infield. As he passed the Cubs' shortstop, who stood with an amused smirk on his face, Bones imagined fielding a grounder on this very spot.

"I want your job someday," he shouted as he passed.

Then he made a beeline for the dugout. The Cubs players parted as they dashed into the tunnel. Suddenly, they were in a locker room. Marcus found a stack of towels, and the boys quickly wrapped them around their waists.

"Now what?" Marcus said.

"We wait for Albert to wake up, I suppose," Kyle said.

Albert covered his face. "This is not happening. I'm only dreaming. This is not happening."

Marcus studied Kyle and Bones. "How come you two know what's going on?"

Kyle started to answer, but Marcus grabbed his arm. "What is *that*?"

Bones sensed it before he turned—a prickle of goose bumps across his shoulders. He followed Marcus's gaze to a mirror stretching the full length of the wall.

They couldn't see their own reflections, though. They could only see the rising shadow of something enormous, something hunched and hideous and coursing with fury. As they stood frozen in horror, cracks spiderwebbed across the glass. Thick, dark blood seeped between the splinters. In mere seconds, the mirror would shatter, and the monster would be upon them—

Bones opened his eyes. The rising sun cast enough light to reveal he was in Marcus's spacious bedroom. He could sense from the tension in the air that the others were also awake.

Marcus broke the silence. "Man, I had the wildest dream."

"Technically, it was Albert's dream." Kyle rolled over. "Don't worry, Albert. I did some research on dreams yesterday, and nudity isn't unusual at all."

Albert went pale. "I have no idea what you're talking about." He shot an arm out of his sleeping bag, pulled a T-shirt from his backpack, and slipped it over his head.

"You're already wearing a shirt," Kyle pointed out.

"I'm cold, OK?" Albert yanked a hoodie on next.

"But it's July. It's warm in here. You're in a sleeping bag. And—"

"Kyle. Shut. *Up*."

"We were all there, Al," Bones said. "Wrigley Field. Naked."

Marcus sat up. "Wait, *what*?" He scratched his head. "How?"

"It happened to Bones and me at Bones's house too," Kyle said. "But we weren't naked."

Albert unleashed a muted scream into his pillow.

"It's nothing to be ashamed of," Kyle said. "The article I read said a naked dream only means you might be feeling vulnerable or insecure, or maybe you have a fear of being exposed, but those are common—"

"Would you *stop talking*?" Albert whacked Kyle with his pillow. "This doesn't leave this room. Never mention it again. Starting right now."

The silence lasted two seconds before Marcus snickered. Then Bones lost it completely. He buried his laughter in his pillow to avoid waking Marcus's family.

"I hate you guys," Albert muttered.

"Aw, you don't mean that," Marcus said. "Honestly, Al, we're sworn to secrecy." He looked at Kyle and Bones. "But how did we have the same dream? What's going on?"

Kyle looked at Bones, who shook his head slightly. But Marcus caught it.

"Come on, guys. What are you not telling us?"

After a long silence, Bones relented. "If we tell you, you have to promise to keep it secret. And you're not allowed to think we've lost our minds."

"We think it's the Alien Zombie Librarian Effect," Kyle jumped in. "We call it the AZL Effect for short."

Albert snorted. "Well, I need to hear more before I can promise not to think you've lost it."

Bones and Kyle launched into an explanation of the past week: Wade Elliott and his journal, the strange behavior of so many adults, the encounter with Walter Boone, the break-in, and the shared dreams.

When they finished, Albert rubbed his eyes. "None of this makes sense. Wait, I know. I'm still dreaming. It's a dream within a dream. Soon I'll wake up and nobody saw me naked and it's all going to be OK." He lay back down and pulled his sleeping bag over his head.

Bones turned to Marcus. Albert's skepticism didn't surprise him, but he desperately wanted Marcus to believe him—or at least not to think he was a lunatic.

Marcus sat cross-legged in his bed. "We did all have the same dream. That can't just *happen*, right?" He paused in thought. "Mr. Haddad at Supreme Pizza was acting real strange on Thursday night. Remember, Al? He didn't say a word. We always talk baseball. But the other day it was like he didn't even see me. Something felt wrong."

"So you believe us?" Bones asked.

Marcus exhaled. "Yeah. I don't think you two would make this up. And I know what I saw in the dream." He shivered. "The thing in the mirror. That felt like it came from somewhere else."

"It—" Kyle cut himself off. He carefully avoided Bones's gaze, and Bones knew why. His own cheeks flushed.

Kyle wasn't wrong. As the shadow surfaced in Albert's dream, Bones had steeled himself to step in front and stop it from reaching the others. Because instinctively he knew—

He knew it was following him. He knew it was his to face.

"We should focus on the most important thing," Kyle said, thankfully changing the subject. "We need to figure out the source before things get worse."

"Maybe you're overreacting," Albert countered. "If this is for real, why would it be happening in Langille?"

"That," Kyle said, "is the critical question."

14.
EXPOSURE

After he said goodbye to the others, Kyle was surprised to find both of his parents at the Robesons' front door, chatting with Marcus's mom and dad. The way they paused their conversation and waved when they saw him made him suspect they'd been talking about him. He slipped on his shoes and thanked the Robesons for their hospitality.

"Any time, Kyle," Coach said. "It was a pleasure having you."

In the car, his parents beamed at him.

"Two sleepovers in one week! You're a regular man-about-town now," his dad said.

"I'm so proud of you, honey," his mom said. "You were right about baseball. I'm glad you're connecting with the other boys."

"I had fun," Kyle said. "I definitely think differently than everyone else, though. Did you call our doctor yet?"

His mom drew a breath. "Not yet. I'll call tomorrow."

The car fell quiet.

"Nothing bad happened," Kyle added. "I'm just noticing things."

"What kind of things?" his dad asked.

Kyle knew he couldn't explain how odd it had felt to be inside Albert's dream. The experience wasn't real, but it gave him a glimpse into how Albert's mind worked differently from his own. He could see more at once without feeling overwhelmed, but the details also seemed muted, like he'd lost access to a dimension of depth. The experience was fascinating but unsettling, and he'd been glad to wake up back in his own body.

"I don't know how to describe it yet," he told his parents. "But I'd like to know more."

"I'll call tomorrow," his mom said. "I promise."

His dad cleared his throat. "In the meantime, we thought we'd take you to get a phone. Then maybe we can go for burgers at Woody's."

"That sounds good," Kyle said.

Downtown Langille was busier than usual for a Sunday at noon. A crew in matching black T-shirts was setting up sound gear in the square across from Town Hall.

"Oh, right, it's Jamboree Week," Kyle's dad said cheerfully. "The big centennial."

His mom sighed. "I hope people behave themselves. Harold and Gus still give me dirty looks for booking them after their fight at the lobster supper last year."

"Harold and Gus?" His dad laughed. "Those two are best buds. They're probably telling whoppers together at Tim Hortons right now."

"Well, you can thank me for ending their feud. They're too busy hating me to stay mad at each other. Hopefully, they won't try to shove lobster claws down each other's throats this year."

"You don't mean that literally, do you?" Kyle asked.

"Unfortunately, I do. Some of the men in this town, I swear."

They parked and walked half a block to Northeast Electronics. His dad waved to the man behind the counter as they entered.

"Afternoon, Randy. How's business?"

Randy didn't look up from his magazine. "Good as it looks."

Kyle surveyed the empty store.

"It's the summer lull," Kyle's mom offered. "Things will pick up when students come back in the fall."

Randy grunted. "The new MegaMart by the highway isn't doing us any favors either. I should have sold this place when things started changing around here. Everyone wants the convenience of big-box stores, and they never think of the little guys."

"Well, you've still got us," Kyle's dad said. "We're here to buy Kyle a phone."

"I can help you, Professor Specks." A young woman stepped out of the stockroom and waved them toward the back counter. Kyle knew her as one of his father's students from last semester. Her name was Dara, and she'd organized a campus rally about Fluxcor's impact on the environment. Kyle had wanted to go, but his mom was nervous about him "marching with college kids."

Dara smiled. "What are you looking for?"

Kyle had done his research, and he told her the exact model he wanted.

"Great choice," she said. "That's the phone I have now. I wish all our customers were as decisive as you."

As she walked his parents through the fine print, she glanced toward the front of the store. "Don't mind Randy," she said quietly. "He gets like that sometimes, but he's been extra morose the last few days. I'm not sure what's eating him." She yawned, then covered her mouth sheepishly. "Don't mind me either. I don't know if it's the humidity or what, but I haven't slept well this weekend. I've had the most disturbing dreams . . ."

"Like what?" Kyle asked.

Dara and his parents stared at him. Kyle lowered his eyes.

"Sorry, rude question," he mumbled.

"No problem." She smiled again, but it faded as her eyes went glassy. There was an awkward silence, until Kyle's father coughed.

"If you want to finish ringing my card through . . ."

Dara snapped back to attention, cheeks reddening. "Of course. Sorry. No bingeing *Legends of the Undead* tonight, that's for sure."

Randy merely grunted as they left the store with Kyle's new phone. Kyle's mom frowned. "Someone needs a vacation."

They backtracked a few blocks to Woody's, then took their burgers and fries to a picnic table at the edge of the town square. The sound crew had finished setting up, and a man with an acoustic guitar played folk songs as people ate or wandered through the square. A line had formed at a booth near the stage, where people were handing out boxes. Kyle excused himself from the table and edged closer to read the banner above the booth.

A sleek black router sat on display on the table. Kyle's fingers tapped his thigh. An elusive thought swirled in his mind, so close to revealing itself he could almost physically feel it. He ran through a catalog of details from the past week.

Wade Elliott. Fluxcor. Ms. Vanderpol. The library. Ms. Malone. The Langille Record. *Walter Boone. Town Hall. Mr. Haddad. Supreme Pizza. Randy and Dara. Northeast Electronics. Serenity exposure.* Record *accepting free Fluxcor Internet . . .*

"I'll be right back," he called to his parents. "I remembered something I forgot to check at Northeast."

They gave him a puzzled look, but they were both still eating, so they let him go by himself. Kyle jogged back to Northeast Electronics. Randy didn't look up when he entered, so he was free to scan the store until he spotted it: a black FluxBox fixed to the wall high above the front counter. Blue lights on the box flashed in a rhythmic pattern.

"Kyle?" Dara called. "Did you forget something?"

He hurried to the back counter. "When did Randy's bad mood start?"

She rubbed her forehead. "I'm *really* tired. Why are we talking about this?"

"It's hard to explain right now, but it's important."

Dara sighed, but she thought it over. "It's hard to tell with him sometimes, but I remember he kept snapping over the smallest things on Thursday."

"And your nightmares?"

She frowned. "Kyle—"

"I'm sorry. I'm not trying to be nosy. I'm trying to understand something. Please."

Dara hesitated. For a moment, Kyle was afraid she'd ask him to leave. But finally, she said, "I had a bad one Thursday night. Friday was fine; then I had another one last night."

"Did you work all three days?"

"No, I had Friday off. Kyle, what's this all about?"

Kyle forced himself to take a breath. "Just one more question. When was that installed?" He pointed to the FluxBox at the front of the store.

Dara squinted. "What day did they have the big announcement? Monday? Some Fluxcor guy dropped it off a couple days later. So Wednesday, I guess."

"Thank you. Sorry to bother you. I'll leave you alone now."

He hurried out of the store, back toward the town square— until a sign caught his eye. He checked for cars, then dashed across the street to Supreme Pizza. He pulled the door open and quickly scanned the shop. There it was, on a shelf beside the stereo system: a FluxBox.

"Ugh, not this kid. What are you even doing here?"

Startled, Kyle jumped. A chorus of laughter rang from the older boys sitting along the counter by the window. In the middle was Tony Spezio.

Kyle's chest tightened. Without a word, he turned and left. Another wave of laughter followed him out the door.

He was out of breath when he reached the square. His parents rose from the picnic table.

"Kyle?" his mom said. "Is everything OK?"

He swallowed. "I'd like to go home now."

That night, he tracked the timeline on his whiteboard. It all lined up: He and Bones started noticing the AZL Effect on Tuesday, the day after the library announcement, and almost everyone who'd been AZL'd had been near a FluxBox. Kyle was almost certain he'd find one of the routers in Walter Boone's office if he went back to Town Hall.

It seemed too solid to be a coincidence. But to be sure, he opened the journal and revisited the Serenity experiments. As he leafed through, two more pages fluttered free.

Kyle read them over and over. With twitching fingers, he booted up his new phone.

"We need to talk," he said when Bones answered on the second ring.

"Dude!" Bones exclaimed. "You got a phone?"

"Listen." Kyle dropped to a whisper. "The AZL Effect isn't in the water. It's in the Wi-Fi."

15.
SELLOUT

As Bones watched his mom drag herself around the kitchen preparing for work, he was torn. He wanted her out of her room and didn't want her to risk losing her job, but work didn't seem safe either. Bones hadn't followed all of Kyle's rushed explanation of the AZL Effect, but he caught the most important part: Fluxcor's Wi-Fi was behind it, and his mom was being exposed at work.

"Are you going on assignment today?" he asked. "Maybe you could hang out in a coffee shop or something? Interview people about the Jamboree?"

She shot him a weary look. Most of her looks were weary recently. "You're my editor now?"

He didn't know what to say, so he threw his arms around her. "I love you, Mom."

After a beat of surprise, she hugged him back. She held on tight, and for a moment she was there, really *there*. Relief flooded through him. He was tempted to tell her everything, to let her know her suspicions about Fluxcor might be right. Maybe she'd snap out of her funk and into reporter mode and figure out what to do.

But a darker thought crossed his mind. He remembered her saying that her editor was golf buddies with the town big shots.

Maybe this was bigger than Fluxcor. Maybe his mom's boss was in on it. They'd clashed at least once. He was probably keeping an eye on her. Maybe, for now, she was safer in AZL mode. If she started digging again, she might be in more danger.

His mom let go and blinked slowly. "Everything all right?"

"I'm fine, Mom."

Her eyes went misty. His heart fell as a cloud drifted back across her face. "I haven't been there for you lately, have I." She pressed a hand to her forehead. "Oh, Bones—"

He shook his head. "Don't worry, Mom. We're good. We should get going."

As Mrs. Spezio stared catatonically at the television, Bones acted on a hunch and searched the Spezios' house. He found what he was looking for in the basement rec room: a black box with blinking blue lights, as Kyle had described.

This was why he and Raury shared a dream, and why Raury was also growing quieter and more withdrawn. They were being exposed at the Spezios'.

"What do you think you're doing?" Tony appeared at the foot of the stairs, glaring at him. "Put that down."

Bones returned the device to the shelf. "Where did you get that? It's new, right?"

Tony sneered. "Why? Jealous? Can't afford the Internet at your house?"

Bones laughed. "This was free, Tony. Did you get it at the library last week?"

Tony looked away, telling Bones he was right.

"This thing is messing up your mom," Bones said. "You notice she's glued to the couch, right? Did she move at all last weekend? She might be growing moldy."

Tony crossed the room in three strides. "Watch your mouth, you little—"

"What?" Bones planted his feet as Tony bumped his chest. "Try me, Tony. You don't scare me."

Bones held eye contact. From point-blank distance, he studied the older boy. Tony's pale skin seemed more translucent than usual, and dark rings shadowed his eyes.

"You look rough too," Bones said. "Been having nightmares?"

Tony's eyes widened for a split second.

"You're not even worth it," he spat. He turned and stomped toward his bedroom.

"You'll get rid of this box if you have any sense," Bones called. He touched the router one more time. He was tempted to trash it, but he suspected the Spezios would find a way to blame him for saving them.

But after checking that Tony was gone, he did unplug the thing.

Langille is weird, he thought. *And it's probably going to get weirder if we don't figure this out soon.*

"The Fluxcor Falcons? The *Fluxcor Falcons*?"

Bones pinched the new jersey Marcus had handed him by its shoulders and held it at arm's length, as if it were a pee-soaked sheet he'd peeled off Dillon's bed. The button-up top was a crisp navy blue. *Falcons* ran across the chest in stylized white letters outlined in silver. A fierce-looking falcon's head curved from the flat side of the *F*. It would have looked fine, except for the Fluxcor logo on the left side of the chest. *FLUXCOR* also crossed the shoulders at the back, above his number 2.

A few of his teammates eagerly tried on their new tops. Bones scowled.

"Is this a joke?"

Marcus shook his head. He didn't look any happier.

Kyle refused to even touch his new jersey. "What if Fluxcor placed some sort of nanotransmitter in the fabric? I'm not wearing it until it's been properly scanned."

Albert sighed. "It's a jersey, Kyle. What's the big deal?"

"Hey, leave him alone," Bones jumped in, before Kyle could respond. They hadn't told anyone else yet about their Wi-Fi discovery, and Bones wasn't sure he wanted to tell Albert. "Did your dad do this? He's a Fluxcor guy, right? I saw him talking to Coach on Saturday."

Albert's eyes narrowed. "My dad's in finance. He's not in charge of marketing. Or conspiracy theories."

Bones stepped toward him. "It's like that now? You're going to pretend we didn't all see the same thing?"

Marcus slid between them. "Guys, chill. *Please.*"

Bones's anger cooled slightly—only slightly—as he took in Marcus's troubled expression.

"Where's Coach?" Bones asked. "How could he let this happen?"

"He ran back home. He forgot the bats . . . and he yelled at me, like it was my fault." Marcus exhaled. "Bones, I think he's—"

Before Marcus could finish, Coach rounded the corner and dropped the bats against the fence. He scowled at the boys rooting through the box of uniforms.

"Let's go," he barked. "You're wasting time. Hit the field."

Everyone froze. No friendly greeting, no jokes, no comment about their win on Saturday, just straight to business? That wasn't like Coach.

"But Coach," Bones protested. "What's the deal? Why would you let Fluxcor—"

"Was I not clear?" Coach folded his arms. "You owe me a lap. Want to make it two?"

Bones shrank back, face flushing. Adults snapping at him was nothing new. He heard it from teachers, principals, Mrs. Spezio. He'd caught grief from his father so often it became routine, like brushing his teeth. But Coach wasn't like that. Coach was different.

Or so Bones thought. Maybe he was wrong.

No one moved.

"One lap." Coach's voice was quiet, but thick with danger. "Now."

Silently, they started jogging around the edge of the field. Bones pulled ahead, wishing he were invisible. Marcus caught up with him.

"I was trying to tell you. Today he woke up like . . ."

Bones went cold. "You mean—?"

Marcus nodded miserably.

Coach had been AZL'd.

This was bad. If the AZL Effect could take down Coach, who was safe?

"Is your mom messed-up too?" Bones asked.

"She said she wasn't feeling well, but she's not as bad as Dad." Marcus swallowed. "He's . . . I don't even know what to do."

"Pick it up!" Coach hollered from home plate.

The rest of practice was awful. Coach barely spoke, except to shout orders or call out mistakes. Flustered by his change in temperament, the boys messed up more than usual. Kyle was so shaken he kept drifting closer to the outfield fence, as if he might scale it and run away. Bones stewed. For the first time since he'd moved to Langille, he didn't want to be on the field.

He was still in his thoughts when Coach sent a sizzling grounder toward second base. Startled, he was a step slow in reacting. The ball whizzed past his glove and into center field.

Coach dropped the bat. "Come on! Wake up out there! If this was a game, you just turned a double play into a run for the other team. Where's your head, Quentin?"

Quentin? Nope. This isn't happening.

"Where's my head?" Bones shot back. "Where's *your* head, Coach?"

Everyone froze. No one ever yelled at Coach. Mostly because he never yelled at them.

"*Excuse* me?" Coach stepped toward him. Bones followed suit. They met at the mound.

"Where's the guy who told us it's not about winning or losing, it's about growing as a team?" Bones hollered. "Where's the guy who said he was on my side? Where's the one guy in this town who wouldn't become a total sellout for Fluxcor?"

Bones was aware of everyone watching him, of the *whoa* whispers rippling through his teammates, but he only saw Coach. For the briefest instant, Bones caught a flicker of pain in his face, the shadow of the man who'd been nothing but kind to him until that morning.

Then those soft brown eyes turned hard and cold.

Coach pointed toward the dugout. He didn't raise his voice, but his words pierced like a blade.

"Fix your attitude or get off my field."

Bones balled up his right fist and pressed it into his glove. He stomped past Coach, toward the dugout. "Quentin!" Coach yelled, and Marcus called for him to stop, but he didn't look back.

He didn't even change out of his cleats. He stuffed his sneakers and his water bottle in his bag.

He paused long enough to throw the awful new jersey toward the trash can and punch the dugout wall in frustration. *Thud. Thud.* The second shot left a dent in the green wood paneling. The sound hung in the air as Bones stormed away.

His throat tightened, but he didn't cry. He didn't let anyone make him cry. He'd had far nastier things shouted at him. He'd once taken a punch in the stomach from Jake Volkering, shaken it off, and then dropped the older boy with one right hook.

But this was different. Coach's dismissal hurt worse than being socked in the gut. It even hurt worse than anything his father had done, because this time Bones hadn't seen it coming. Because he'd let himself hope—

Forget it. He'd pull it together and look after himself, same as always.

He heard footsteps and voices calling his name, but he didn't slow down.

Marcus and Kyle pulled up on either side of him. When Bones kept walking, Marcus reached for his shoulder.

Bones spun around. "I don't want to hear it, all right? If you came to tell me he didn't mean it or whatever, it doesn't matter. I don't care."

"I want to help." Marcus's voice cracked. "Whatever you and Kyle are doing, whatever you need, I'm in." He swiped at his eyes with the back of his hand. "That's not my dad. I want my dad back."

Then Marcus Robeson sat down on the curb and cried.

All the rage deflated from Bones's chest.

Kyle ran a hand through his hair. "What do we do now?"

Bones looked at Marcus, who had his face buried in his hands. He wasn't mad at Coach anymore. He wanted Coach back too. Like he wanted his mom back.

"We need to figure out how the Wi-Fi is AZLing people and who's behind it." Bones folded his arms across his chest. "Then we stop them."

16.
HIGH ROAD, LOW ROAD

Kyle paced, shaking out his hands as if they'd fallen asleep. His room hadn't felt the same since the break-in, as if the radiation from that chaotic energy still pulsed in the walls and collected in the closet. Kyle didn't believe in ghosts, but he was no stranger to the haunting power of memory.

Bones kept telling him to relax, which made him pace more, until finally Kyle asked if he could have a moment alone. He could hear Bones in the kitchen now, scavenging in the Specks' fridge.

Marcus and Albert would be here any minute.

Once Marcus had calmed down, looking sheepish, he volunteered the Robesons' pool house as home base for their operations. But Bones insisted they use Kyle's house. The Robesons lived on the hill across the river, and Bones didn't want to be so far away from his brothers.

"Besides," Bones had said, "Kyle already has whiteboards."

Marcus looked puzzled. "Whiteboards?"

Bones grinned. "Trust me. It's awesome."

Kyle wanted to protest, but Bones made good points, and he knew he wasn't going to win an argument with Bones. Now he had to prepare for a further intrusion. He trusted

Marcus, but Albert was an unknown variable. Bones felt the same way. It took Marcus a while to convince them Albert was trustworthy.

"We'll see," Bones grumbled, but he gave in.

The doorbell rang. As Kyle readied himself to answer, he heard Bones greet the others. He pushed aside a flash of irritation. Bones was spontaneous, even in someone else's house. He didn't have to think through the steps of a routine; he just acted.

That's not his fault, though. It's what typical people do, right?

Focus. Kyle had to sort everything in order so it would make sense. He had a lot to tell. Including the latest he'd learned from Wade Elliott's journal.

Albert plopped into Kyle's desk chair while Bones and Marcus sat on the bed. Albert's eyes drifted to the whiteboard.

"Holy Sherlock Holmes. You guys are really taking this seriously."

"It *is* serious," Bones snapped. "You saw Coach. This isn't a game."

"Easy. I'm not arguing," Albert said. "I've never seen Coach like that, and if Marcus thinks this . . . whatever . . . is behind it, I'm in."

"Oh, so you believe Marcus," Bones muttered.

Marcus exhaled. "Guys. We're on the same team here." He turned to Kyle. "Break it down for us, Specks."

Kyle closed his eyes for a second. All these conflicting per-sonalities added to the tension, like particles zinging around his room. *Stick to the facts*, he reminded himself. He tried to explain all the lists and connections on his whiteboard, but the others fell into silent confusion.

$$\text{Serenity (inverted)} \rightarrow \text{enhanced fear response}$$
$$+ X* = AZL \text{ Effect}$$

Albert's forehead wrinkled. "What? Can you explain without using math?"

"I'm getting there." Kyle ran a hand through his hair. "You see, when you're afraid, the neurological response begins in your amygdala—"

"I said no math," Albert interrupted.

"That isn't math. It's biology."

"OK, well, can you try not to sound like a textbook?"

Bones groaned. "God, Albert, shut *up*."

Kyle paused. He found an empty space on one of his white-boards and drew two roads, one above the other.

"I read an explanation like this. When something scares you, your brain follows two roads. The low road is instant panic. You're alone at night and you hear a noise in the backyard, you assume you're in danger, your body reacts." He looked around. "Following?"

The others nodded. Kyle pointed to the high road.

"On this high path, your brain is more logical. That noise is probably just the wind. It's a slower process, but eventually you calm down. Most people do, anyway. But sometimes people get stuck on the low road. So Wade Elliott was working on a way to help them. He called it Serenity—a cure for fear."

"Whoa," Albert said. "Is that even possible?"

"Probably not completely," Kyle said. "And even if it was, it wouldn't be safe. A healthy amount of fear keeps us from walking in front of cars or doing other risky things that might get us killed."

Albert's gaze locked on Bones.

"What?" Bones snapped. "I'm not dumb enough to play in traffic."

Albert held up his hands. "I didn't say anything."

"You were thinking it, though!"

"Well, you are—"

"I'm *what*?" Bones rose from the bed. He stared down Albert, who stopped twirling in the chair and stared right back.

"Can you two *please* let Kyle finish." Impatience crept into Marcus's voice.

After a moment, Bones sat back down. Marcus nodded at Kyle, and he resumed.

"Dr. Elliott's work focused on the kind of fears that seriously hinder people's lives, like anxiety disorders and major phobias."

"So like you swallow some Serenity and then you're not afraid of dogs?" Albert's cheeks reddened. "Not that I'm afraid of dogs. Not really. They just . . . never mind."

"It's not medicine." Kyle looked at Bones. "You know how the notebook talked about Serenity exposure? I was able to read more last night. Dr. Elliott was experimenting with ultrasonic transmission."

Marcus leaned forward. "Like a Wi-Fi signal?"

"Exactly! It sounds great in theory, but the problem is—"

"Serenity inverted." Marcus looked at the whiteboard. "Someone turned it upside down."

"That's it." Kyle smiled, pleased that someone was following him. "Instead of limiting fears, I think the Wi-Fi signal in the FluxBoxes is amplifying them. Among younger people, it seems to affect us most while we're sleeping—to the point we can experience each other's subconscious fears if we're close enough. But the effects seem more lasting on adults. And it's turning them into Alien Zombie Librarians."

"Weird," Albert said. "Shouldn't it be the opposite, since adults are less afraid than kids? I mean, what does Coach have to be afraid of?"

Marcus frowned. "I don't know why it's gotten Dad so bad. Or *how* it's gotten him. We don't have a FluxBox."

"Neither do we, but the Spezios do. Maybe Coach got infected somewhere else." Bones leaped to his feet. "Someone at Fluxcor has to be behind this, right? We have to stop them. But we need to protect ourselves before it gets any worse."

"I've considered that." Kyle picked up a roll of aluminum foil from his desk. "I think if we line our baseball caps, that'll help. I've tried it already. It takes some adjusting, but it's manageable."

Albert snorted. "Tinfoil hats? You've got to be kidding me."

"I can't guarantee it will work, but it's worth a shot."

"This is bananas."

"You'd rather have more naked dreams?" Bones asked.

Albert shot him a look, but he held his tongue.

"Next," Kyle said, "we should determine the scope of the problem."

"What are you thinking, Kyle?" Marcus asked.

Kyle outlined his plan to inspect the shops and public spaces in Langille, searching for FluxBoxes. They could go door-to-door to determine how many families were using them, like the Spezios. In reality, the idea of approaching that many strangers terrified him, but he didn't want to compromise the mission with his own fears.

Marcus stared at the floor. "I can't do that."

"Really?" Kyle said. "I thought you'd find it easiest. You're very friendly."

"It's not that."

"Then what?"

Albert sighed. "You're really going to make him spell it out?"

Kyle looked around, puzzled. Even Bones seemed agitated. Kyle's stomach buzzed. This was clearly one of those situations where everyone else had a map but he was lost.

When Marcus spoke, his words were heavy. "I'm a tall Black kid, Kyle. I can't go knocking on people's doors, asking if they have a FluxBox."

"Someone would call the cops," Bones added sourly. "Or worse."

"But that's ridiculous," Kyle blurted. "You're one of the nicest people in Langille."

Marcus smiled but still looked sad. "Thanks. But remember that?" He pointed to the drawing on the whiteboard. "When some people see a guy like me, they get stuck on the low road."

A somber quiet fell over them. Kyle hung his head, feeling like he'd drifted a hundred miles away from the others. He knew they didn't look like most kids in town, including him. But it struck him as such a superficial difference compared with something like the wiring of the brain. They could sort the world in proper order without getting lost in the details. They didn't have to give themselves a pep talk every time they left the house. In Kyle's view, they were more alike than different.

Bones placed a hand on his shoulder. "Don't look so bummed, Specks. The real problem is that not everyone is as sensible as you."

Kyle looked up. Marcus and Bones were smiling at him. The mood in the room lightened a bit.

"Did you find anything else about the key?" Bones asked, shifting back to business. "The first page of the notebook mentioned getting back a key. Do you know what that means?"

Kyle shook his head. "If Dr. Elliott explains it, I haven't been able to read that part yet."

"Why is this stuff always so mysterious?" Albert griped. "If you're out to save a town from turning into alien zombies, you think you'd write clearly and keep your instructions in a waterproof bag."

Bones groaned again. Albert ignored him. "If any of this is true, we should tell the police." He looked at Kyle. "Your mom's a cop, right?"

"We can't," Bones insisted, before Kyle could reply. "We don't know who's been AZL'd, or who's in on it. Ray Giraud's a powerful dude, right? The mayor and the police chief might be on his side."

"Now we're back in conspiracy territory." Albert turned to Marcus. "What do you think?"

Marcus scratched his chin. "I'm with Bones. We should be cautious. For now, anyway."

Bones gave Albert a triumphant grin.

Albert scowled. "Fine. But we can't run around asking everyone if they have FluxBoxes either. People will know we're up to something. We have to be stealthy."

Bones nodded. "That's the first smart thing you've said all day."

As they figured out how to canvass the town without looking suspicious, they moved their discussion—and its ensuing arguments—into the kitchen. Kyle never knew when to weigh in once they started talking over one another, especially as Bones and Albert continued to bicker.

The door opened, halting the conversation. Kyle's mom stepped into an awkward silence.

"Oh. Hello, boys. Nice to see everyone." Her eyes moved from face to face, landing on Kyle. Was she upset he had guests over unplanned? Happy he was being social? He wasn't sure.

"Hello, Mrs. Specks," Marcus said. "We just stopped to visit. We're not staying long."

That seemed to be the right thing to say. Kyle's mother eased. "Oh, it's no trouble, Marcus. Make yourselves at home."

"Why are you home?" Kyle asked. "You could have let me know you were coming."

This came out more bluntly than he'd intended. She flinched. "I messaged to say I was stopping by. I guess we'll have to get used to this texting thing now that you have a phone."

Right. His new phone was in his backpack, where he'd stored it during practice. In the rush to chase Bones, he'd forgotten about it.

His eyes fell on the brown box his mother had set on the counter. "Is that a FluxBox?"

"Is that what they're called? The chief had extras at the station to take home. I don't know if we needed it, but I figured you could set it up, if you want. That's your and your father's domain, not mine."

The boys looked from the box to each other. They all tried to tell Kyle something with their faces, but they were all doing different things. What should he say? Obviously, he wasn't going to set up the FluxBox. He didn't even want it in the house. But this was an opportunity. He could take it apart, maybe discover how it worked.

"Thanks, Mom. I'll look at it." This was true. He wasn't lying.

Then an alarming thought struck him. "Are these set up at the police station?"

She shrugged. "I think they were hooking some up this afternoon."

"Are you going back there today? Are there any near your desk?"

He couldn't help the urgency in his voice. The other boys did frantic things with their expressions, but he didn't care. This was his mom. He couldn't let her get AZL'd.

"Well, I have to go back to finish my shift," she said. "Kyle, what—"

"He was telling us about, uh, this scientific study," Bones jumped in. "If you sit too near a Wi-Fi router for too long, you, um—"

"It messes with your ovaries," Albert blurted.

Kyle's and Bones's eyes widened in horror. Marcus covered his face.

Kyle's mom raised an eyebrow. "Well. I guess it's good I spend most of my time on the road." She rested a hand on the box. "Should I take this back?"

"No, leave it," Kyle said quickly. "Let me look at it, anyway."

His mother paused again, like she wanted to ask something else. Instead, she set her hat on the Fluxcor box and headed to the bathroom. An idea flashed in Kyle's head. As soon as the bathroom door closed, he grabbed her hat and raced to his room.

"*Kyle*," Bones said, but he didn't stop. He only had about two minutes. In his room he eyed the aluminum foil and instantly ruled it out. Too clunky and obvious. He retrieved an old science kit from his closet and found three thin, flexible strips of metal as wide as his thumb. He carefully slid them beneath the band running along the inside of his mother's hat. He tried it on. The metal wasn't noticeable.

Hopefully, it would help.

He left his room, holding the hat, as his mother stepped out of the bathroom.

She gave him a funny look. "What are you doing with my hat?"

He handed it back. "The insignia was crooked. I straightened it for you."

The words prickled as they left his mouth. Kyle hated lying. He hated how often people said one thing when they meant another. It turned a conversation into a jigsaw puzzle with missing pieces. Now he was doing it too.

She examined the hat and set it back on her head. He held his breath, but she didn't seem to notice anything unusual. Not about the hat, anyway.

"I called our doctor this morning for a referral to the autism specialist," she said quietly. "She thought that was a good idea. And they called me at lunch, surprisingly. They had a cancellation, and an appointment opened up next week."

"Oh." Kyle stiffened, caught off guard by the turn in conversation. "That's . . . good."

His mother exhaled. "I hope your father and I haven't made you feel like there's anything wrong with being autistic, or that we'd be disappointed, because we wouldn't be. Not at all," she said firmly. "We just . . . well, we were trying to do what we thought was best, but things can be more complicated than they seem."

Kyle wrinkled his nose. Her vague language was confusing. "Can we talk about this later?"

"Right. Of course." She paused. "Remember to be a good host. Ask your friends if they need anything."

He followed her back to the kitchen, where she bade the boys goodbye and headed back out. As soon as the door closed, the others leaned forward.

"What was that about?" Bones asked. "You didn't tell her, did you?"

Kyle shook his head. "I just lined her hat with metal. But she didn't notice."

Bones's eyes widened. "You did what? That was risky."

"She's my mom," Kyle insisted. "I'm not letting her get AZL'd."

The room hummed. Marcus broke a tense silence. "I get it, Kyle. It's OK."

"It's a good strategy," Albert added. "If we find actual evidence of a fear-zombie conspiracy, we'll have to tell someone. We need to make sure your mom isn't affected."

"Yeah, we need to protect her ovaries," Marcus said, laughing. Bones snickered.

Albert reddened. "I don't know why I said that. It just came out."

Kyle's shoulders loosened in relief.

Bones didn't give him much time to dwell on it. He stood. "We should get moving if we still want to scope out downtown."

17.
THE WEIGHT OF SILENCE

The boys canvassed Langille using a strategy Albert came up with, which Bones grudgingly had to admit was brilliant. They wandered around town with phones in hand, gauging where they could pick up a Wi-Fi signal. If anyone questioned them, they pretended they were doing an online scavenger hunt. After two hours, they regrouped at the Tim Hortons coffee shop downtown. They unfolded a town map that Marcus had snagged at the tourist booth near the river and plotted their findings.

The news wasn't good. Every street had at least one hot spot. Downtown and the university campus were almost completely blanketed, which caused Kyle to start worrying about his father in the Royden Science Center. Among Langille's businesses, the lone holdouts were J&B's Appliance Repair and Woody's Burgers.

"I asked Woody if he had Wi-Fi, and he lectured me for five minutes that we all walk around with phones up our noses and are forgetting how to enjoy life," Albert relayed. "He told me to go build a tree fort in the woods."

Marcus grinned. "Woody's the best."

There wasn't much else to smile about, though. Bones observed another trend that the others corroborated: Fluxcor's name and logo were spreading around town. FLUXCOR appeared in a larger font than LANGILLE on the Jamboree banners and posters. The electronic bulletin board outside the community center boasted of events "presented by Fluxcor," and every restaurant but Woody's had a Fluxcor Jamboree Special. Even the Tim's they were in offered a limited-time Jamboree doughnut with a stylized Fluxcor logo in the icing.

"I bet the secret ingredient in the cream filling is pure evil," Bones muttered.

Marcus pointed out the window. "Check it out."

Across the street, Ray Giraud walked out of Town Hall with a tall man in a police uniform.

"That's Chief Schofield," Kyle said.

The men shook hands on the top step. The chief headed to the parking lot, while Giraud slid on his sunglasses and started across the street.

"See?" Bones declared. "Giraud and the chief are working together. Maybe they were visiting the mayor. They probably have an Evil Rich White Guy Club."

"We don't know that," Albert replied. "You make a lot of assumptions, you know."

Bones started to argue, but Marcus shushed them as Giraud strode through the doors, pushing up his sunglasses onto his head. He waved to a handful of patrons and strolled to the counter.

"What's his deal, anyway?" Bones whispered. "Why would a super-rich tech guy come back to Langille?"

"To be worshipped as the town savior, probably. Seems like he loves attention." Marcus shredded a napkin to bits as he watched the man place his order.

"See? Marcus doesn't trust him either," Bones pointed out.

Marcus dipped his head. "He just has such a giant ego. He was so mad when Dad convinced the Town Council not to call the Common 'Fluxcor-Robeson Park' or whatever. He wanted his name on it so bad. And he's so petty that now he calls Dad *Carl*, like he pretends he doesn't know his name is *Carlos*."

The boys watched as Giraud stepped away from the counter and took a sip of his coffee. He froze, and his eyes narrowed. He pivoted on his heel.

"Janice. *Darling*." He slid his cup across the counter toward the cashier. "We seem to have a mix-up on our hands. I think you gave my coffee to someone else."

"Hmm?" She glanced at the markings on the cup's lid. "You ordered a single-double, right? Your usual?"

He tapped the lid. "I did indeed. Same thing I've ordered hundreds of times. Yet my taste buds tell me this is not my usual. Too sweet."

Janice hesitated. "Sorry. I'll make you a new one, Mr. Giraud."

He flashed a grin. "You're a peach, Janice."

At the boys' table, Marcus and Bones rolled their eyes.

"OK, so he's kind of petty," Albert admitted. "That doesn't mean . . ."

He trailed off. Ray Giraud was headed their way. Bones discreetly slid the map into his lap.

"Afternoon, boys." Giraud's eyes settled on Marcus. "Carl's youngest, right? Malcolm?"

"*Marcus.*" The reply came through clenched teeth.

"Right. I can never keep you all straight. How many are you again? Five? Six?" Giraud gave a too-big laugh. "Nice win on Saturday. I can't wait till we turn on the FluxBoard at the Jamboree Game on Thursday. You're going to love it." His gaze fell on Bones. "Pulled any more dramatic rescues lately, shortstop?"

Bones swallowed. "Uh, no."

"Well, take it easy, boys."

Giraud wandered off to chat up a group of seniors three tables away. When Janice called his remade order and he finally stepped out of the shop, Marcus made a face like he was going to be sick.

"Dude is greasy," Bones agreed. "He's definitely a suspect."

"You judge people awfully fast," Albert said.

Bones gave him a steely look. "Sometimes it doesn't take long."

Kyle suddenly sat up. "The FluxBoard! Bones, let me see that map again."

Bones spread the map back on the table. Kyle took his pen and drew a triangle near Langille Beach to the northeast.

"Fluxcor built a new cell tower out here. Bones's mom has lots of notes on it. There's also one on the Fluxcor property." He drew a straight line from the northeast tower to the Fluxcor campus, southwest of downtown. "And right in the middle . . ."

Kyle drew a circle around Langille Common. The baseball field.

"Oh shoot!" Marcus said. "The FluxBoard."

Kyle nodded. "I think it's a hub for the AZL Effect. When it turns on—"

Bones leaned over the table. "What if it's already on? Think about it. We had a shared nightmare after our game on Saturday. Coach is AZL'd. The field is the one place we all could have been exposed."

"You're right," Kyle said. "It's probably affecting us already. But whatever it's doing, I think it's about to get worse at the Jamboree Game." He stiffened. His eyes shifted around the restaurant. "Wait. Do you feel that? Do you hear it?"

"Hear what?" Bones wasn't sure why, but he matched Kyle's whisper. "I don't hear anything."

"That's the thing." Kyle whispered, fingers drumming on the table. "It's too quiet."

They listened. The tinny strains of a country tune wafted from the sound system, but otherwise the half-full shop had fallen silent. Every conversation ceased. No one moved.

Then, in the same instant, all the adult customers lifted their coffee cups, took a sip, and set them back on their tables in perfect unison.

Bones shivered.

Two seconds later, the spell broke. People blinked. Some touched their heads. Chatter resumed, hesitant at first, as if no one could quite recover their train of thought.

Albert hunched over the table. "That. Was. *Freaky*. Can we get out of here?"

Marcus rose. "Gladly."

Bones looked out the window. Giraud slipped into another shop a few doors away. As he entered, Bones thought he saw the man smiling.

An impulsive thought grabbed him. "We should split up again. Let's catch up later."

Marcus gave him a funny look. "Bones, what—"

"Later." He was already on his way out the door.

Bones leaned against a wall a safe distance away and pretended to be absorbed in his phone as Ray Giraud emerged from a real estate office, whistling. The businessman continued down Front Street and ducked into the post office.

What is he up to?

Bones moved closer to the real estate office. He pretended to study the listings posted in the window as he peered inside. But with the glare of the sun, he could only see the shape of a receptionist sitting behind a desk. He thought about finding some excuse to slip inside and see if the woman seemed AZL'd, but he hesitated. When the boys had covered the town, Bones had avoided this block on purpose.

His father had sold houses. He'd worked constantly and taken calls at all hours. He could speak in a cheery, professional tone to a client on the phone even as he shot a furious glare at one of the boys for making too much noise. Then, as soon as the call ended, the pleasant pretense vanished.

"Thinking of buying a house, are you?"

Startled, Bones turned. An elderly man with a British accent smiled at him, not unkindly. Bones mumbled he was just daydreaming and moved on. Out of the corner of his eye, he noticed Giraud leave the post office and cross the street to the Save-Easy.

Surely a zillionaire didn't buy his own groceries. He had to be up to something. Bones waited a beat before he followed him into the air-conditioned supermarket. The Save-Easy was just big enough that he could trail at a distance without seeming too suspicious. He picked up a copy of *Sports Illustrated* off the magazine rack as a cover. He browsed the aisles, trying to keep tabs on Giraud. The man wandered briefly, flashing his megawatt smile at anyone who recognized him. As he passed the butcher's counter, he looked upward. Bones followed his gaze to a black box with a blinking blue light, nestled in the beams of the ceiling. When Bones looked down again, Giraud was slipping through a door marked *Store Personnel Only*. Bones crept closer. He slid his foot in the door before it shut. After a pause, he opened it far enough to poke his head in. Giraud was climbing a set of stairs at the end of a hallway.

Bones was tempted to follow, but he hung back. He had no idea what might be upstairs and whether he'd have any cover or escape route. Reluctantly, he let the door close. He paced the meat section, feigning interest in brands of bacon and hoping he didn't look sketchy.

Then his neck prickled with a sense of déjà vu. A moment later, all movement and chatter ceased. Everything was dead silent except for the hum of the fluorescent lights. To Bones's left, a woman with a package of hot dogs in her hand stood perfectly still, staring blankly at him. A single tear dribbled down her cheek.

Almost as soon as it began, the moment passed. Cart wheels squeaked as people resumed shopping. The woman blinked. She set down the hot dogs, frowned, then picked them up again and placed them in her cart.

Bones shuddered. No one acknowledged the eerie moment. He scratched his head and felt the crinkle of foil in his baseball cap. Maybe Kyle's protection was working. Maybe he was the only person in the store unaffected.

As he thought it, Giraud emerged, whistling. Bones doubled back, dropped the magazine in a bin of discounted deodorant, and made for the exit. He heard a woman calling, "Hey, you!" behind him, but he didn't pay attention until a security guard stepped in front of the doors, blocking his path.

"Hold up, son," the man said sternly.

Bones frowned. "Why?"

"You stole a magazine. I saw you." The woman who had been shouting caught up and stood beside the security guard, hands on her hips. She wore a yellow cardigan over her red Save-Easy T-shirt and glared down at him behind her crooked glasses. "You kids always think you can get away with it. But not today! Not on my watch."

Heat rose in Bones's chest. "I didn't take anything. I picked it up, but I changed my mind." He spread his arms wide. "Where am I going to put a magazine?"

The woman glared. "I bet you tucked it into your shorts. Lift up your shirt."

"What? No." Bones folded his arms.

Her face went red. "We can either do this here or in the manager's office."

Passing shoppers, all of them white, stopped and gawked. A man in suspenders whispered to his wife. She stared at Bones and clucked disapprovingly. Bones felt their judgment sink in like it was being tattooed on his brown skin.

"I'm not a thief," he said, trying to keep his voice calm.

"I saw you too." The woman with the hot dogs spoke up. "You had a magazine."

They all stared at Bones with vacant, half-focused eyes, like they were looking through him. He pinched his own leg to make sure this wasn't all just a bad dream. But it was all too real.

"I had a magazine, but I put it down. I could show you where it is. I never—"

"You calling her a liar?" Suspenders Man growled. "I don't like your attitude, boy. You're not from around here, are you?"

The security guard stepped closer. "Just hand over the magazine, kid."

"I don't have it! You're all brainwashed!" Bones threw his arms in the air in frustration. Half the crowd recoiled. One person even screamed. The guard's eyes bulged.

"We have a thief, possibly dangerous!" he shouted into the radio pinned to his collar. He lunged. Bones saw it coming and sidestepped. The man tumbled to the floor. Bones tried to break for the exit, but Suspenders Man and two others blocked the doors with their carts. Bones turned and ran back through the store.

He sprinted down the pasta aisle with a mob on his heels. A man in a Save-Easy shirt jumped out at the end of the aisle and braced as Bones approached. Without breaking stride, Bones snagged a package of linguine off the shelf and threw the hardest fastball he could manage. It struck the man in the chin and he staggered backward with a yelp. Bones dashed past him. He skidded around a cooler full of discount margarine and stopped. Suspenders Man approached from his left. Bones turned, but the crowd had split in half and was closing in from both sides.

His mind raced. *How is this real? Langille was supposed to be quiet and boring. Not a place where a horde of zombie-brained white folks mobs me in the grocery store.*

"Stop!" he pleaded, backing toward the cooler. "I didn't take the stupid magazine! You've all gone loopy because of—"

The group pounced. A hand knocked his hat off his head. Another grabbed the collar of his T-shirt. On instinct, Bones dropped to the floor and slid right out of his shirt. He scooped up his baseball cap and crawled through the jumble of legs. The mob piled on with such frenzy that they didn't notice he'd slipped away.

He hurried toward a set of swinging doors near the bakery. Behind him, he heard the *SSSSKRTCH* of ripping fabric as the frenzied horde tore his shirt to pieces.

Bones slipped through the doors, bolted past a startled baker, and crashed out of a service exit. He leaned against the building, catching his breath.

"Running shirtless through the Save-Easy? You lose a bet or something?"

Ray Giraud stood ten feet away in the alley behind the grocery store, smoking a cigarette.

Bones swallowed hard and tried to compose himself. "Something like that."

Giraud laughed. He dropped the cigarette butt and crushed it beneath his polished leather shoe. "Don't tell anyone. Dirty secret of mine." He popped a candy in his mouth and extended the package to Bones. "Mint?"

Bones shook his head. He turned to leave.

"I like watching you play, Quentin," Giraud said. "You've got a nice swing, and a killer arm. Scrappy too. I like scrappy." He chuckled again. "But you and that long-haired Specks kid think you're a regular couple of Hardy Boys, don't you? I heard you stopped by the library and Town Hall, asking questions."

Bones tried to keep his face even. Was Giraud watching them?

"Shame about Wade, by the way." Giraud shook his head. "Brilliant man. Or he was, until his mind turned on him. Doesn't look good, unfortunately." He inched closer. "He say anything when you hauled him out of the river?"

Alarms sounded in Bones's head. Giraud definitely knew more than he was letting on. Did he know about the journal? Maybe he *was* behind the break-in at Kyle's house. But Bones couldn't accuse him, or he'd give himself away.

Bones kept his face stony. "Like you said, dude was a mess. He kind of mumbled a bit, but none of it made any sense."

"Huh." Giraud's face tightened. "Well, if anything comes to mind—"

"I already told the police all I know," Bones said. "I should really catch up with my friends. Nice seeing you, Mr. Giraud."

He'd taken two steps away when the man spoke again.

"Your mom's a smart lady. Asks tough questions. Too talented to be working at a rag like the *Record*, if you ask me." His razor-like grin returned. "How is she, anyway? I didn't see her at the ballpark the other day. I hope she'll be able to come out to the Jamboree Game."

Bones's senses sharpened. The remark felt like a threat: a subtle one—Giraud chose his words carefully—but a threat nonetheless.

"My mom's fine," he said, icy cool in his words. "She just was feeling sick—picked up the flu or something. Seems to be going around. But she'll be fine. She's got me to take care of her."

Giraud chuckled. He started down the alley in Bones's direction. Bones held his ground as the man passed and patted him on the shoulder.

"You seem like a good kid," he said, close enough for Bones to smell the nicotine and spearmint on his breath. "Stick to baseball, eh? Go easy on your poor mom's nerves."

Bones waited until the man released his arm before he clenched his fists. Giraud rounded the corner and disappeared.

When he was gone, Bones pulled out his phone and texted Kyle, Marcus, and Albert.

We can't let that FluxBoard go live. We have to stop it before the game.

18.
OPERATION SABOTAGE

Albert folded his arms. "No way. Not unless someone can explain how we won't get arrested for this."

Bones scowled. The Jamboree Game was two days away. They'd been arguing in the Robesons' pool house for an hour over what to do about the FluxBoard, and they were still stuck. Bones wanted to scale the board in the dead of night and figure out how to disable it. But even after he described how he'd been mobbed the previous afternoon, Albert still wouldn't budge, and Bones could tell the others weren't totally on his side either.

"Come on, Kyle," he insisted. "You took apart the box your mom brought home yesterday, right? You know this is our best chance to stop the FluxBoard."

Kyle fidgeted. "I don't know," he mumbled.

"Maybe we could disconnect the power source," Marcus offered.

"They'd fix that in thirty seconds," Bones shot back.

"And if we vandalize it, they'll know it was us in thirty seconds," Albert said. "For how expensive it is, there has to be a camera up there or something."

Bones shrugged. "That's a risk I'm willing to take."

Albert rolled his eyes. "Are there any risks you *aren't* willing to take?"

"Albert, easy," Marcus cautioned.

A familiar heat built in Bones's chest. He clenched and unclenched his fists. He was sick of talking. None of them were taking this seriously enough. None of them had been chased by a horde of zombies through the Save-Easy. None of them had to watch their only reliable parent fall apart. He had to get out of the room before he said or did something he'd end up regretting later.

"I'm going for a walk," he announced. "I need some air. Alone."

Before he reached the door, Kyle stood up. "I'm scared, Bones."

Bones stopped. "What?"

Kyle pushed his hair from his face. "You're right. We have to stop the FluxBoard. And the best way to stop it is at the source, like you said. But I'm scared. I don't like heights. I don't want to go up there. And I'm scared of getting caught."

Kyle's confession sucked all the pent-up heat out of the room. The boys fidgeted, not quite meeting one another's eyes.

"Yeah, me too," Marcus admitted. "Obviously I want to stop the AZL Effect and help Dad, but . . . I'm scared too."

Bones looked at Albert. Albert's cheeks reddened.

"I already told you I don't want to go to jail," he mumbled.

"We're not as fearless as you, Bones," Kyle said.

Bones exhaled. He sank into an armchair in the corner. "Look, I'm scared too, OK? You think I'd be doing this if I wasn't afraid of what's happening to my mom? If I wasn't worried about Raury?

Moving here was supposed to make things better. We were supposed to be safe, away from Dad. But now it's all a mess."

Kyle let out a tight breath. "Your scar is from your dad, isn't it?"

Rage surged in Bones's belly. Kyle was bringing that up *now*? He almost snapped, but he stopped. Kyle had risked telling him the truth about his own fear. Kyle always told him the truth.

Bones sighed. "Yeah. I told you, my dad's the worst. He didn't like me very much."

He couldn't explain why he kept talking. He usually hated telling the story. He hardly told anyone. Maybe it was the way Kyle looked at him, or how Marcus crossed the room and put a hand on his shoulder. But he let himself recall how his father had changed most nights after his mom left for the evening shift at the *Express*. The smallest grievances set him off: Muddy cleats in the foyer. Milk left on the counter. Homework—always homework. Bones was never smart enough, never tried hard enough, never did anything right. One night when he was ten, Bones had enough of the yelling and yelled right back. His father's face went lava-red, and his hand lashed out before Bones could duck.

Bones told them the truth, strange as it seemed: That was the night he decided he couldn't afford to be afraid anymore. He made his choice. It would always be him, never Raury or Dillon. If his father so much as glared at his brothers, Bones stepped in like a lightning rod. Said something. Broke something. Whatever it took to redirect his father's wrath.

He never told anyone—especially not his mother. It could never be her either. It was the only way he knew how to protect his family, until it no longer worked.

The beginning of the end had come a year ago. He'd heard his father yelling at Raury after his bath. Bones raced down the hall and shoved his father so hard he fell in the still-draining tub, bringing the shower curtain down on his head. Arnold Emmerson climbed from the mess and hurled Bones into the mirror. It shattered, slicing his back open. In a panic, Dillon ran outside screaming. The neighbors called 911.

At the hospital, as a doctor stitched his shoulder and a police officer asked him questions and his mother hurried into the room and immediately burst into tears, Bones made another choice. He knew that if he intervened with his father again, the ending would likely be worse. So he told the officer enough, and the police arrested his father.

"Did he go to jail?" Kyle asked.

Bones shook his head. "Not right away."

His father was a well-connected man with an experienced lawyer. A judge granted him bail and ordered him to stay away from his family. He heeded the order for three nights. On the fourth, he showed up, stumbling and slurring, and set the house on fire.

I built this life for you, he raged. *I gave you everything. I can take it all away.*

Bones could still smell charred wood and melting plastic, feel the heat, hear the crackle of flames and his mom's panicked cries. Even just the memory made his heart pound. As his mom guided his brothers through the smoke, Bones's fear of losing them hardened into fury. Without thinking, he grabbed a baseball. He veered from his family in the yard and stalked down the driveway toward his father. When the man rushed at him, Bones wound up and drilled him in the forehead with a fastball. His father crumpled.

This time, his father didn't make bail. At the trial, a judge gave him a sentence that would keep him locked up for years, until Bones was an adult. Bones's mom filed for divorce, returned to her maiden name, and decided it was time to start over somewhere new.

When Bones finished telling the story, the air had changed. He felt both lighter and more exposed, as if he'd shed some weight he wasn't sure he'd been ready to give up.

"Oh, Bones," Marcus said softly. "I can't even imagine."

"No kidding," Albert added. "Your dad sounds like a monster."

Bones winced. He didn't want pity. He'd hated the *you poor kid* looks, the soothing consolations of counselors who expected him to crumble. That wasn't how he rolled.

He coughed awkwardly. "Story time's over."

Kyle was still watching him. "You are definitely the most interesting person I know," he said.

Bones laughed. Only Kyle would react that way, and it was the only reaction he'd ever received that didn't make him squirm. "You're the best, Specks."

Kyle blinked. "Really?"

"Yes, really. Now, are we going to blow up the FluxBoard or what?"

"We're not going to make it explode," Kyle said. "That would be too dangerous."

Bones looked around. "But we *are* going ahead with Operation Sabotage?"

"That's a useless code name," Albert scoffed. "We might as well call it *Operation Look We're Doing a Crime*."

"But we're in," Marcus said. "Right, Albert?"

He sighed. "Yeah, we're in."

They regrouped at the field at midnight and huddled by the trees beyond the left-field fence to go over their roles. Bones and Kyle would tackle the FluxBoard while Marcus broke into the scorer's booth to deal with the control panel, and Albert would serve as lookout.

"You sure you want to go up?" Bones asked Kyle.

Kyle let out a shaky breath. "I have to. I took our FluxBox apart. I'm the only one who knows how it works."

"You could tell me what to do over the radio," Bones offered.

"I don't think I could explain it without seeing it. My brain doesn't work that way."

Marcus handed out a set of two-way radios. "My sisters are a few blocks away, keeping an eye out for us too."

Bones's eyes widened. "You told your sisters?"

Marcus lowered his head. "I had to. They know something's wrong with Dad, and they wanted to help. And they have triplet powers, man. I can't keep secrets from them!"

"They'd better not tell anyone else," Bones said. "Come on, let's move."

Albert went to find a sheltered lookout spot, while Marcus headed for the clubhouse. Bones gestured to the metal ladder attached to one of the FluxBoard's support poles.

"After you," he said to Kyle.

Kyle nodded, swallowing. He was pale and trembling, Bones noted with alarm. But he started up the ladder. Near the top, his foot slipped. He caught himself and hugged the ladder. But he advanced no farther.

"You all right?" Bones asked.

"I can't do this," Kyle whispered.

"Yes, you can. Don't panic."

Kyle didn't move. He rested his forehead against a rung. Bones could hear his labored breathing.

The radio crackled. "How's it going?" Marcus asked.

"Not great," Bones answered. He had to do something.

"Thirty-eight," he called to Kyle.

Kyle squinted down at him. "What?"

"That's how many stitches it took. For my back."

Kyle's eyes opened wider. "Did it hurt?"

"Of course it hurt." Bones grinned. "And it looked so bad. I told the kids at school that I got attacked by a bear."

"Did they believe you?"

"No."

Kyle went *heh*. With a deep breath, he climbed the last few rungs of the ladder and crawled onto the catwalk. Bones scrambled up the ladder and sat beside him.

"You good?" he asked.

After a moment, Kyle nodded. "Thanks. Your story helped."

Bones held a flashlight as Kyle opened his backpack and pulled out a cordless drill to remove the panel on the FluxBoard. Once it was off, Kyle studied the wiring inside.

"Hmm. This is more complicated than the FluxBox." He stuck his head inside the guts of the FluxBoard. "I'm not sure I can reach the signal emission unit. My plan was to disable it while leaving the rest of the scoreboard intact, but—"

The radio crackled. "Shayla just texted," Marcus said. "A police car is turning off Church Street, heading this way."

"We need to go to Plan B," Bones said. "Just cut the wires."

Kyle sighed. "Pass me the needle-nose pliers from my bag."

"Oh *crap*!" Albert's frantic whisper shot through the radio. "That cop car just turned in to the parking lot. Everybody hide!"

Kyle went stiff. "Be cool," Bones said. "I'll yank a couple wires and we'll be done." He took the pliers and stuck his arm inside the FluxBoard.

"Bones, wait. If you cut yellow first—"

"Yellow? Got it."

"No, *don't*!"

Bones attacked the thickest yellow wire he could find. The board went *CRACK!* and a shower of sparks flashed in his face. The shock tossed him backward, over the waist-high railing.

He was falling.

A hand closed around his left wrist. Kyle cried out as Bones's weight and momentum slammed him into the railing, but he held on. Bones dangled in midair for a dizzying second before his right hand found the rail of the ladder. Once he planted his feet on the ladder, he let go of Kyle's hand. Kyle fell to his knees. Bones scrambled back to the catwalk.

"Are you all right?" he asked.

Kyle shook his head, too rattled to speak.

Bones slumped beside him. "You saved me from a few broken bones, at least. But you really should have worded your warning differently."

Albert squealed in the radio. "Whatever you just did, the cop saw it. He's coming your way!"

Kyle clutched his side where he'd crashed into the railing. Between his banged-up ribs and his fear of heights, he was in no shape to run.

"You guys stay hidden," Bones said in the radio. "Kyle, lie low. I'll lead him away, and if he catches me, I'll say it was all me. Just don't move. You'll be fine."

"Forget it!" Marcus insisted. "There's no way we're bailing on you."

"Uh, yeah," Albert mumbled, with far less conviction. "What Marcus said."

Bones set the walkie-talkie next to Kyle and started down the ladder. Kyle sat up.

"What are you doing? Didn't you hear Marcus?"

But Bones kept going. "I'm not getting you in trouble, Kyle. This is on me."

Kyle protested and picked up the radio. Bones knew he had to hurry. He hopped off the ladder and hit the ground running.

He only managed three strides before a flashlight beam hit him in the face.

"Don't move!" a male voice said beyond the blinding light. "You're under arrest."

19.
THE END OF A LONG DREAM

The metal bench in the gray-green holding cell was clearly designed to be uncomfortable. Worse still, it squeaked every time Albert bounced his knee.

"Albert, can you *not*?" Bones snapped.

Albert's knee didn't slow. "Give me a break. I've never been arrested before."

Bones scowled. He still couldn't believe the others had gotten caught so easily. At the Common, he'd tried to convince the officer he was alone, but then Kyle knocked the pliers off the catwalk. The officer shone his light upward and spotted Kyle instantly. As the man marched them to his cruiser, Bones groaned. Marcus and Albert were there, waiting to turn themselves in. Albert looked like he might either faint or vomit. Marcus stood with arms folded, nervous but resolute.

It was noble of them not to ditch him, Bones had to admit. But foolish.

Now the four of them were crowded in a holding cell, waiting. Marcus, Albert, and Bones sat on the bench while Kyle leaned against the wall, rubbing his side. He had slipped into withdrawn silence. Bones wanted to ask if he was all right, but he suspected it wouldn't help.

"How long have we been here?" Albert said. "Do you think they'll keep us all night? Is that legal? Shouldn't we get a lawyer, or a phone call?"

"Relax," Bones said. "It's a tactic, like in the principal's office. They make you wait and hope you'll get nervous and crack. Don't let them faze you." He stretched his legs.

Albert's knee bounced faster. "I've never been sent to the principal's office either." He leaped up and went to the door. "Hello? I have to pee."

Bones yawned. "Just go in the corner. Don't be shy. We've already seen you naked."

Albert whirled. "How can you joke right now?"

"It's better than stressing out. Look, when they come, let me handle it. You'd spill your guts in a second."

"We just need to be honest," Marcus offered. "If we tell them—"

"Quiet," Kyle said, startling everyone. It was the first time he'd spoken since they'd been arrested. "They might be watching. Or listening."

He glanced at the dark reflective dome on the ceiling. Next to it was a black FluxBox.

Kyle slumped against the wall and rubbed his side again.

"How bad is it?" Bones asked.

Silence.

"Kyle. Let me see." Bones moved toward him. Kyle relented and lifted his shirt. A large purple bruise was forming like an island across the side of his ribs. Bones winced. That was his fault.

"That's a good one," he joked weakly. "Something to brag about."

Kyle didn't smile. Before Bones could apologize, the door opened and Chief Schofield walked in. Bones was surprised to see the chief, but he hid it.

"Before you start, Albert needs to pee," he said. It was important to speak first and show he wasn't intimidated.

Chief Schofield glowered at him. "Sit." He studied them all. "I have to say I'm shocked. Shocked and disappointed. What were you boys thinking?" He stared at Marcus, then Kyle. "What will your parents think?"

Kyle twitched. Bones worried he might crumble.

"We didn't do anything wrong," Bones said. "We were just playing hide-and-seek."

Chief Schofield's forehead creased in annoyance. "And *you* have quite the history, Quentin Malone. I had a look at your school records. You certainly didn't waste time making your presence known in Langille."

Bones grinned. "You went to that much trouble this late at night? Wow, I'm flattered."

Chief Schofield's gray eyebrows furrowed. "Drop the tone, Mister. Maybe it worked in the city, but in Langille we have zero tolerance for hooliganism. You were caught vandalizing a brand-new, *expensive* public landmark, and that's not something we take lightly. You'll cooperate if you know what's good for you."

Bones studied the man's bleary eyes. "How much is Ray Giraud paying you?"

Albert let out a strangled whimper. Blood crept upward from the chief's neck.

"*Excuse* me?"

"You expect us to believe the police chief got up in the middle of the night because four kids maybe—allegedly—messed with a scoreboard?" Bones shook his head. "Naw. Giraud's crooked, and you're helping him. So what's in it for you?"

Chief Schofield spluttered. "How dare you make such—such slanderous accusations! Speak to me like that again and—"

The door opened. The officer who'd arrested the boys stuck his head inside. "Sorry to interrupt, sir, but Mr. Giraud is here. He said you'd want to see him."

Bones smirked. The chief glared at his subordinate officer.

"Not a good time, Constable. Tell Ray—Mr. Giraud—I'll be with him shortly."

"OK, but—"

"Gentlemen." Giraud pushed breezily into the room. Despite the hour, he was still sharply dressed in a golf shirt and pressed khakis.

The chief scowled. "You can't be here, Ray. This is official police business."

"Oh, come on, Bill. All this isn't necessary. I'd like to drop the charges."

Chief Schofield looked almost as shocked as Bones felt. "This isn't a TV show, Ray. It's not your decision. That scoreboard is on municipal land. These boys destroyed public property."

"It's not that bad." Giraud waved in Bones's direction. "Not like the time this one smashed up his father's real estate office with a baseball bat. That was really something, I hear. Got some anger issues under the surface there, eh, shortstop?"

Bones went cold as his friends stared at him. How could Giraud possibly know about that? He'd done it a few days after the fire. His family was salvaging what they could from the wreckage, and Bones had lost it. He biked to his father's office and unleashed his rage in a flurry of fractured plastic and broken glass. But he was eleven, too young to be charged. He was coping with extraordinary trauma, a psychologist said. He sat through a few counseling sessions and the whole thing was supposed to disappear. There was no way Giraud should have been able to find out about it.

Giraud flashed a piercing smile. "But this? This is nothing. Just a few wires. I sent a tech guy to look. The FluxBoard will be fixed by noon, at the latest. We'll still be good to go for the grand unveiling on Thursday."

Bones tried not to betray his disappointment. Not only had they failed, they'd tipped their hand to Giraud. Clearly, he understood the boys hadn't been out to commit a random act of vandalism. His smile remained, but his eyes sized up Bones as a fox might scout a squawking chicken, wondering whether to eat it now or later.

Chief Schofield cleared his throat. "With all due respect, we have to send a message to the town. If we let vandals run amok—"

"A moment outside, Bill?" Giraud cut him off. The chief hesitated before following him, shooting one more withering look at Bones.

As soon as the door closed, Albert leaned past Marcus and poked Bones in the chest. "Have you *lost it?* Insulting the chief is your idea of *handling it?*"

"I wasn't wrong," Bones shot back. "Why's Giraud here if they're not working together?"

"Well, now Giraud knows who we are too." Albert folded his arms. "This was a bad idea. I know you've been through some awful stuff with your dad—"

Bones's ears began to ring.

"Albert," Marcus cautioned.

"I'm just saying, maybe we shouldn't let the guy who tries to smash his way through everything be in charge," Albert insisted. "Like, if you'd just told your mom about your dad—"

Bones lunged. Marcus caught him before he could swing at Albert.

"You don't know the first thing about me!" Bones shouted as he struggled against Marcus's grip. "You're a spoiled, *scared* rich kid who only worries about himself!"

Albert retreated to the opposite wall. His voice trembled, but he looked Bones in the eye. "You don't know the first thing about me either," he shot back. "I'm here, aren't I? I didn't bail, even when things got bad. But I'm tired of it. You need therapy or something."

Bones lunged again, but Marcus held him tighter.

"Guys, *stop*," Marcus pleaded. "We have to stick together. We're all we've got."

The door opened again. They all froze as Chief Schofield stepped stiffly into the room. Even in their agitated state, they noticed the change in his eyes. He blinked twice and swiveled his head robotically.

"I'm going to let you boys off with a stern warning." His voice sounded far away, as if it belonged to someone else. "But I won't be so lenient next time. So don't pull any other stunts."

He was letting them go? That was good news, but Bones didn't feel comforted. Not with Ray Giraud leaning in the doorway.

"It's settled, then," Giraud said. "Let's all go home."

He held the door open for Chief Schofield and gestured for the boys to go next. As Bones filed out last, Giraud leaned close and whispered.

"Strike two, shortstop. Watch yourself."

Bones didn't flinch. He squared his shoulders and followed the others out, with Giraud on his heels.

It took more effort not to react when he saw his mom in the lobby.

"Ms. Malone has graciously agreed to drive you all home," Giraud said. "Here they are, ma'am. None the worse for wear, and maybe a little wiser. We've put it behind us, though. Right, son?"

Son? Bones tried not to scowl. His eyes were on his mother.

She stood, slowly. Her expression didn't change. She looked right through him.

Silence blanketed the car like smoke, thick and suffocating. Bones stared out the passenger window. Too many emotions swirled in his chest—rage at Albert; embarrassment that the others were seeing his mom like this; concern for Kyle, who'd stopped talking altogether. As much as he hated to admit it, beneath it all was a nagging fear that Albert was right. Attacking the FluxBoard was a mistake. They'd shown their hand, and Giraud had given them a glimpse of his—demonstrated how much power he really had. He'd clearly brainwashed the chief into letting them go. But why?

Maybe it was a warning, or a way to pressure them into silence. The message was clear: Fluxcor was the law in Langille, and the boys had to watch their step.

"Thanks for the ride, Ms. Malone," Marcus said timidly as they turned in to his street. "You can let Albert and me out here."

She stopped. The boys climbed out. Marcus hesitated, clearly wanting to say something to Bones, but he quickly mumbled, "We'll talk later," and started down his street.

Bones's mom pulled a U-turn and headed back across town, where they dropped Kyle at the foot of Maple Street. He bolted without a word.

Now that they were alone, Bones braced for his mother to yell. He *wanted* her to yell. He gladly would have taken *What on earth were you thinking?* Or *Have you lost your mind?* Or even *You have no idea how much trouble you're in, bucko*. But she said nothing.

He couldn't handle the silence any longer.

"You're not even going to ask why? You think I did it for fun?" He had no business coming at her angry, but he was too tired to hold back. "Are you in there at all? Hello?"

Nothing. Blank stare. He slumped against the car door.

"We should leave."

It was less than a whisper, so soft he barely caught it. He leaned toward her. "What?"

She blinked, eyes fixed forward. "We should leave. Get your brothers and go. Tonight."

His relief at hearing her voice was immediately snuffed out by the hopelessness it carried. "Go? Where? Why?"

"I don't know. Anywhere but here."

He might have jumped at the idea once, but not now, not like this.

"Maybe you should go," he said. "Just for a bit. Take the boys to Grandma's. You could use a break, Mom. I have baseball and stuff. I have to stay."

She shook her head. "Then they'll take you."

"What?"

"They'll take you away. They think I'm a bad mother."

His heart sank. "Mom—"

"The fights. The river. This thing with the scoreboard. You run wild, all over town."

"Mom, I'm not—"

"It's not your fault. It's mine." As they passed through the glow of a streetlight, he saw the path of a tear winding along her cheek. "Everybody knows. I haven't—I'm not a good mother. I failed you."

Bones's stomach plunged. "That's *ridiculous*. Stop it."

She didn't look at him. "I let him hurt you for so long. I should have known. I *did* know, deep down."

"Mom, stop. *Please*." He sat up in alarm. She was speeding up. She sailed past their street. "You just missed—"

"I'm a journalist, for crying out loud." The engine rattled as the old car accelerated. "It's my *job* to notice things. And I didn't see what was happening in my own house. I refused to see—"

"Mom, slow down!"

She seemed entranced. They barreled east, away from the heart of town. "Every night, I went to work and left you with *that man*—"

"Mom, *please*—"

"How could I not see? How?"

"LOOK OUT!"

A deer stood in the middle of the road.

The car was traveling far too fast to stop. Bones reached over and jerked the wheel to the right. They missed the deer by inches. The passenger-side tires dipped onto the gravel shoulder, sending a spray of rocks thunking against the undercarriage. His mom gasped. She yanked the wheel to the left and stomped on the brakes. With a screech and an acrid streak of melting rubber, the wheels locked and the car spun. For an awful second it seemed they might go airborne. Bones dove to his left, as if shifting his skinny frame might make all the difference. They teetered on the brink of disaster, until the car came to a halt facing back toward town.

They sat still. Bones's heart pounded. The deer bounded off into a field.

"How did I not see you?" his mom whispered.

Bones knew in his heart she wasn't talking about the deer.

He swallowed. "Mom. Listen."

Her gaze stayed locked on the spot where the animal had stood. He unbuckled his seat belt and took her face in his hands, so she had no choice but to look at him.

Albert's words echoed in his head. *If you'd just told your mom—*

He'd buried this thought a thousand times, pushing it back down every time it tried to surface, but it never left him alone.

"It wasn't your fault. You didn't see because I didn't let you," he finally said. "I know it was a mistake, but I thought I was doing the right thing."

He couldn't keep the quake out of his voice. Her eyes watered again.

"I'm your mother. I should have known—"

"Mom, *stop*. I never blamed you. Never."

She touched his cheek. He looked into her eyes. A dam broke and she started sobbing, holding him tight. He wrapped his arms around her, and maybe he cried too, but it was the middle of the night and who could blame him?

A horn blared as a car sped past from behind, shaking them from their bubble. His mom straightened up and wiped her cheeks. She looked as if she'd just stirred from a long dream. She shifted the car into drive and started back toward home.

She made it a block before she pulled over and turned to face him.

"Boy, what in the *world* possessed you to climb that scoreboard?"

Bones nearly cried again for sheer joy. That was his mom talking.

He was so relieved he couldn't stop the story from spilling out, even the part about sneaking onto her computer. Her eyes narrowed.

"I know it sounds wild," he said.

She held up a hand. "My weasel detector went off the second I heard Ray Giraud open his lying mouth. I have no doubt that man is shady as the day is long."

Bones grinned. That was *definitely* his mom talking.

"What do we do now?" he asked.

The look on her face made his heart sink. He knew what was coming before she said it.

"*You* won't do anything. Hear me perfectly clear, Bones. You've put yourself in far too much danger already."

"But Mom—"

"I am not playing. You and your friends need to back off. Immediately. Understand?"

"Fine," he grumbled. "But what are *you* going to do? You have to be careful, Mom. Giraud is controlling Chief Schofield. Maybe even Mayor MacKenzie. There aren't many people in town we can trust."

"Don't worry about me." She threw the car into drive with forceful conviction. "It won't be the first time I show a man he can't pull one over on Rachel Malone."

20.
OVER THE EDGE

Kyle spent the brief walk up his street trying to rein in his jumbled thoughts. He knew he had to tell his mother everything. Chief Schofield was AZL'd and under Giraud's control. The police department wasn't safe.

Explaining would be difficult. There was so much to tell, it would all sound ludicrous at first, and his mom would be shocked to hear what he'd already done. But he'd make her understand. He had to.

He wasn't expecting to find her at the kitchen table, staring at the phone as if willing it to ring. His phone was set to silent in his pocket. He wondered how many times she'd called.

She looked up, and her eyes contained a storm of emotions.

"Kyle Peter Morgan Specks, where on earth have you been?" She used the tone where she tried not to show any emotion at all, which was the tone that made him most anxious.

He tried, but the words got stuck. Fatigue and stress overwhelmed him. This last surprise—her waiting in the kitchen—was the least jarring of the night, but it tipped him over the edge. He pushed at his hair once, twice, three times. His limbs were electric, and he couldn't corral them.

"I'm waiting," she said.

He ran to his bedroom. He was under the covers before she caught up with him. He buried his head beneath his pillow and sobbed. He was sweaty and his ribs hurt and normally he hated going to bed in his clothes—he even still had socks on—but he needed the pressure of his weighted blanket cocooned around him. His body coursed with heat as it sought a regulating rhythm. Tears flowed and he wrestled to catch his breath.

He hadn't physically melted down so severely in a long time. His mother's muffled voice shifted from stern to pleading to alarmed. "Kyle, what is it? Talk to me. Please." But he didn't emerge from the blankets. He heard his dad enter, and then they both tried to talk to him. When that didn't help, they started to talk to each other. Eventually, they moved their conversation into the hall and pulled his door closed.

Twenty minutes later, he felt soggy and drained but reordered enough to lie still. He threw off his blankets, welcoming the cool air. The hall was quiet. His parents had returned to their room. He peeled off his sweaty T-shirt and used it to wipe his face and chest. He took off his socks and changed into pajama shorts. Then he sat on his bed, flexing his toes, feeling his skin breathe.

Bones, he thought.

Hearing Bones describe the awful things his father had done and seeing his pain as he argued with Albert made Kyle's heart ache so much he could hardly bear it. His own father made him feel safe. He couldn't imagine how awful it would be if his father was the most terrifying person in his life. Just considering it made him anxious.

Parents were supposed to take care of their kids, and people were supposed to take care of one another—and the planet too—but it didn't always work that way. Everything was always in flux. Some people were willing to break everything for money, or power, or because they were broken too.

He couldn't forget the new page he'd read near the end of Dr. Elliott's notebook that afternoon, the words that convinced him trying to stop the FluxBoard was the right thing to do.

I'm afraid I may have made a terrible mistake. Today I arrived at the lab and a test was already underway in Room 2B. Security wouldn't let me observe. When I asked why they were testing without administering Serenity first, when I asked who they were testing, I was escorted from the observation room. Before I left, I heard the most horrible scream.

I called Ray, but he didn't answer. I went to his office, and his assistant told me he was out. I think he's avoiding me. I desperately hope I'm wrong, but I'm beginning to fear that a much different project than the one I envisioned is unfolding in Room 2B. Oh, my dear James, I think you were right about all of this.

The AZL Effect was no accident. They had to stop Fluxcor, to bring back Coach and Bones's mom and to protect the town. To protect his own parents.

He had to tell them. He couldn't bear the thought of losing them.

He had begun to pace without realizing. His bedroom door creaked open.

"Kyle?" his dad said softly. "Sounds like you're still up. Do you want to talk?"

It was the middle of the night, and his dad had waited up for him.

Kyle felt such a rush of gratitude he flung his arms around his dad, nearly knocking him backward. Startled, his dad took a moment to recover and rub his back. When Kyle let go, his dad examined him closely, drawing in his breath at the bruise on Kyle's side.

"What happened, kiddo?"

Kyle still couldn't find the right words to explain it all. "Please don't be mad," he pleaded instead. "Please don't change."

"Oh, Kyle." His father squeezed him tight. "Whatever's going on, it's going to be all right. How about we work it out in the morning, OK?"

He let his father guide him back to bed. *In the morning*, he decided, yawning. He would tell them everything then.

21.
CLOWNS

It seemed like mere minutes after Bones had finally fallen into bed when his mother flicked on his light. He groaned and threw an arm over his face.

"Mom. It's early. What's going on?"

"I need you to take the boys to Eileen's. I'm going into the office. I need to get on this Fluxcor thing."

She didn't sound right—too frantic, as if she were making up for lost AZL time by shifting into overdrive. She zinged around his room, closing half-open dresser drawers, scooping dirty clothes off the floor. Just watching her made him exhausted.

He yawned. "Slow down, Mom."

"No time." She kissed his forehead and hurried for the door. "Eat something before you go," she called over her shoulder. "Lock the door behind you. Stay out of trouble. And stay away from Fluxcor!"

"You too!" he hollered back, but she was gone. Sighing, he slowly rose and dragged himself to the kitchen. His brothers sat dazed in the wake of their mom's whirlwind departure.

"What's with Mom?" Dillon asked. "Is she better?"

Bones yawned again. "She's . . . better than yesterday, I think."

He recalled the scene in the car, the shift in her eyes. Only a few hours had passed, but it all felt like a distant memory, or a dream. Still, thinking about it made him feel raw all over again.

"She's still acting weird." Raury's lower lip trembled. "Where were you last night? I woke up and you weren't here."

Bones squeezed his shoulder. "Did you have another bad dream?"

Raury nodded.

"Don't worry. I'm here now. We'll be all right, buddy, OK? I promise." Bones didn't know how, exactly, but he hoped it was true.

He was so tired. The Spezios' house was quiet when he and his brothers entered through the back door, which was always unlocked. Tony was sleeping, and Mrs. Spezio was rooted to the couch. Dillon settled in to play video games and Raury dug into his book, so Bones had time to himself. He knew he should answer Marcus's texts or call Kyle. Of course, he had no intention of heeding his mother's order to drop everything. But the night had drained him. He slipped into the spare room and flopped on the bed to rest his eyes, just for a minute . . .

An eerie refrain drifted on the air, muffled and out of tune. Bones gathered his bearings. He stood in a long-abandoned amusement park at dusk. The strings of party lights that crisscrossed between attractions hung limp and dark. Half the bulbs were smashed. A breeze sent faded hot dog wrappers skittering across the cracked pavement. In the distance, a cage at the top of the dormant Ferris wheel shifted in the wind.

Squeak. Squeak. Squeak. Squeak.

Beneath it all, music droned in endless repetition—a circus ditty that warbled from crackling loudspeakers. The short phrase cut off abruptly and looped to the beginning over and over, never resolving. Bones rubbed his temples in irritation as the demented tune wormed into his brain. He set out to get away from the sound.

As he passed a booth, it sprang to life.

"Step right up, step right up! Test your strength! Test your skill!"

Bones jumped, then laughed sheepishly as he spotted the source of the voice: an animatronic carnival barker beckoning him to play its game. The smiling robot's paint had faded, its jaw hung loose at one cracked hinge, and its left eye was missing, giving it a ghoulish appearance. At the back of the booth, tin targets popped up and disappeared in a random sequence. A baseball dropped from a slot at the front of the booth and rolled to Bones's feet. He picked it up, set his fastball grip—and whipped it at the robot. The ball struck it square in the forehead, and the head snapped backward with a *crack*. The display stuttered to a halt.

Satisfied, Bones looked around. What was this place?

"Bones?"

He turned. Raury stood on the walkway, hugging himself.

"Raury!" Bones hurried toward him.

"Where are we?" Raury said. "How did we get here?"

"I think this is another one of your nightmares," Bones said.

Raury shook his head, wide-eyed. "This feels different. It's weird."

A figure barreled around a corner and hurtled toward them. Tony. Bones stepped in front of Raury and braced himself, but as Tony drew closer, he saw that the older boy's face was twisted in terror.

"No no no no no," Tony gasped. "Stay away from me!"

He wasn't after them. He was fleeing something else.

As Tony passed in a sweaty blur, his pursuers rounded the corner. Bones counted nearly a dozen vicious-looking clowns, dressed in garish stripes and polka dots, faces painted with exaggerated menace. They moved surprisingly quickly despite their oversized shoes that squeaked and quacked with each step. They might have seemed amusing, if they weren't also armed with hacksaws, machetes, a rusted scythe, and a stuttering chain saw. They looked like they were itching to use their weapons—and some looked like they'd been recently used. Bones usually chose fight over flight, but he didn't see any gain in confronting a bloodthirsty mob of clowns, especially not with Raury in tow. He grabbed his brother's hand and ran after Tony. They caught up as they passed the Scrambler.

"You're afraid of clowns?" Bones exclaimed.

Tony gaped at them without slowing down. "What are you doing here?" He managed to sound annoyed and terrified at the same time.

"Don't fight it, Tony!" a clown shrieked behind them. "You're one of us! It's time for your surgery!"

"It won't hurt a bit, we promise! We'll fix you up just right!" The clowns broke into squeals of high-pitched laughter.

Bones shot Tony a sideways look. "You're more twisted than I thought."

"Shut up and help me get out of here," Tony wheezed.

They zigzagged through the fairground, past the Gravitron and the haunted house. Bones peeked over his shoulder. The clowns were out of sight. He shoved Tony through the nearest doorway, and they stumbled forward in utter darkness. Bones felt his way around one turn and then another, until his hands met a cool, smooth surface. A dead end.

"Why did you drag us in here?" Tony whispered frantically. "They're going to find us."

"They will if you don't quit freaking out," Bones shot back.

A light flipped on, illuminating the room. Tony covered his mouth to stifle a scream. They'd landed in a hall of mirrors. Everywhere Bones looked, his reflection was cast in distorted shapes: short and squat, long and stretched, warped in squiggling waves.

"Toooo-ny," a voice called. "Come out and plaaaaay."

Raury squirmed, and Bones wrapped an arm around him.

"We know you're in there, Tony the Phony."

Whispers. Giggles.

"They're coming," Tony whimpered.

"Phony Tony. You're a fake. An actor. A clown."

Footsteps drew nearer. *Squeak. Quack. Squeak. Quack.*

"You can't hide from us. You're one of us."

Tony hunched over with his hands on his knees. "This is your fault," he moaned. "We're trapped, and they're going to cut me up and turn me into a clown."

Bones balanced on the balls of his feet, fists clenched. It was a terrible room in which to face a horde of killer clowns: only one exit, no weapons, nowhere to hide. Nothing but mirrors.

Mirrors. Goose bumps rose on his neck.

A shadow slid across a mirror to his left; he glimpsed it from the corner of his eye. He turned, but it jumped to the next mirror. Bones wound in a circle, trying to keep pace with the shifting shape. He knew in his gut it was a familiar force, the specter that stalked him from dream to dream. Anger surged in his belly.

"Show yourself! Quit hiding!"

Tony sat up in fright. "Stop yelling! You're going to lead them right to us!"

Bones didn't care. He was tired of the awful anticipation.

There. In the mirror behind him. He spun around in one smooth leap, but it was behind him again.

No—it was inside the mirror.

"Let's do this! No more running!"

Even as he spoke, a crack appeared in the mirror. Deep crimson liquid seeped from the crevice. Tony grabbed him in fright, but Bones shook him off. He ran straight at the mirror—

Bones lurched upright in the Spezios' spare bedroom, fists cocked. After a flash of confusion, anger surged through his chest. He stormed to the basement.

Raury sat up on the couch, rubbing his eyes. He'd drifted off while reading, Bones realized. He looked exhausted, just as he had for days. Worse, the Spezios' FluxBox was active, blue lights flicking in rhythm. He yanked the unit free of its plug and marched into Tony's room, throwing the door open with a bang that startled Tony so badly he tumbled out of bed.

"I told you!" Bones yelled, tossing the FluxBox on the bed. "I even unplugged it for you. I should have known you're so dense you wouldn't listen. And now you dragged poor Raury into your messed-up dream!"

Tony scrambled to his feet, half-asleep and hopelessly confused in just his boxers. "What the—"

"Clowns, Tony? Clowns with chain saws? Lay off the horror movies, you creep."

Tony was too rattled to cover his shock. "You couldn't . . . that's impossible."

"It's not impossible. It's that stupid box. It's messing you up, and it's killing your mom. I warned you. Get rid of it."

Tony sunk onto the bed. "It was so real. They're all so real."

He buried his face in his hands. As he hunched over, Bones could see the outline of his spine. Tony had lost weight. His shoulders curved as if he were curling into himself. Sitting there undressed, he looked vulnerable. Scared.

Bones felt a pang of sympathy. He took a step closer.

Tony looked up, and his face twisted with rage and shame.

"This is *your* fault. Mom and I were fine until you and your whiny brothers showed up." He grabbed the FluxBox and hurled it at Bones's head. Bones ducked. The unit struck the wall and cracked open before crashing to the floor.

Bones saw red. He was about to go off when his brothers burst through the doorway.

"Bones? What's going on?" Dillon took in the scene, wide-eyed. He giggled at Tony. "You're in your underwear!"

"Get out!" Tony's voice cracked. "If you're still in my house in five minutes, I swear to God—"

Bones put an arm around Dillon's shoulders. "Come on, guys. Get your stuff. We're leaving."

Bones's knee bounced impatiently as he sat on a bench by the Common playground, eyes darting from his brothers to his phone. He had the creeping sense that the parents there were watching him. But he couldn't afford to become paranoid. It was a lingering effect of falling asleep near the FluxBox, he decided. He should have been more careful.

At the baseball field, a Fluxcor crew worked on the scoreboard. Bones turned away. He made accidental eye contact with a mother who frowned and hovered closer to her girls.

Finally, Marcus arrived. Bones was caught off guard when Marcus greeted him with a clasped hand and a one-shoulder hug.

"You good?" Marcus asked. "Last night was rough."

Touched, Bones dropped his eyes to his sneakers. "I'm fine. You?"

"Yeah. My sisters gave me heat for getting caught, but they ran interference with Mom." He scuffed at the grass with his shoe. "Albert felt pretty bad about . . . you know."

"I bet," Bones muttered.

Marcus exhaled. "Look, I know Albert can be—"

"A constant downer? A pain in the butt?"

"Cautious," Marcus finished, shooting Bones a look. "But you have no idea how huge it was that he even came with us last night. He was the new guy too, you know. Two years ago. And some kids were real jerks at first. Like, singling him out for being Chinese and stuff. They were super racist."

"Been there," Bones retorted.

"Albert's not like you, though," Marcus said, not unkindly. "He hates being the center of attention. You saw his nightmare."

Bones recalled Albert's dream: an entire stadium booing him, kids from school pointing and laughing. He could see how getting arrested would stress Albert out. But that still didn't excuse the awful things he'd said.

Not even if some of them were maybe, possibly, a tiny bit true.

He changed the subject. "Have you heard from Kyle? He hasn't answered my texts."

Marcus shook his head. They both looked away, toward the FluxBoard, just as the crew was descending the ladder.

"I guess it's fixed," Bones muttered. "Today just keeps getting better."

"What happened?" Marcus asked.

Bones explained about his mom and about Tony.

"Come to my house," Marcus said. "You'll be safe there."

"What about your dad?"

Marcus sighed. "He's mostly keeping to himself. We can hang out in the pool house."

Bones hesitated. "Can you take my brothers? There's something I have to do first."

He ignored the voice of doom in his head as he walked back up Maple Street. It was past noon, and Kyle was still ghosting him. Kyle's mother answered the door when Bones knocked. She didn't look surprised to see him, nor as angry as he expected. Still, he knew in one heartrending instant how their conversation was about to unfold.

He tried anyway. He put on his most polite voice. "Is Kyle home? I was hoping to talk to him."

She sighed. "I don't think that's a good idea."

His defenses wilted. "Chief Schofield talked to you."

"Yes. But Kyle talked to me first."

"Did he tell you everything?"

"I certainly hope so. I can't possibly imagine there's more." Her brow wrinkled. "You both should have told me much sooner. Withholding evidence was a terrible idea."

Bones's jaw dropped. "He gave you the journal?" He pressed on as her eyes narrowed. "You have to believe him. Kyle wouldn't lie. He's the most honest person I know."

Mrs. Specks paused in surprise. "You're right. He's very honest. Which is why I'm shocked he's been sneaking around and keeping so many secrets."

Bones swallowed. The implication was clear: He was a bad influence.

"It's my fault." He forced himself not to look away as her jaw tightened. "But we know what Fluxcor can do. It's already happened to my mom. We didn't want it to happen to you too."

"That's what Kyle told me. But you're just boys. I'm a police officer."

"Yeah, but you're at more risk! Chief Schofield is compromised. We saw it last night. Ray Giraud can control him. And I don't have a lot of reasons to trust the police."

He knew it wasn't the smartest thing to say in the moment, but it wasn't wrong either.

"Bones." She set her hands on her hips. "This needs to stop. I won't have you dragging Kyle into this any further. Last night he—"

She stopped and swallowed hard. A car passed down Maple Street. Its driver offered a friendly toot, oblivious to the heartache unfolding on the Specks' doorstep.

"He is not a typical boy," she said quietly, her voice wobbling. "You can't just tell him things or make promises and—"

"Hold up." Bones blinked away the heat springing to his eyes. "You think I'm messing with him? You think I'd do that?"

She grimaced. "That's not what I meant. But he has limits, and I don't want him to get hurt. I won't *let* him get hurt."

Bones set his hands on his head, trying to breathe. He took a step backward, onto the walkway. Mrs. Specks's eyes pooled as he retreated across the lawn, but she didn't budge from the doorway. His eyes went to Kyle's window. The curtains were closed.

"You're right," Bones said. "Kyle isn't typical. He's smarter, and braver, and practically the only guy worth knowing in this whole crappy town. I'm not a perfect kid—maybe I'm not even a good kid—but I'd never hurt Kyle on purpose. I wouldn't do that to my friend."

She drew in her breath. But before she could say anything, Bones hurried away.

22.
RECKLESS

Bones tugged at the front of his new jersey as he stood with his teammates along the first-base line the next evening, waiting for the opening ceremony of the Jamboree Game to begin. He'd balked when Marcus handed him the Fluxcor-branded top before the game.

"Dad says we have to wear them or we don't play," Marcus said.

"Fine," Bones retorted. He started to walk off the field, but Marcus stopped him.

"Please. We're a team. We have to stick together." Marcus's voice slipped to a raspy whisper. "Please."

Reluctantly, Bones buttoned the jersey over his undershirt. Kyle took as much convincing when he showed up, but eventually he did the same.

Now Kyle stood four players away in line. Bones had fought the urge all day to text or call him, growing more restless as the clock ticked toward the Jamboree Game. He kept hoping Kyle would reach out and say he'd come up with some last-minute plan to stop the FluxBoard, but he hadn't. They'd exchanged an awkward "hey" during warmups, then Kyle glanced toward his parents in the stands. It stung, but Bones got the message. If that's how it was going to be, fine. Whatever. He had other things to worry about anyway.

The bleachers were full—the biggest crowd the Falcons had seen all year—but they were also eerily quiet. Most of the adults sat still, not making small talk, simply waiting. Bones spotted his mom in the back row, eyes hidden behind sunglasses and a ball cap pulled low on her head. For once, he'd begged her to stay home, but she'd insisted on coming.

"Ray Giraud's going to be there to unveil that scoreboard. I have to be there to keep an eye on him," she'd said.

He'd talked her into wearing sunglasses and lining her cap with foil, at least. He worried what the FluxBoard might do to her—to all of them.

His eyes drifted to the board, now covered with a giant blue tarp as they awaited the grand unveiling. Two security guards stood at the base of the ladder, and Bones assumed there was at least one more on the catwalk behind the board. For a moment, he allowed himself to imagine a giant rock falling out of the sky and smashing the board to bits. Where was an actual meteor strike when you needed one?

As his gaze returned to the bleachers, a flood of adrenaline shot through him when he spotted one of the couples who'd mobbed him at the Save-Easy sitting three rows below his mom. Did they recognize him? Did they even remember what they'd done? Before he left for the field, Bones had to fight a tug of dread that he shouldn't go out at all. Maybe Langille was too dangerous for him now. But he shoved it away, scolding himself. He couldn't help anyone if he let this messed-up town make him afraid.

Not that he could do much to help right now. The FluxBoard would go live any minute, and there was nothing they could do to stop it.

Next to Bones, Marcus stared straight ahead, looking unusually grim.

On Marcus's other side, Albert shifted his weight. "This is so creepy," he muttered. "I wish they'd get it over with."

Bones didn't answer. He wasn't sure he wanted to talk to Albert yet.

Finally, a set of bagpipes started up in the parking lot, making Bones cringe. Nothing good ever began with bagpipes.

He rolled his eyes as a parade of dignitaries trailed the piper onto the field. He tapped his foot through Mayor MacKenzie's monotone speech about heritage and tradition and the timeless joy of baseball as a metaphor for the spirit of small-town life, or something like that. Then at last, the mayor introduced Ray Giraud, and the Fluxcor boss stepped forward. He was dressed in an expensive suit, with his eyes hidden behind mirrored sunglasses.

"Ah, the Jamboree Game," he said as he took the microphone. "I had the privilege of playing in it myself, twenty-five years ago. Time really does fly. Looking at you kids makes me feel old." He chuckled at his own joke. "Of course, we didn't have a field this nice back then, and I didn't get to play for an actual *major leaguer*—" He shot Coach Robeson a grin that grew tight as people in the stands interrupted with polite applause. Coach gave a quick nod, barely acknowledging the crowd.

"But baseball is baseball," Ray Giraud continued. "And I'm still young enough to remember how annoying it is when the adults won't shut up when you just want to play ball. So without further ado, it's my pleasure to present the state-of-the-art scoreboard for the greatest little town in Canada. Allow me to introduce the FluxBoard!"

The blue curtain fell away. The crowd gasped.

If not for its scaled-down size, the high-definition scoreboard could have belonged in a major-league stadium. It was massive overkill for a youth baseball field in a town the size of Langille. The words *LET'S PLAY BALL* scrolled across the screen, and digital fireworks appeared to pop out of the display in a dazzling 3D effect.

Bones would have been impressed, if he hadn't known the scoreboard's real purpose.

The opening display culminated in a bright blue flash of light. Then the screen went dark, and the slogan *FLUXCOR: LIVE THE FUTURE*™ slowly materialized.

People in the bleachers rose and began to clap, but it felt eerie—too synchronized, like they'd been programmed by a metronome. Bones shuddered.

"This isn't good," Kyle whispered.

Before he left the field, Ray Giraud waved to the Falcons players and flashed a grin.

"Have a great game, boys. I'll be watching. Do the town proud."

It was hard to be sure behind his sunglasses, but Bones was convinced Giraud was staring right at him.

As the dignitaries left the field, Bones and his teammates gathered in front of the dugout, where Coach Robeson read the starting lineup in a weary mumble. Bones felt worse with each name. Gavin Caraway was batting leadoff. Jack Andrews was starting at shortstop. Coach hadn't mentioned their fight at the last practice, but clearly he hadn't forgotten. Bones was benched.

Marcus gave him a sympathetic slap on the shoulder before he jogged to first base. Bones walked past Coach with his head down and slumped at the edge of the dugout.

The game felt like a waking nightmare. The Falcons had solidly beaten the Truro Bearcats three weeks earlier at an away game, but tonight, nothing was going right. On the mound, Riley Campbell couldn't find the strike zone. When he did, the Bearcats laced his fastball all over the field. Albert let a pitch bounce between his legs, and the FluxBoard flashed a bright red "1" as Truro scored. The board flashed twice more before the Falcons came to bat, trailing 3–0. But they weren't off the field long. Even Marcus struck out as Langille went three up, three down.

Bones leaned against the dugout's protective fence, feeling like a caged hamster as the innings rolled by. The eerie silence from

Coach and the spectators wore on the players. Hardly anyone spoke in the dugout. Marcus looked like he was fighting back tears. And the whole time, whenever the FluxBoard flashed the score or fancy 3D animations, Bones wondered what it was doing to the brains of everyone in the stands.

In the fourth inning, Kyle lost a fly ball in the evening sun, allowing two more runs to score. Bones couldn't remember Kyle missing a ball like that all season, not even in practice. When the inning mercifully ended, Kyle practically ran off the field and sat in the corner of the dugout, fingers drumming against his thigh.

Bones inched down the bench closer to Kyle. "Hey," he said. Kyle didn't answer.

"It's not your fault," Bones said. "Everyone's a mess tonight. It seems rough out there."

Kyle still didn't speak. Bones couldn't tell if he needed space, if he was following his mom's orders, or if he was mad about how things went down on Tuesday night. Whatever the case, he clearly didn't want Bones's company. Bones started to slide back down the bench.

"I should have figured it out earlier," Kyle said.

Bones stopped. "What?"

"The Wi-Fi. The FluxBoard. Maybe we could have stopped it, if I hadn't frozen on the ladder. We could have protected Coach, and everyone else."

Bones slid closer again. "Kyle. That was *definitely* not your fault. You did the best you could. You've done more than anyone in town."

Kyle's twitching fingers slowed. A moment later, Marcus sat on Bones's other side, and Albert sat beside Marcus. No one spoke, but Bones felt a little better.

Things didn't improve in the game, though. Before the top of the seventh inning, with the Falcons trailing 7–1, Coach finally looked down the bench and said, "Malone. Go for Caraway."

Bones rose slowly. "But . . . Gavin was in right field."

Coach stared, unblinking. Bones grabbed his glove and hurried onto the field. Kyle looked at him in surprise as they trotted to the outfield together. Bones had never played right field, a distant outpost from the action at shortstop. But he made it through the inning without anyone launching a fly ball his way, and he raced back to the dugout to grab a bat. Langille had one last shot, and he was up third.

The two batters ahead of him struck out. But Bones stepped up and ripped a double down the third-base line, sending a flutter of life through his teammates. Albert dug into the batter's box. As the pitcher started his windup, Bones took off for third base. Albert watched a curveball go by and Bones slid into third safely, ahead of the catcher's throw. But he was left standing there when Albert hit a soft liner back to the pitcher, who caught it and pumped his fist. Game over.

As Bones trudged off the field, Coach waited with arms folded. "I didn't give you the steal sign. You don't try to steal third with two outs. That was reckless."

Bones was too stunned to speak. He had tried his hardest to start a rally, and Coach was going to lecture him for it?

"Don't take reckless risks. That's how people get hurt." Coach's eyes went glassy. "You don't understand. I don't want you to get hurt."

Before Bones could figure out how to respond, Coach sighed and walked away.

The Falcons looked at one another in confusion. Marcus swallowed hard.

The boys were still gathering their gear when Shayla and Jayden burst into the dugout.

"We have a serious problem," Shayla said. "Dad's obviously a mess, and you should have seen what it was like in the stands tonight. These people are half-gone. It's creepy!"

Marcus sighed. "We *did* see. And we know we have a problem. That's why we tried to shut down the FluxBoard. But it obviously didn't work."

Jayden surveyed the four boys. "Well, your first mistake was cooking up that ridiculous plan on your own. No more scheming without us."

"No more scheming period," Albert grumbled. "All we did is get in trouble, and we didn't even stop the FluxBoard. It's over."

"No, it's not."

They all turned to Kyle.

"The FluxBoard isn't the end," he said. "If I'm reading Dr. Elliott's journal right, there's one more step before Ray Giraud has most of the town under his control. And now I think I know when it's coming."

23.
STRIKE THREE

Bones listlessly tossed a baseball with Marcus and Albert in the Robesons' backyard, while his brothers played in the pool with Jayden and Shayla. His mom had dropped them off at the Spezios' early again that morning, and Mrs. Spezio was still AZL'd, so Bones and his brothers had slipped away and made the long walk to the Robesons' before Tony woke up. Marcus kept casting his eyes toward the house, as if he expected his dad to appear. His uneasiness brought back bad memories of nights when Bones had crept around his old house, wondering when his smoldering father might ignite.

Sometimes he'd lit the match on purpose, just to get it over with.

Bones checked his phone again. Nothing from Kyle. He said he'd show, but Bones wasn't convinced his parents would let him. Bones thought about texting, but things still felt off-balance, and he didn't know what to say.

Finally, Kyle came around the side of the Robesons' house, still catching his breath from the uphill bike ride. Bones immediately beckoned the others to the pool house. Jayden and Shayla hopped out of the pool.

"No scheming without us, remember?" Jayden called. They grabbed towels and followed the boys into the pool house.

"How did you convince your parents to let you out?" Bones asked Kyle when they were situated.

Kyle fidgeted. "I didn't. I'm not supposed to be here. I had to wait until Mom started her shift. Dad went to Halifax to try to see Wade Elliott. He took the journal. He wanted me to go with him, but . . ." Kyle exhaled. "I got upset."

"Oh." Bones didn't make him elaborate. "But . . . your mom didn't turn in the journal as evidence? Does that mean she believes us?"

"She didn't say that, exactly. But I think she's realized that a lot of people aren't acting like themselves lately, including Chief Schofield."

"So what's the plan? What's this next step you mentioned?" Marcus asked.

Kyle pulled out his phone. "I scanned the journal before I gave it to my parents. Listen to what Dr. Elliott said in his last entry."

My worst fears are true. Serenity is but an afterthought for Ray. Maybe he was truly interested at first, but I'm afraid I inadvertently opened the door for him to distort my work into something monstrous. He doesn't want to alleviate fear: He wants to exploit it. His reasons are so coarse that I won't stoop to describing them here.

He's discovered that prolonged exposure to Serenity's vile opposite renders a subject increasingly susceptible to outside influence. If one knew how to manipulate an exposed subject with the right input, well, the potential is horrific.

The one saving grace is that Ray and his team don't yet understand the key variable that determines a person's vulnerability to this awful technology. But I understand it far too well. And I must make sure Ray never does.

I must leave Langille. I know Ray suspects I'm onto him, and I doubt James and I are safe here any longer. I don't trust anyone in town enough to reveal what I know. They're too indebted to Fluxcor. Hopefully I can at least convince authorities elsewhere that something truly catastrophic is brewing here. I know I will be doubted, for money talks far louder than one foolish scientist who made a grave mistake. But I have to try.

Kyle finished reading. "Do you understand? Dr. Elliott thinks Giraud is learning how to control people. If they're AZL'd long enough, he can manipulate them into thinking what he wants them to think. We saw that with Chief Schofield the other night. I don't think he's figured out how to make it work on kids yet, but I think he'll try the next wave on adults at the lobster dinner and dance tonight."

"That makes sense," Shayla said. "Most of the town will be there."

Albert grew pale. "This isn't good. My dad, he was fine until yesterday, but . . ." He swallowed. "I thought we were safe. Dad works there. I didn't think he'd zap his own people."

Bones leaped to his feet. "You've been a pain in the butt this whole time because you didn't think this would affect *you*? Of all the selfish—"

"That's not fair," Albert protested. "I helped. I hated seeing Coach so messed-up. And—and I'm sorry. But . . ."

"But it's real now, isn't it," Bones said bitterly.

Albert buried his face in his hands. Marcus patted his shoulder. Bones was annoyed with Marcus for being so forgiving, but as they sat in silence, his anger weakened. Marcus had a point. Even if Albert was a pain in the butt, he did keep showing up. And watching your parents change in front of your eyes was awful. Bones wouldn't wish that on anyone.

"So how do we stop this?" he asked Kyle.

"We have to figure out what kind of signal Giraud will use to trigger full control and shut it down. I think we need to disable the Wi-Fi at the community center."

"What about the rest of the town?" Jayden said. "We should go on the offensive here. While adults are at the dance, we can take out the other FluxBoxes in town."

Bones grinned. "I like your thinking."

"But there are only six of us," Marcus objected. "And we

need to focus on stopping this next wave at the community center, right?"

"The six of us will handle the dance," Jayden said. "The squad will handle the rest."

Kyle frowned in confusion. "What squad?"

Shayla whipped out her phone and started texting. "Leave that to us. You focus on how we're shutting down the community center."

Kyle shifted. "The five of you will have to do it. I can't."

Bones stared at him. "Kyle, you have to!"

"Are you grounded?" Albert asked.

"I'm definitely not supposed to have anything to do with Fluxcor. But it's not that." Kyle drummed against his thigh. "I hate the lobster dinner. It's too crowded and hot." He closed his eyes. "And I can't stand seeing cooked lobsters. I know it's weird."

"It's not weird," Marcus said. "Lobsters are creepy. They're basically giant sea bugs."

"I love lobster," Albert said. "But yeah, they're freaky looking," he added under Bones's glare.

"It's not how they look," Kyle said. "People boil them alive. It's barbaric. And it reminds me how we're poisoning the oceans and destroying the world. We're causing a catastrophe."

Bones recalled Kyle's dream: panic as the ocean swelled in vengeance, drowning a city.

"Whoa," Albert said. "If I thought as much as you, maybe I wouldn't like seafood either."

"So stay out of the lobster boil," Bones told Kyle. "We can try to disable the Wi-Fi while everyone else is eating."

"It's not just the lobsters!"

Everyone paused at the sudden rise in Kyle's voice. He stared at the floor, fingers drumming on his thigh.

"Kyle." Bones approached slowly and set a hand on his shoulder. "I hear you. Honestly. But we need you. What if you wore your earplugs, like you do in games? Then it won't feel so noisy." He pointed a thumb toward the others. "They'll keep an eye on the crowd, and you and I can sneak around behind the scenes. OK?"

Kyle pushed at his hair. He didn't look up, but he nodded. "I'll try."

"Great," Bones said. "Let's do this."

Langille had always struck Bones as a strange little town, and its contradictions were on full display at the lobster dinner. Men and women with weather-lined faces worked through plates of lobster in businesslike fashion—cracking, splitting, prying meat from claws—while two tables away, Fluxcor software developers and Royden teaching assistants sipped craft beers. Little kids darted through the mix with hot dogs and cans of pop. Langille's past, present, and future jostled against one another, people who worked the land and sea bumping elbows with those who trafficked in ideas and virtual reality.

That wasn't the only explanation for the feeling that something was *off* in the sweltering hall. Some people looked dazed, while others were aggressively upbeat, laughing too long and loud as their eyes darted in panic, like they feared something terrible would happen if they stopped having fun. Albert's parents were among the manic. Every time his normally reserved father's high-pitched laughter cut across the room, Albert looked ready to burst into tears.

Bones thought of his mother. She hadn't come home yet when he dropped off his brothers before heading to the community center. Be there in 10, she assured him in a text. Bones felt awful leaving the boys alone, but he didn't dare bring them to the lobster dinner in case anything went wrong.

"You're ten," he assured Raury. "Mom will be home any minute. You'll be fine. And you can call me if you need anything."

His phone hadn't rung yet, so hopefully everything was fine. He scratched his head. He felt conspicuous in his double-lined baseball cap and cheap, yellow-tinted sunglasses that Kyle thought might counter any blue flashes, but the adults were too AZL'd to care. The only one who might notice was—

"Oh, look," Jayden said. "Captain Big Shot has arrived."

Ray Giraud stepped through the door, shaking hands as he worked the room.

"That's our cue," Bones said quietly. He texted Kyle.

Giraud's here for dinner. Meet you by the back doors.

Bones lowered his head and kept his distance from Giraud as he slipped out to the back stairwell, where he let Kyle inside.

As he updated him on what they'd observed already, Kyle's eyes darted constantly and his fingers bounced on his leg.

"Are you all right?" Bones asked.

Kyle shook his head. "You smell like seafood. It's going to be crowded in there. What if Giraud is expecting us? This might be a trap."

"Kyle, easy," Bones said. "It'll be OK. We'll just figure out where the Internet connection is, shut it down, and get you out of here."

Kyle took a shaky breath. "The Internet hub might be in the main office."

"Cool. You know this place better than me, so lead the way."

They crept down the hall. As they rounded a corner, it became clear it would be trickier than they thought to get into the main office. Three people in Fluxcor T-shirts stood by the door, chatting away. Through the window, they could see another woman at the main desk, talking on the phone.

"Shoot," Bones said. "All the techy stuff is probably in the back somewhere, right? Maybe we can sneak in another way." He pointed to an unmarked door along the same wall as the office. "Maybe that's a back entrance." He patted his pockets. "Do you have a coin on you?"

"Why?" Kyle asked.

"Just trust me."

Kyle checked his wallet and handed Bones a dime.

"Perfect. Follow me, and act casual."

They strolled down the hall. The people by the office glanced their way and went back to their conversation. As they neared the unmarked door, Bones flicked the dime at the windows near the main entrance. It struck the glass with a sharp *ping*, and everyone in the foyer turned to look. While their heads were turned, Bones grabbed Kyle and pulled him through the door.

Into total darkness.

"This is not a back entrance to the office," Kyle said.

Bones sighed. "No kidding." He fumbled for his phone and turned on the flashlight. They stood in a narrow storage closet stocked with cleaning supplies, toilet paper, brooms, mops, and other odds and ends. As he scanned the room, he pointed to a vent just below the ceiling.

"Maybe we can get to the office through there."

Kyle recoiled. "I'm not crawling through a vent."

"I'll do it, then. I'm small."

"This is a bad idea." Kyle backed up and reached for the door handle. It didn't budge. He tried it again. Nothing.

"Bones?" Kyle's voice shot up an octave. "The door's locked. We're stuck."

"What? Why would it lock like that?" Bones tried the handle. "Oh. Oops. Maybe I should try the vent after all."

"I don't like being stuck." Kyle pushed at his hair. "This room is too small. We need to get out of here."

"OK, no problem. Marcus will get us out in a minute." Bones texted Marcus and told him where they were.

Be there soon, but you'll have to sit tight for a minute. Everyone's headed to the gym for the dance. Lobby's full.

Kyle turned toward the door, as if willing it to pop open. They waited in tense silence until Marcus freed them. Kyle rushed out into the foyer and shook out his hands.

"You OK?" Jayden asked.

He nodded tightly. "I just don't like being stuck."

"I take it you guys didn't figure out how to shut down the Wi-Fi," Albert said.

Bones rolled his eyes. "Has the dance started? We need to get in position."

They headed for the gym and fanned out in the darkened room. Shayla and Jayden monitored the dance floor and the main doors. Marcus and Albert kept an eye on the tables around the edges of the gym and the back doors that led outside, which were propped open to help counter the heat. Bones and Kyle covered the hallway to the bathroom and the side door leading onto the stage. Kyle wanted to camp in the hallway, but Bones convinced him that would look suspicious. As the music thumped, Kyle hung close to the wall, flattening himself if anyone drew too close. He tugged at the neck of a T-shirt that was dampening in the muggy air.

"Stay here," Bones whispered. "I'll get you some water."

Kyle nodded tightly. When Bones returned, Kyle downed his drink in one go. He wiped his mouth with the back of his hand.

"The lights," he said.

"What?" Bones had to lean close as the music swallowed Kyle's strained voice.

"The next wave. I think it's in the lights."

A laser show pulsed above the crowd in time with the booming beat. A few people reached high in the air, trying to touch the beams. A digital screen at the back of the stage shifted in psychedelic patterns. Bones watched, mesmerized. His head felt light.

He forced himself to look away. "I think you're right. We have to shut it down."

Kyle stared at the stage, eyes wide. "There's a pattern. A sequence."

"Don't look at it. Hey." Bones pinched his arm. Kyle blinked and shook his head.

"This is bad. We have to warn the others and get them out of here."

Bones messaged the others.

Don't look at the stage. The lights are evil. Kyle and I will shut them down. Be ready to go.

Near the main doors, Shayla flashed him a thumbs-up. He scanned for Marcus and Albert, but he couldn't see them. He and Kyle slipped along the edge of the crowd toward the door nearest the stage. A guard stood there, arms folded across his chest, eyes hidden behind sunglasses even in the dark of the room. Bones turned to Kyle. *How would they get past?*

Even as he thought it, Jayden and Shayla rushed toward the guard. "Oh my gosh, I have to pee so bad!" Shayla yelled over the music. "Is this the way to the bathroom?"

The guard tensed. "This hallway is closed. You can use the one in the locker room at the back of the gym."

"I can't. Someone threw up in there and it's nasty." Shayla did a dance of desperation. "Pretty *please*! I'll be quick."

The man stood firm.

"I told you, hold your nose and use the other one!" Jayden yelled. "You're such a drama queen."

"Me?" Shayla hollered back. "This is *your* fault!"

They launched into a full-on shouting match. Bones grinned. The guard wavered, but he finally lurched from the door when the girls started shoving each other. As he tried to break up their squabble, Bones grabbed Kyle and they slipped out behind the guard's back.

The hallway was an instant change of atmosphere, cooler and clearer. Bones started for the backstage door, but Kyle held up a finger. He was sweating buckets. He slumped against the wall and wiped his forehead.

"Maybe you should sit this one out," Bones said. "You look awful."

Kyle shook his head. "I—just a moment."

"We don't have much time."

Kyle gulped and pushed off the wall. Bones crept to the stage door and cautiously tried the handle. It was open. He and Kyle slipped into a dark alcove by the stairs. The music was muffled backstage behind the speakers, but a consistent thud pulsed against Bones's chest. He checked the wall behind him. They stood beneath an electrical panel.

"Stay here," he whispered. "Be ready."

He sneaked toward the stairs. He made it up two steps before he heard a voice approaching. He dove forward and ducked behind a massive speaker at the edge of the stage. The reverberations rattled his teeth. Sandwiched between the speaker and the stage curtain, he risked a peek at the crowd. The view of the dance floor turned his stomach.

Everyone moved in rhythm. Left-right, left-right they swayed, like seaweed rooted to the ocean floor, pulled back and forth by the waves.

"Everybody put your hands in the air," the DJ commanded. They responded on cue.

"When I say *Fluxcor*, you say *rocks*. Fluxcor!"

"Rocks!" the crowd bellowed.

"Fluxcor!"

"Rocks!"

Watching the sea of people, eyes vacant in the flashing lights, Bones felt as if he'd stumbled into another nightmare.

The cords trailing from the speaker caught his eye. They disappeared under a ridged floor guard and reemerged at a sound board in the wings of the stage. Two men worked the consoles, nodding in time with the beat.

A plan formed in his mind. He texted Kyle.

Are you still by the electrical panel? Count to 5, then kill the power.

Bones hit send. He braced himself and counted in his head. As he reached five, he prepared to spring—but nothing happened. *Was Kyle all right? Had he been caught, or—*

The music died and the room went black. People screamed. The room exploded in panicked chatter, crashes, people thumping against the doors. Bones darted across the stage in three bounds and yanked as many cords from the consoles as he could. He could hear the men shouting as they tried to sort out what had happened.

As Bones headed back for the stairs, a light from a phone flashed in the alcove. The security guard from the gym appeared, with Kyle in tow.

"What do you think you're doing, kid?" Bones heard him growl at Kyle. "You're in big trouble."

Another light flashed behind him. "There's two of them!" one of the men from the DJ booth yelled.

The guard tucked his phone between his teeth as he tried to hold Kyle with one hand and turn the electricity back on with the other. Bones reacted in an instant: He jumped forward, snatched the phone from the guard's mouth, flung it at the DJ, and slammed the electrical panel door shut.

"Hey!" the guard hollered, at the same time the DJ said "Ow!"

Bones grabbed Kyle's arm. "Come on!"

He pushed Kyle out the side door, into a stampede flooding the hall. They were separated immediately. Bones tried to keep his eyes on Kyle as the crowd swept him along. Ahead of him, the bathroom door opened and closed. He fought through the tide of humanity and shoved his way into the bathroom just as the lights came back on. Inside, Kyle cowered by the sink as Tony hovered over him, rubbing his jaw.

"Watch where you're going, weirdo," Tony snarled. "What are you even doing here?"

"Hey!" Bones slid between Tony and Kyle. "Leave him alone."

Tony looked from Kyle to Bones, smirking. "Of *course* you two are buddies. How cute. The two biggest rejects in town."

Heat surged in Bones's chest. The words came out before he considered them.

"Don't ever talk about Kyle again, you clown."

Tony's pupils dilated to pinpricks of rage. Bones braced for the larger boy to swing at him, but Tony didn't throw a punch. He did something worse.

His mouth twisted in a snarl. "I saw you too, you know. You're afraid of your own reflection. You can't even look at yourself in the mirror. Probably because you're so—"

He didn't finish. Bones shut his mouth with a left hook.

Tony went down, and Bones dove after him. He barely heard the door open behind him. He landed one more shot before a hand clamped on his shoulder. On instinct, he shifted his weight and shoved his new assailant as hard as he could. The sound of rushing air filled the room as the hand dryer clicked on. He ignored it and prepared to take another cut at Tony.

"Stop!" Kyle shouted.

Bones froze. Slowly, he turned. ·

Albert and Kyle were staring at him in horror. Marcus sat beneath the dryer, holding a hand over his left eye.

Marcus. He'd shoved Marcus face-first into the hand dryer.

The dryer switched off, draping the room in silence. Tony swore and covered his bleeding lip. A chill of dread spread through Bones's veins. He let his fists uncurl.

Albert glared at Bones as he squatted to check on Marcus. "Honestly, there's something wrong with you. You don't even think."

A dozen thoughts jumbled in Bones's mind. He didn't dare look at Kyle. He wanted to say it was an accident, and he was sorry. But none of that came out.

"We need to go, before that security guard finds us," he mumbled. "We should split up."

Without waiting for an answer, he ran. He hated himself for it even as he burst out the door and took off toward home. He wasn't a coward. He didn't run away. But this was the smartest move, right? They were better off splitting up, using the chaos they'd caused to their advantage. They could regroup later, and he'd apologize to Marcus. Everything was messy, but they'd stopped the brainwashing and that was the main thing, right?

As he crossed the bridge, his phone rang. He'd barely answered before his mom was in full stream.

"Bones? I'm onto something, and I have to work late—maybe all night. Your brothers are at Eileen's, and I've dropped off a bag for you."

Bones groaned. "Mom, we can't—"

"Gotta go. Be good, OK? See you in the morning."

The line went dead. Bones tried calling her back, but she didn't answer. He swore in frustration. Maybe she was working on a story on Fluxcor, but she sounded frantic, almost out of control. She hadn't fully shaken the AZL Effect. What if the next wave still got her somehow?

And he had a more immediate problem: There was no way he could spend the night at the Spezios' house. Not after what he'd done to Tony. But he couldn't leave his brothers there either.

His phone dinged with a text. When he checked, he nearly dropped his phone in the river.

I know it was you, shortstop. That's strike three.

24.
FIREWORKS

Bones's heart thumped. The text had to be from Ray Giraud. How did Giraud get his number? How did Giraud know *everything*? And what did he mean by *strike three*?

Whatever it was, it couldn't be good.

Bones slipped through the Spezios' unlocked back door. He wrinkled his nose. Dishes were piled on the kitchen counter, and the sink smelled of rotten food. He poked his head into the living room, where Mrs. Spezio was still rooted to the couch, staring at the TV. The stench in there was worse, like an animal carcass slowly decaying. He found his brothers huddled in the spare room. As soon as they saw him, Raury broke down crying, which set Dillon off too. Bones hugged them both.

"Don't worry, it's going to be OK," he said, but he felt less sure about that than ever. "Get your stuff. We can't stay here." He knew Tony might be back any minute now.

"But . . . where will we go?" Dillon asked.

"I'm working on it."

Where could they go? Heading home didn't feel right. Their mom would be mad if she found out, but worse, Giraud's text left Bones unsettled. If the man had his number, he probably knew where they lived as well. Maybe he even had people watching their house. He hated to admit it, but he didn't want to be there alone. The Robesons' was out too. Bones tried not to picture Marcus in the bathroom, holding his injured eye.

He recalled that Kyle's mom was on the night shift and his dad had gone to Halifax. The city was two hours away; maybe he'd stay overnight. Maybe they could stay at Kyle's house.

As he hustled his brothers toward the door, he called a quick goodbye to Mrs. Spezio. Silence. Bones was halfway out the door when he paused, sighed, and returned to the kitchen. He found a pen and wrote a note on the back of an unopened bill on the counter.

Tony, I'm sorry I hit you. My bad. Fluxcor is the reason you're having nightmares and your mom is a zombie. My friends and I are trying to stop them. We're trying to help your mom, and everyone else. –Bones

Before he could leave, his phone dinged again, with another text from Giraud.

Can't wait to see you in the parade tomorrow. Be there or else.

Bones cursed. Amid everything else, he'd forgotten the Falcons were supposed to march in the Jamboree parade tomorrow. Clearly, Giraud would be watching.

He hit *block* on the number. His anger swelled. If Giraud wanted a showdown, he'd get it. One way or another, it would end tomorrow.

Kyle's house was dark. Bones rang the bell, waited, knocked, waited some more, and rang again. Kyle hadn't answered his texts. What if he hadn't made it home? What if the security guard had caught him?

He tried the door. It was open. "Wait here," he told his brothers. He tiptoed inside.

"Kyle?" he half whispered. "Are you here?"

A light glowed from Kyle's room. Bones found Kyle on his bed, hugging his knees, staring into space. Bones's relief quickly faded. Kyle looked zombified.

Bones hovered by the door. "Are you all right?"

Kyle didn't answer.

"You're not a zombie librarian, are you?" Bones joked weakly, trying to prompt a reaction. Any reaction. Kyle cinched himself tighter.

"Kyle, I'm sorry. Tonight was a mess, but we stopped the lights at least, right?" Bones paced in agitation as Kyle stayed silent. "But it's not over yet. I got these texts—I think it's Giraud. He's threatening me about the parade. We need a plan. And my brothers and I need a place to sleep."

Kyle closed his eyes.

"Come on. Pull it together," Bones urged. "I'm in serious trouble here."

"I *can't!*" The words burst from Kyle with such force that Bones stepped back. Kyle pulled at his hair.

"You say you get it but you don't. You push and push and I *can't*. I knew it would be too much and I went because you needed me but the lasers and the lights, and it smelled, and I could hardly breathe, and now my head hurts *so much*. I need to be alone. I can't."

Kyle had gone rigid, eyes squeezed tight. Bones's stomach swirled helplessly. He wanted to go to Kyle, comfort him somehow, but where did he even start?

"OK. Um . . . We'll just sleep in the living room? We'll talk in the morning."

"My mom wouldn't—"

"Your mom wouldn't want you to throw us out in the street," Bones insisted.

Kyle rocked back and forth. "You don't listen. It's always your way."

A desperate anger surged in Bones's chest. "Look, I shouldn't have dragged you there tonight, but we did break up a zombie dance party, so what do you want me to say? I need your *help*, Kyle. Are you my friend or not? Friends don't abandon each other when it's tough."

Kyle pressed his fists against his head. "Friends aren't supposed to hurt each other either!"

Bones reeled. Kyle's words slashed through his heart. He stormed out, slamming the door hard enough to rattle the wall. Behind him, he heard the crash of one of Kyle's whiteboards falling to the floor. He didn't slow down. He rounded up his brothers and left. Dillon peppered him with questions as he marched out the front door, down Maple and across Robie, veering onto the path to the river. He didn't say anything. He wanted to hit something so badly. Why did his mother drag them to this awful town? Now she was AZL'd or in overdrive or *whatever* was happening—and he couldn't count on a single person to help. Everyone always let him down. He always wound up fighting on his own. People rolled over and let the bad guys win because they were too scared, too selfish, too indifferent, too—

"Bones! Where are we *going*?" Dillon hollered.

He turned and yelled right back. "I don't *know*, OK? I don't know what to do anymore! I hate it here!"

He picked up a fist-sized rock and hurled it into the river. It wasn't enough, so he threw another, and another.

His brothers slumped on a bench beside the trail. Bones stood with his back to them, staring toward the river, a black rippling ribbon in the night.

Then the sky exploded in light. A split second later came the *BOOM*. The sound made them all jump. Bangs echoed as Langille lit up in bursts of color. Fireworks.

The celebration went on. Maybe the dance had continued too. Maybe the sound crew plugged back in and picked up where they'd left off. Maybe people had filed right back inside, willingly dancing to their own destruction.

Every explosion in the sky was a high-definition reminder that Fluxcor was winning, and he'd failed.

Who was he kidding? This was how it always went. He screwed up. He hurt people.

He hurt Tony, with his words and then his fists. He didn't mean to hurt Marcus, or Kyle, or his mom, but he did it anyway. He said the wrong things. He did the wrong things. He never stopped to think, just like Albert had said. He drove people away.

His last conversation with Noah surfaced in his mind.

"You're moving? That sucks," Noah said, voice heavy with disbelief and maybe something else. Bones tucked his hands in his pockets.

"Not really," he answered gruffly. *"I hate it here. I won't miss one thing about this dumb place."*

Noah blinked, clearly hurt. Bones wanted to amend this declaration to clarify what he meant—that Noah was the one exception, and it already hurt to think about how much he'd miss him—but he didn't. He couldn't. He stood silent as Noah shuffled away.

That was the last time they spoke.

Other words from that old life flooded his memory. He pictured his father's snarling face.

"I've given you so much, and you're so ungrateful. It's like you take a sick pleasure in sabotaging everything. It's your own fault, Quentin. You make me do this. You do this to yourself."

Bones heaved another rock into the river. He couldn't even take care of his brothers. They sat in darkness in a strange town where almost everyone had been brainwashed, and he had nowhere to take them. No way to protect them. He was a failure.

He was so absorbed in the fireworks and his own misery that he didn't notice the footsteps on the path until Dillon cried out. He spun around.

Someone had scooped up Dillon. Someone else reached for Raury. Bones took one explosive step forward—and stopped as he realized his brothers were hugging the two figures. Dillon had leaped into Jayden's arms. Shayla rubbed Raury's back.

Jayden cast a wary eye at Bones's fists. "Easy, Hulk. No more punching tonight."

Marcus stepped out of the shadows. "Hey."

"What are you doing here?" Bones mumbled.

It wasn't the greeting Marcus deserved, but he shrugged it off. "Kyle called me. He didn't make a ton of sense, but he said something happened to your mom and we needed to find you."

Bones felt a flash of relief, but then he remembered how he'd yelled and slammed Kyle's door, and he felt lower than ever.

"Come on," Shayla said. "Joel's waiting in the car. You're coming to our place."

Jayden started up the path, with Dillon riding piggyback. Bones couldn't have protested even if he wanted.

He had no idea what he wanted. He only knew what he didn't deserve.

As they packed into the Robesons' vehicle, Bones noticed Marcus's eye was swollen and purple. Bones said little on the drive. He hung back as Jayden and Shayla tucked his brothers into bed on the pullout couch in the pool house. He mumbled a sheepish thanks when Joel set up an air mattress and a sleeping bag for him. He tossed restlessly as his brothers dropped off to sleep.

The pool house door opened, and Marcus slipped in, carrying his pillow and a sleeping bag.

Bones sat up. "What are you doing?"

"You had an awful night," Marcus said. "I thought you might not want to be alone."

Bones swallowed. "Why are you still being nice, after what I did?"

"What, this?" Marcus pointed to his bruised eye. "This is nothing. Do you know how many family wrestling matches I've been in? Being the youngest is rough. Jayden has a black belt in judo. I grew this tall for self-defense."

Bones felt a sliver of relief. At least Marcus didn't hate him.

"Still, um." He scratched his chest. "I'm sorry."

"I know," Marcus said. "But thanks for saying it."

Bones settled into his sleeping bag. Despite everything, sleep came more quickly than he expected. He dreamed of a wasteland where bleached skeletons lay scattered across cracked earth. *Lifeless* was the only way to describe it. Nothing had lived there for generations or would ever live there again. Even the air felt stale and dead.

"Anyone here?" he called out, but his words fell like stones.

He'd never felt more alone.

He walked for what seemed like hours, but the landscape barely changed. Finally, on the horizon, he spotted a figure seeking shade beneath the ribs of some long-dead animal. Somehow, he knew it was Marcus. When he drew near, Marcus looked up with sunken eyes. As Bones reached for him, smoke poured from the broken ground and gathered in an enormous shadow that swirled around them and blotted the sun.

Bones jolted awake. Marcus was already sitting up beside him.

"It seems silly, doesn't it?" Marcus sounded distant, still half-asleep. "We traveled a lot when Dad was still playing, but I couldn't go anywhere without holding Mom or Dad's hand until I was, like, seven. I had this weird fear they'd lose count and leave me behind by accident. It's probably Shayla's fault. She liked to mess with my head." He gave a wistful laugh. "Ironic, huh? I live in a house full of people who drive me nuts sometimes, but I don't like being alone."

Bones yawned. "If I had your family, I bet I'd feel the same way."

Marcus turned to him, eyes heavy. "Do you worry your dad will look for you someday?"

Bones tensed. "I stopped being afraid of him a long time ago."

Marcus nodded, accepting this as truth. "But you worry about your brothers. And your mom."

After a silence, Bones swallowed. "Yeah."

Uttering that one syllable felt like unclasping a padlock from a rusted gate. He wasn't ready to let it swing open, but for the first time the idea did not seem unthinkable. He didn't mind as Marcus wrapped a long arm around his shoulders. He let himself lean against the taller boy. A pang still gripped his chest when he pictured Kyle, or his mother out there somewhere, still not herself. And anger swirled in his stomach when he thought of Giraud. But his troubles didn't press as heavily as they had by the river. He still felt certain he'd be walking into a lion's den in the morning. But he wouldn't be making the walk alone.

25.
THE OCEAN AND THE KEY

The sound of the whiteboard crashing to the floor echoed on repeat in Kyle's mind. His worst memories of the night ran on a loop: Being trapped in the storage closet. The security guard's rough hand squeezing his shoulder. Tony's disgust when they collided in the bathroom. The awful *smack* of Bones's fist striking Tony's face. Bones's desperation as he stood next to Kyle's bed, begging for help.

"Friends don't abandon each other when it's tough."

Kyle wanted so badly to help, but he couldn't.

Marcus's text that he'd found Bones brought some relief, but it also made Kyle feel worse. He'd called Marcus because he knew Marcus would do the right thing. He was a good friend. Kyle wasn't. When Bones needed him most, he'd failed. Bones might never forgive him for that.

Kyle would gladly face a thousand nightmares for a do-over, one chance to bend time and escape his own limitations. A thousand nightmares would hurt less than the twisting knot in his stomach, the fear that his failure could never be undone.

Wait.

That's it.

This was worse than a nightmare. Worse than fear.

He leaped out of bed. "Of course. Of course, of course! How did I not see it?"

He rushed to his computer and opened his scans of Wade Elliott's journal. The answer stared at him on the first page. The missing piece fell into place. Now he understood why the AZL Effect hit adults harder, and why some felt it worse than others. He understood the key. He needed to tell the others.

He had his phone in hand before he realized it was 1:17 A.M. He couldn't call now. But there was little chance he would sleep.

As he considered what he'd come to understand, another idea unfolded. He flipped through the digitized journal. Other things were clearer now. Kyle grabbed a sheaf of paper and sketched some of the scientist's diagrams, filling in gaps and the blurred or damaged parts with his own knowledge of what he'd learned and seen. Once he was satisfied, he dug out the disassembled FluxBox from beneath his bed.

He'd figured out how to neutralize the AZL Effect, but he'd been hesitant before to risk going a step further. But now he was ready to try. After an hour of tinkering, and a trip to the basement for his dad's soldering iron, he took a deep breath and plugged in the device.

Its lights didn't flash blue. Instead, they glowed a soft, steady green.

Kyle threw his arms in the air and laughed. He felt silly, which made him laugh harder. But he'd done it!

Well, maybe.

There was only one way to know.

He set his alarm. There was much to do in the morning, and he couldn't risk oversleeping. He wasn't convinced he'd sleep at all, but it was better to be safe. He eyed the machine warily as he settled into bed, also not convinced he wasn't making a foolish mistake. But sometimes science required risks, and this risk might be the key to saving Langille.

Eventually, despite the tumult in his mind, his bleary eyes drifted shut.

The ocean felt so soothing against his skin, like a warm bath. He was underwater, yet he breathed freely. He was weightless, able to glide in any direction he wanted. He stretched and floated, savoring the stillness of his senses. So often the noise and chaos of life overwhelmed him, but here, underwater, everything was peaceful.

Serenity.

Rays of sunlight gleamed through the water, casting golden beams all around him. Schools of fish darted past in rippling patterns. The vibrant yellows, blues, and reds of their scales hummed with life. The entire experience was so delightful that when his alarm clock trilled, cutting through the bliss and returning him to his bed, his first feeling was melancholy. The humid air, the chirping birds outside his window, the damp sheet tangled around his torso all came as a disappointment. He wanted to go back.

As he came fully awake, he hopped out of bed in triumph. He'd slept barely four hours, but he felt more refreshed and clearheaded than he had in ages. Ideas buzzed. There was so much to do.

26.
THE UPRISING

Thick clouds, gray as wet cement, gathered above Langille as Bones picked at a bowl of cereal in the Robesons' kitchen. He had little reason to be cheery, but the fact that the heavens were poised to rain on Ray Giraud's parade was a small blessing, anyway.

His phone dinged. Bones checked it and found a cryptic text from Kyle.

Found the key. Have a plan, sort of. Meet at 9:45 by the Science Center.

Bones showed Marcus, who grabbed his own phone and started texting. "I'm telling the whole team," Marcus said. "This has hit all our parents now. We're doing this together."

"We'll bring the squad too." Jayden cracked her knuckles. "That bleach-headed slimeball messed with the wrong town."

"Who all's in the squad, anyway?" Bones asked.

"Everybody," Shayla said. "You'll see."

"Shh," Marcus cautioned, eyes flitting toward the door.

Coach Robeson entered, looking as if he hadn't slept. Bones ducked his head, but Coach didn't comment on his presence.

"Ready for the parade?" he asked, with all the enthusiasm of a man headed for dental surgery. Bones snuck another look at him.

Coach had skipped the previous night's festivities, so even though he still appeared AZL'd, maybe he wasn't full-on brainwashed.

"We're going early," Marcus said. "We'll meet you at the start."

Coach shrugged and shuffled out. Marcus's jaw tensed. Bones had no doubts Marcus or the other Robesons were willing to risk whatever it took to bring their dad back.

In the foyer of the Science Center, Bones checked his phone. Still no word from his mom. He'd written to let her know he and his brothers had stayed at the Robesons', and she'd sent back a thumbs-up emoji. That was it. He had no idea if she'd show up for the parade, or if she was still at the office, or what was going on with her.

The team arrived early, as Marcus requested. When Albert showed up, he gave Bones a tiny nod, and Bones nodded back. As the Falcons gathered, so did dozens of other kids. Some were in Scout and Cadet uniforms or sports jerseys, ready to march in the parade. Others showed up in regular clothes, ready to help. Even Tony and his buddies rolled in, dressed in tank tops and shorts. Tony had a swollen lip.

"I told you," Jayden said. "Squad assembled."

Albert gaped. "This is like half the kids in town!"

"Never doubt our influence," Shayla said.

But there was still one kid missing: Kyle. As Bones grew antsy enough to check his phone, Kyle burst through the Science Center doors.

"Sorry I'm late. The Dollarama opened half an hour later than I thought."

Bones blinked. "Dollarama? Why—"

"I'll explain later." Kyle looked around. "Where did all these people come from?"

"Jayden and Shayla," Marcus said.

Bones feared this twist might throw Kyle off, but Kyle smiled. "Perfect. We could use the help." He checked his watch. "Bones, can I talk to you outside for a second?"

Bones followed Kyle outside. He knew they needed to talk, but he wasn't looking forward to it. Once they stepped outside, he started. "Hey. Last night, I—"

Before he could finish, Kyle hugged him. Startled, Bones froze before he hugged Kyle back.

"Sorry, I should have asked first," Kyle said after he let go. "I just felt terrible. I'm sorry I abandoned you. I'm sorry I'm not a good friend."

"Are you kidding?" Bones blurted. "You're the best friend I've ever had."

Even as he said it, he realized it was true.

Kyle stared in surprise. "I am? What about Marcus?"

Bones scratched his neck. "Don't get me wrong, Marcus is great, but I have more fun breaking the law with you."

Kyle studied him, puzzled. Recognition flashed in his eyes. "You're making a joke, because you're afraid of seeming emotional."

Bones elbowed him. "Jeez, thanks for calling me out like that." He swallowed. "But seriously. You're a great friend. And you were right last night. I don't always listen when you tell me what you need. I pushed you too far, and I hurt you. I'm sorry, Kyle. I'll try to do better."

Kyle blinked. His eyes were misty. "I know you try really hard, Bones. And you're the best friend I've ever had too."

The door behind them squeaked open. Bones and Kyle turned. "Hey, I hate to break up your moment, but it's almost parade time," Shayla called.

Kyle and Bones shrugged sheepishly and headed back inside. As they returned, Jayden let out a piercing whistle that silenced the room.

"Right," she said. "So let's hear your reports on last night."

A teenage girl in a soccer kit stepped forward. "Our team got thirty FluxBoxes—from our own houses plus the places where we were babysitting."

"We got sixteen, including two at the Legion and one from the Quik-Mart," said a kid in a Cadet uniform.

A few others ran down how many FluxBoxes they'd unplugged. Bones grinned.

"This is awesome. I didn't realize so many people knew Fluxcor was rotten."

Another girl stepped forward and lifted the sash draped across her chest to reveal a Fluxcor logo near the shoulder of her green shirt, which read *Wayfarers* across the front. "We knew something was up when Pastor Todd gave us these new youth group T-shirts. They're an abomination." She scowled. "Pastor Todd sold us out. No one can serve God and the capitalist machine at the same time. We might as well tattoo the mark of the beast on our foreheads too!"

"Easy, Sarah," Jayden chuckled. "But good work, everyone."

"Yeah, it's great," Kyle said. "But taking out individual Flux-Boxes isn't going to be enough. Between Fluxcor's own towers, the FluxBoard, and all the hot spots on town property, they still have Langille covered."

"Who put you in charge?" Tony hollered from the back.

Bones was ready to snap at him, but Jayden beat him to it. "Kyle knows what he's talking about, Tony. So zip it!"

Surprisingly, Tony listened. Jayden turned to Kyle. "So . . . what's the plan, then?"

"We have to break into Fluxcor," Kyle said. "I know how to reverse the effect. I rewired a FluxBox last night and tried it on myself, and it worked. But we have to go inside and get to the source."

"You figured out how to reverse the effect? And you want to break into Fluxcor?" Bones laughed maniacally. "Kyle, you're a wizard!"

"Wow." Jayden's gaze lingered on Kyle. "Congrats, you're definitely the smartest of Marcus's friends."

"Oh, by a long shot!" Bones grinned. He didn't even mind the indirect insult. He was enjoying how Jayden was looking at Kyle, and the way Kyle's cheeks went pink in return.

Albert sighed. "We're really doing this, huh?"

Marcus slapped his arm. "You bet."

They threw together a hasty plan: At the end of the parade, the other kids would create a distraction so Bones, Kyle, Marcus, and Albert could slip away and sneak into Fluxcor. Then they sent everyone out of the Science Center in smaller groups, so they didn't look suspicious. By the time the Falcons reached the marshaling station, the rest of the parade had already assembled. Kids shuffled uneasily as the adult participants—veterans from the Legion, the ladies' auxiliary, a marching band—stood stiff and silent, like robots rolled off an assembly line. Coach Robeson barely blinked as his players joined him. The only adult showing any sign of life was a young man wearing a Fluxcor golf shirt and a headset.

"Let's hustle, kids!" he called. "You were supposed to be here three minutes ago. We're running a tight ship. Mr. Giraud values punctuality."

"Ask me if I give a flux what that man values," Jayden muttered.

"Onto the truck, girls," Pastor Todd monotoned, eyes on his feet. "Remember, happy faces all around. The Lord loves a cheerful heart."

The difference between his words and his tone was so vast that Kyle squinted. "He's quite far gone, isn't he?"

"Tell me about it." Shayla shook her head. "Good luck. Be ready."

Jayden and Shayla joined the Wayfarers, who were right in front of the Falcons in the parade. Half the girls rode a float on the back of a pickup truck, while the others planned to walk behind, handing out candy. As everyone took their places, the Fluxcor aide snapped to attention.

"Look sharp! Grand marshal on deck!"

Ray Giraud strode alongside the parade lineup, hands clasped behind his back, a satisfied grin on his face. He wore a gold sash over his suit identifying him as the grand marshal. Bones kept his head down as the man neared.

"Good morning, children," Giraud said. "I'm sure you're proud to represent your town today. Maybe you Wayfarers can lift up a prayer that the rain holds off."

Jayden whispered a prayer that lightning would strike a specific part of Giraud's body.

Giraud stopped in front of Bones. Even as he averted his gaze, Bones felt the man's eyes boring into him.

"I'm sure you'll all be on your best behavior today," Giraud said. "Your parents are watching. Most of them, anyway."

Bones knew he shouldn't, but his impulsiveness won out. "If you knew me as well as you thought," he murmured, "you'd know I'm not great at following orders from ego-tripping dudes in suits."

To Bones's surprise, and unease, Giraud smiled.

"Let's get this show on the road, shall we?" The man strode to the front of the parade. Not long after, Bones heard bagpipes at the head of the procession. They were moving.

Along the sidewalks, children hovered near their parents' legs, cowed by the unusual solemnity of the affair. Adults stood motionless, eyes vacant. The overwhelming majority seemed fully brainwashed, Bones noted with dismay. As pipers played, drummers pounded out a militaristic beat, and everyone walked in stoic lockstep, the parade felt less like a celebration and more like a funeral procession.

Ahead of him, the Wayfarers tried to stir the oblivious crowd. The girls on the truck sang along to upbeat songs blaring from speakers on the truck bed. Shayla trotted to the sidewalk and pressed a lollipop into a young girl's hand.

"Here you go, sweetie." She cracked her knuckles. "God loves you. Your parents are sheep. Smash the patriarchy." The girl's eyes widened as she glanced back at her spaced-out parents.

Bones stayed on high alert. As they passed through an intersection, Chief Schofield stood beside his cruiser parked there, stopping traffic for the parade. He looked square at Bones and spoke into his radio.

The police were watching him? *Great. Things keep getting worse.*

Even as he thought it, the skies opened.

Rain poured down in dime-sized drops, splattering the pavement so furiously that in moments a small stream gushed along the curb. Kids watching the parade hollered and sought shelter under storefront awnings, but most adults remained frozen, seemingly unaware of the water coursing through their hair and dripping from the ends of their noses. Bones shivered.

Jayden spread her arms and looked skyward. "Thank you!" she hollered. She grabbed a megaphone from the back of the truck.

"People of Langille, wake from your slumber!" she bellowed. "Fluxcor would lead you to doom, but it's not too late to turn from your ways. Awake! The time is now!"

She stared at Bones and Kyle. "Awake! The time is *now!*"

She was giving them a signal. So much for waiting until the end of the parade.

"Marcus!" Bones called. "Now!"

Marcus pulled off his Fluxcor-sponsored jersey, revealing his old Falcons top underneath. Their other teammates followed. Bones ripped off his jersey and tossed it into the rain gutter.

"Fluxcor sucks!" Gavin Caraway yelled. "Fluxcor sucks!"

The chant spread through the team. The Wayfarers picked it up, raising their fists in the air as they bellowed from the back of the truck.

Pastor Todd stopped in the middle of the parade route and climbed out of the truck's cab. "Children, please," he begged. "This is highly inappropriate."

"No more worshipping corporate idols!" Jayden shouted at him through the megaphone. "We won't sell our souls to Fluxcor!"

The girls grew louder. They tore off their green Wayfarer shirts, revealing black T-shirts underneath. Kids on the sidewalks picked up the chant, giggling. Adults who'd been at the dance misheard them and began hypnotically mumbling "Fluxcor rocks." The two mantras clashed, with kids emphatically shouting down the adults.

"Fluxcor rocks."

"FLUXCOR SUCKS!"

Other kids in the parade joined in, shedding Fluxcor-emblazoned jerseys and uniforms. One young Scout pulled off his khakis and lofted them overhead, screaming "FLUXCOR PANTS ARE A PRISON OF LIES!" Chief Schofield abandoned his post and started barking at the Scouts to stop stripping to their boxers.

As the bottlenecked parade descended into rain-drenched anarchy, Jayden hurried to the boys. "Now's your chance. Get back to the Science Center and grab your bikes."

"Or we could take this truck. It's faster."

They turned. Tony stuck his head out of the driver's window of Pastor Todd's truck.

"No way," Albert said. "You guys, *no*."

Bones looked to Kyle. They had lots of reasons not to trust Tony.

Tony scowled. "Look, I want to stop these creeps as bad as you do. Come on, already."

"It's definitely faster than going back for our bikes," Kyle agreed. He started for the truck.

"This is a terrible idea," Albert protested, but he followed the others when they climbed into the backseat. Tony inched the truck forward, then pulled a hard left onto a side street and took off. They watched in the rearview mirror as Pastor Todd threw his arms in the air. He faded from view as the truck sped away.

27.
SCARE-IN

As they raced toward Fluxcor, Albert's knee bounced so violently that Bones felt it in his seat.

"We're so dead," Albert moaned. "The chief warned us not to cause any more trouble, and we stole a truck. We stole a *pastor's* truck. That's a crime *and* a sin. We're going to jail, and I'm not going to get into a good college, and I'm going to spend my life cleaning dog poop off the sidewalk in Langille—if my parents don't kill me first!"

"Get a grip, Al." Bones was drenched, but he couldn't stop grinning. He turned to Tony. "Do you even have your license? I didn't think you were sixteen yet."

Tony kept his eyes on the road. "I got my learner's permit yesterday. On my birthday."

Bones winced. "Your birthday was *yesterday*? Sorry I—"

"Yeah, I saw your note," Tony cut him off. He pulled another hard left, sending Bones reeling against the passenger door.

"Um . . ." Albert began, when they'd all straightened out. "If you only got your permit yesterday, does that mean you've never actually driven before?"

"Relax. I've been practicing with Mom's car for weeks. She's not using it. She barely leaves the couch." Tony's expression hardened. Once again, Bones felt a pang of sympathy.

Marcus leaned between the front seats. "Listen, I know we have a lot happening here, and I'm so glad this plan worked. But can we just take a minute to talk about how my sister definitely has a crush on Kyle?"

"You noticed too?" Bones grinned back at Kyle. "Jayden was giving you The Look."

"What look?" Kyle said.

"The look where she was like, *Kyle Specks is extremely smart and brave and I* like *him.*"

"Yeah, I saw that too, at the Science Center," Tony agreed, to Bones's surprise. "She digs you."

Kyle stared at the road. "She barely knows me. If she did, she'd probably think I was weird."

The car fell quiet. Rain thundered against the roof.

"Kyle, what? That's not true," Marcus said. "I mean, it's *definitely* a little weird to think about Jayden liking you, but I'm not surprised. She has high standards, and you're awesome."

"This is like the third illegal, town-saving thing you've done all month," Albert pointed out. "You're basically a rebel action hero."

"After we shut down the AZL Effect, the town's going to throw another parade, just for you," Bones said. "The streets will be lined with people chanting *Ky-le, Ky-le, Ky-le.*"

"Now you're being ridiculous," Kyle said. But he smiled.

Albert sat up with a *squelch* as his wet clothes rubbed against the seat. "I know I'm always the downer, but how exactly are we supposed to sneak into Fluxcor? We don't really have surprise on our side right now."

"I considered that," Kyle said. "You said Giraud AZL'd his own employees, so they'll likely have heightened fear responses. We'll scare our way in. That's why I stopped at the store."

Bones turned to reach between the front seats and peeked in Kyle's backpack. He burst out laughing. "Check it out."

He passed the bag to Albert, who plucked out a rubber spider. "You can't be serious." He pulled out a toy snake, a plastic skull, and a windup mouse. "This is like a third grader's Halloween party! We're toast."

"It's the best I could do on such short notice," Kyle said. "We just have to make people jump and let their amygdala do the rest."

"Here, Al. You can wear this." Marcus put on a rubber clown mask.

Albert recoiled. "Aah! Take that off! I hate clowns!"

Tony gripped the steering wheel tighter. "Clowns are the worst."

They crested a hill, and the Fluxcor complex came into view. The grounds held three main buildings: a warehouse, a sleek structure of reflective glass, and a six-story office building. Smaller storage sheds and outbuildings dotted the grounds, and a cell tower rose from the southwest corner. A fence surrounded the entire property, with a security booth by the main gates. The rain had eased, and in its wake a dense mist swirled in the valley below, making Fluxcor appear even more ominous.

"How do we get past security?" Albert asked.

"I have an idea," Bones said. "Pull up to the gate. Marcus, be ready."

The boys braced themselves as Tony approached Fluxcor's main gate. A security guard stepped out of his booth.

"Can I help you?" He frowned. "Geez, you're a kid. How old are you? What are you doing here?"

As the man leaned in the window to question Tony, Bones threw a handful of rubber spiders at him. One struck him in the forehead, and he let out an earsplitting scream. As the man frantically brushed at his face, Marcus hopped out, dashed into the security booth, and switched on the automated gate. He dove back into the backseat as Tony sped through.

"Wow. I didn't think that would work," Albert said as they propelled across the Fluxcor lot. "I guess the lesson is when you're out to conquer a town in a reign of paralyzing fear, you shouldn't zap the people who guard your evil lair." He sighed. "Also, my dad needs a new boss."

Tony pulled up behind the glass building. "Good luck," he said as they climbed out of the truck. "I'm not going in there. I'll do some doughnuts to distract them. Go break stuff."

He peeled away with a screech, leaving a streak of melted rubber on the pavement. Bones watched him go and thought about how strange it was that Tony Spezio had just helped their getaway. But he didn't have time to dwell on it. The boys snuck around the corner and crouched behind the bushes near the entryway of the glass building.

"This is the tricky part," Kyle said. "I imagine they keep the place locked, especially on a Saturday."

"No problem. We can use my dad's key card." Albert held up an ID attached to a belt clip. He shrugged as the others stared. "What? I had a hunch we'd do something dangerous today."

Bones punched his shoulder. "Nice thinking."

"See?" Albert told him. "I'm not totally useless."

"I never said you were useless. I said you were a pain in the butt."

Albert muttered under his breath as he crept to the door. The others hovered in the bushes. Albert swiped the card and pulled the door handle. Nothing. He tried again. It didn't budge.

Bones tensed. A woman approached from Albert's other side, coffee in one hand. He didn't see her coming, and the others didn't dare risk shouting a warning.

"Excuse me, young man," she said. Albert jumped. "Can I help you?"

"Yeah, I, uh . . ." Albert stumbled. "My dad forgot his, um, briefcase. He asked me to pick it up, but his card won't let me in."

"Hmm. Ah, finance is in the main office, not this building. They have different clearance."

As she examined Mr. Chen's ID, Bones spotted her own tag clutched in her hand with her coffee. He reached into Kyle's bag for ammunition, circled behind her, and tossed a rubber snake at her feet.

"SNAAAAAKE!" he bellowed. She screamed and threw her coffee cup at the snake, dropping her ID in the process. The coffee cup exploded on the steps and splashed all over Albert's sneakers. Then she took off running. Once she disappeared around the corner, Bones picked up her ID and pressed it to the scanner. The light blinked green, and the door opened.

"Thanks, I guess," Albert mumbled. "Although now I smell like coffee."

Bones patted his shoulder. "You'll live."

They lowered their voices as they crossed the lobby, an open space with skylights above stone floors and a fountain trickling in the middle of the room. It was deserted. Even the front desk sat empty.

"This is weird," Marcus whispered. "I know it's the weekend, but it seems—"

"Too quiet," Albert finished.

Bones shrugged. "Giraud probably forced his minions to go to the parade and worship him with everyone else." He stepped behind the desk and found what he hoped he'd find: a video monitor displaying four panels, each showing a different camera placed around the building.

"Where should we go?" he asked Kyle.

"I think this is our first stop." Kyle pointed to the top left display. "That looks like the control center. Maybe we can shut down everything from there."

"Should we split up and check out the whole building?" Bones said.

Marcus shook his head. "This place gives me bad vibes. I think we should stick together."

"Definitely," Albert agreed. "Everybody knows that the first guy to wander off alone is the first one to get eaten."

"This isn't Jurassic Park," Bones muttered, but he gave in.

The control room appeared to be on a basement level, two floors underground. They took the stairs, since Albert insisted that boarding an elevator in a villain's lair was also an obvious no-go. At the bottom of the stairs, Bones carefully tested the door. It opened onto a long hallway. The floor, walls, and ceiling were all the same cool shade of white. There weren't any employees here either. They hurried forward until they reached what appeared to be the control room. With fingers crossed, Bones swiped the pilfered key card. The door sensor blinked green.

They cautiously slipped inside—and realized stealth was unnecessary. Computers hummed and screens cast a blue glow, but not a soul was in sight.

"I have a bad feeling about this," Albert said.

The words had barely left his mouth when everything vanished, leaving them in a cavernous room of the same unbroken white as the hallway.

"Amazing what you can do with virtual reality these days, eh? We're really changing the game here at Fluxcor. Living the future, as we like to say."

Even before he turned, Bones knew it was Giraud.

The man was leaning against the doorway, smiling. "Welcome to Room 2B. I had a feeling you'd show up."

28.
THE THINGS YOU'LL CARRY

Bones looked away, but Giraud's devilish grin stayed etched in his mind.

"Aw, man. I knew this was too easy. You set us up," Albert said.

"Now you're getting it. Did you honestly think you were outsmarting me? A bunch of kids?" Giraud walked toward them, his leather shoes barely making a sound on the slick white floor. "Points for creativity, though. I watched your break-in on the security feed in my limo. The spiders cracked me up." He chuckled and turned his attention to Bones. "I've been wanting to get you here for a while, shortstop. I figured out how you work. You always react so quickly. I knew if I poked you, you'd go on the offensive."

Bones cursed under his breath—at Giraud, but mostly at himself. He'd been played.

"I did try to warn you," Giraud said with a shrug.

"Why are you messing with me?" Bones demanded.

Giraud smiled. "I like you. You've got spirit. Not a lick of sense, but lots of spirit. Not much scares you, does it? I'm curious what makes you tick."

Kyle studied the man. "I was right, and so was Dr. Elliott. You're stealing his work, but you don't fully understand it. You don't know why it's not working on kids."

Giraud sneered. "Wade is a fool. He didn't have a clue about the potential of the MindFlux. Why eradicate fear when you could harness it?"

"So you took his idea, twisted it, and tried to drown him in the river," Marcus concluded.

"And gave his work a really corny name," Albert added.

Giraud scowled. "Wade's undoing was entirely his own fault. He ran out of here screaming like a madman one night, then no one saw him again until you boys rescued him. He fell into the river on his own accord."

"You experimented on him, didn't you?" Marcus insisted. "Messed with his head, just like you're doing with people in town."

"And you staged a break-in at Kyle's house to try to get his journal," Bones said.

Giraud offered a sly half smile. "Those are quite serious accusations." He fixed his gaze on Kyle. "But I suppose *you've* sorted out how it works, haven't you?"

He tried to sound dismissive, but there was hunger in his voice. Bones was curious too. He remembered Kyle's text that morning: *Found the key.* He was dying to know, though he didn't want to reveal the answer to Giraud. But apparently Kyle couldn't resist.

"I made the same mistake as you, at first. I thought fear was the key, but it's only the catalyst," Kyle said. "People are most vulnerable when they wish they'd made a different choice in life.

It's still fear, in a way—fear they've made a mistake they can never undo, something that will haunt them forever. It was there the whole time. The key is regret."

Bones pictured the messy scrawl in the journal: *Reget key.* Kyle had been right: The man hadn't made up a word. They'd simply missed a letter, the lowercase *r* bunched up into the *g*.

Regret key.

Regret is the key.

Bones closed his eyes. No wonder his mother was so affected. She was the strongest woman he knew, but she carried guilt like poison in her belly.

"I let him hurt you for so long . . . How could I not see? How?"

He thought he'd been protecting her, but his secret had torn a rift in her heart.

"I'm not a good mother. I failed you."

His throat tightened, but he pushed the emotion away. He had to get out of this room and find her.

Beside him, Marcus hung his head. Clearly, his mind followed a similar trail as he considered why his father had succumbed. *What did Coach regret?* Bones wondered. He had an amazing family. He'd been a major-league All-Star—the best life Bones could imagine. But what brought a man like that to small-town Nova Scotia? Bones recalled his haunted look at their last game. *"Don't take reckless risks. That's how people get hurt."* Maybe Coach carried the ghosts of a tragedy, some moment he wished he could undo.

Bones wondered what he might regret someday. The list was adding up.

Albert must have had a similar thought. "Kids have regrets too," he said. "I've done a few things I wish I could take back."

"It's not the same. Someday you'll understand." There was a melancholy in Ray Giraud's voice. The man's eyes went far away. "Whoever said that time heals all wounds was a fool. Some things you never forget. Twenty-five years from now, you'll still hear the umpire calling, '*Strike three*,' even though the pitch was clearly outside. You'll see the disappointment in your coach's eyes, hear the mocking voices of your teammates. '*What were you waiting for, Gerbil? You always just stand there.*'

"You have no idea about the things you'll carry." He looked up, face hardening. "But now they see. They don't dare mock me anymore."

Albert scratched his head. "Wait. *This* is your deal? Your teammates ragged on you for striking out *twenty-five years ago*, and you're still so mad about it that you decided to brainwash the town?"

"They always treated me like I was nothing. And it wasn't just any game!" Giraud thundered. "It was the Jamboree Game. The seventy-fifth anniversary. Langille hadn't lost a Jamboree Game in twelve years—my whole life. I had a full count with the bases loaded, and the pitch was outside! It missed by a mile! I should have walked in the tying run, but *no*. Walter Boone had to make a big show of calling me out."

"Walter Boone? The old guy from Town Hall?" Bones said. "You hijacked the Jamboree to get revenge on *Walter Boone*? I bet you used the FluxBoard at the field just because you hate Coach, didn't you?"

Albert whistled. "That is some serious grudge-holding. You really are the king of petty."

Giraud laughed coldly. "Give me some credit. Wrecking the Jamboree and messing with Robeson were just added perks. Do you realize how many *billions* I'll make once I work out the last hiccups in the MindFlux? By harnessing people's fears, I can control anything. What they buy, how they vote, who they hate. I'll be the most influential man alive. Corporations and politicians will spend a fortune for that kind of power."

Marcus recoiled. "You're experimenting on all of Langille just so you can get even richer?"

Giraud rolled his eyes. "Oh, spare me. This was a backward little town stuck in the past, and I gave it a future. Besides, you're one to talk. Your father made millions playing a *game*. And apparently he passed his insufferable do-gooder delusions on to you." The man's jaw tightened. "Enough chatter. Hats off."

The boys looked at each other uneasily.

Giraud grinned. "Yes, I know about your little trick. It's cute." His smile faded. "Toss them over. Now."

"Come get them," Bones said.

Giraud glared. "You know, they're still trying to sort Wade out. They've tried medication, electrotherapy—you name it. Poor guy's cooked." He pulled his phone from his pocket. "Three taps, shortstop, and I can jack up the effect all over town."

Bones considered the distance. How long would it take Giraud to activate his phone? How many Fluxcor goons might be waiting outside? He could get in one good shot, grab the phone—

"Bones." Marcus must have guessed what he was thinking. Shaking his head slightly, he took off his hat and tossed it at Giraud's feet. Kyle and Albert followed.

With a sigh, Bones threw his too. "It's me you want. Let my friends go."

To his surprise, his friends groaned.

"Really, Bones? That's not happening," Marcus said.

Giraud grinned again. "Your hero complex is cute. But I can't do that." He waved toward the others. "The Specks kid is too smart for his own good. Junior Robeson needs to be taken down a peg. And the other one? Frankly, he just gets on my nerves."

Despite the situation, Bones smiled at Albert. "Yeah, he does that."

"I'll take that as a compliment," Albert replied.

"Now, put these on." Giraud pulled four black wristbands from his pocket and tossed them to the boys. "They'll monitor your vitals, make sure your hearts keep ticking. We don't want you dying of fright. That won't help the research."

Albert gulped as he fastened his wristband. "What are you going to do to us?"

Giraud picked up their hats and backed toward the door. "You're the next test subjects for the MindFlux 2.0. You'll be the first kids to try it. I can't promise you'll make it through with your minds intact, but who knows. Maybe someday you'll get to regret being foolish enough to cross me. Oh, and friendly word of advice? You might want to sit down. The first bit is rough. Then it gets worse."

He gave a sarcastic wave just before he closed the door.

Before the boys had time to brace themselves, the walls and ceiling turned blue, glowing brighter and brighter until Bones had to shut his eyes. Then everything went dark.

29.
NATURE IS TRYING TO KILL US

The darkness was so complete it erased the bounds of space and time. Bones had the dizzying sense that he couldn't tell up from down, or whether he'd been there—wherever *there* was—for seconds or hours. Someone's hand landed on his shoulder, and he braced to fight until he realized it was Marcus. They both stumbled as Albert crashed into them.

"Sorry," Albert said, righting himself. Bones could hear his heavy, nervous breathing in the dark.

"Where's Kyle?" Bones said.

"Right here. Nobody panic." Kyle sounded less fazed than the others. "We have to remember: Whatever comes next isn't real."

"What's coming next?" Albert asked in alarm. "Where are we?"

"I only have a theory—"

"I don't want another theory! I want to get out of here!"

Bones winced as a foot landed on his. "Come on, Al. Pull it together."

Something growled, low and deep.

The eyes appeared first, eerie spheres floating in the murk. Then slowly, as Bones's eyes adjusted, a pack of wild dogs emerged from the darkness. They were pale gray, with ribs poking against their gaunt flesh. They bared their teeth.

"Oh man," Albert whimpered. "I don't like dogs. Especially dogs that want to eat me."

The creatures advanced, snarling.

"Stay calm," Bones urged. "Dogs can sense fear. So be cool."

"Easy for you to say," Albert squeaked. His breathing grew ragged.

A world began to take shape around them. Moonlight overhead cast the pale dogs in a ghostly glow. Behind the boys, a meadow sloped toward a forest.

"This feels familiar." Albert's voice shook. "Like I've been here before."

"I think this is a super-enhanced version of our nightmares," Kyle said. "Giraud's room is projecting our fears."

Albert backed up. "I don't like that theory. I want to go home."

The dogs saw his movement. They snarled.

"Albert, *don't*," Bones cautioned. "Whatever you do, don't—"

"Run!" Albert shouted.

He took off for the forest. The others had no choice but to follow as the dogs sprang into action. Sweat poured from Albert's face, and his breath rasped as he ran. Bones followed into the woods and caught up to him as they darted between trees. The dogs barked madly on their tail.

"Albert, try to think," Bones huffed. "Remember, this is—"

A low-hanging branch clobbered him in the face. Bones's head exploded in pain, and his legs shot out from under him. He landed on his back, vision blurred with stars. As his eyes cleared, he saw a dog charging toward him. He barely had time to raise his hands before the animal pounced. He managed to get a hand under its jaw and hold it at bay. Saliva dripped on his face as the dog's teeth snapped, inches from his nose. He pushed and pushed, but the animal had momentum on its side, and he couldn't hold out much longer. The teeth closed in.

Then something crashed out of the woods and the animal went flying with a yelp, skidding across the forest floor. Albert stood over Bones, chest heaving. He clung to a fractured tree branch like a baseball bat.

Bones scrambled to his feet. "Thanks. You saved me."

Albert nodded rigidly. Other dogs crept from the forest, circling them.

"This is your dream, Al," Bones said. "Think happy thoughts. Unicorns or something."

The dogs shuddered. Their shoulders broadened and their legs stretched, until they were the size of small horses. Sharp tusks sprouted from their foreheads.

"That's *not* what I meant," Bones said.

"It's a start, at least." Kyle's voice rang from above. Bones spotted him in a tree, ten feet off the ground.

"How did you get up there?" he called.

"I climbed," Kyle replied, as if it were the most obvious thing in the world. "It seems the rules are fuzzy here, like in a dream. We have some element of control over our environment. If you can manipulate the dogs, Albert, you can do other things too. Concentrate."

Albert shook his head wildly, too locked on high alert to speak. Bones stepped forward. If Albert couldn't do it, maybe he could.

"Come on!" he yelled at the horned dogs. "I'm not scared."

The dogs barked. Bones hollered and rushed at them.

Before they could collide, a brick wall sprang up in front of him. Bones slid to a stop just before he ran into it face-first. He was safe. The dogs were gone.

"Ha!" he shouted. He turned to give Albert a high five, but he met another wall. He was closed in on three sides. The walls were too high to see if Kyle was still in a tree, or if the forest still existed. He was alone.

"Hello?" he called. "Guys?"

Nothing. He only had one option, so he followed the wall to the open side. After a few paces, he reached a T-junction. He was in a maze, he realized.

"Guys?" he hollered again. Still nothing. He turned right and kept walking.

He rubbed the goose bumps on his arms. A thick mist gathered in the cooling air, making it harder to sort out where he was going. Sinewy vines snaked along the walls, sprouting from cracks in the mortar. The plants were a sickly gray, their crumbling leaves spotted with pockmarks. They appeared to be dying even as they sprouted, but they grew so fast they soon obscured the brick completely.

The vines spread with a rustling swish. As his ears attuned to the noise, Bones heard whispers.

"You're all alone."

"No one is coming."

"You belong to us now."

He shivered. The air grew colder. The mist was sharp against his skin, tiny pricks of ice. Frost curled the edges of the decaying leaves along the walls.

"Bones!"

He turned. Kyle emerged from the mist, walking with the fingertips of his right hand trailing against the wall. Albert was two steps behind, hugging himself against the cold.

"I figured I'd find you eventually," Kyle said. "Basic maze theory seems to apply here. Keep right and eventually you'll find your way. Have you seen Marcus?"

Marcus. This had to be his fear: total separation, cut off from everyone.

"No," Bones said. "But we need to find him. He's probably scared."

"No wonder," Albert said. "This is creepy."

They followed Kyle, calling Marcus's name. In response, the air grew colder. Wind howled along the maze's passages. Bones's teeth chattered. The vines' whispering grew louder. Their tendrils stretched across the ground.

"Help!" Albert yelped as a vine snagged his ankle. He bent to pull at it and another caught his wrist. The vines swarmed him, dragging him to the ground. As Kyle turned to help, the plants wound around his legs as well.

Bones did an antsy dance, high-stepping to avoid the tendrils clawing at his feet. His friends struggled and cried out as the vines wound tighter around their limbs and stretched toward their faces. His mind raced for a way out.

If we can control this, I could use a machete.

As he thought about it hard enough, a blade materialized in his hand. He slashed at the vines grasping his sneakers. They shrieked and shrank from the machete. He set out to free the others.

"Careful," Albert urged as Bones hacked branches away from his limbs. "Where did you get that?"

"I just imagined it. Kyle's right. We can control some things if we really concentrate."

Bones cut Kyle free and helped brush the leaves from his arms. The vines writhed angrily on the ground. The temperature kept dropping. Kyle's lips were turning blue.

"We need to find Marcus," Bones said. "I'm not sure we can stop this without him."

They pressed onward. Bones slashed at vines as they went, grateful for some small motion to stir his blood. He was losing feeling in his toes—and hope in Kyle's maze theory—when they finally stumbled into the heart of the maze. A human shape carved from a hedge stood in the center of the square, crouched with one hand reaching out.

"Marcus?" Albert called.

Even as he spoke, the horrible truth dawned on them. That was no sculpture. It was Marcus, being swallowed alive.

They ran to him and tore at the vines. Bones dropped his machete. He couldn't tell where the plant ended and Marcus began, so he didn't dare start swinging. His fingers were so numbed with cold he could barely grip the vines. Even as he managed to pull a strand free, two more took its place, tougher and thornier. The boys worked with desperate futility, wincing as thorns drew blood from their aching, frozen fingers. They tugged and yanked and shivered, but it was useless.

"Think warm thoughts!" Bones shouted over the howling wind. "Come on, Marcus. You're not alone. We're right here. We won't leave you. Think about summer!"

Albert joined in. "Pretend we're at your pool! We're all there. Your brothers and sisters, the whole team. Everybody. It's hot out. You can do it."

The wind subsided. The vines went slack. Bones gave a shout of hope and dove in with new energy, ignoring the thorns shredding his hands as he tore the plants away. Finally, Marcus tumbled out and landed on Bones, who staggered and fell backward into Albert. They collapsed in a heap. Once they were sure Marcus was alive and breathing, they hung on to him and slapped his back, giddy with relief.

"Whew." Albert wiped his forehead. "Glad that's over."

The vines shriveled and disappeared. The walls of the maze faded. The temperature reached a comfortable level—and kept rising.

In a minute, Albert was full-on sweating. "Uh, Marcus? You can stop thinking hot thoughts now."

"It's not me." Marcus looked up. A few feet away, Kyle paced and tapped his thigh.

"I'm sorry," he mumbled. "I tried really hard."

The air grew thick and muggy, almost suffocating. Bones knew what was happening.

"Kyle," he said, as calmly as he could. "You know it's not real. You were the first to know."

"I know. But I considered the dogs, and the vines, and how nature is trying to kill us, and it got me thinking—" Kyle tugged at his hair. "I'm trying to stop it. I really am. I'm sorry."

A sound like a dive-bombing jet droned past their heads. The boys ducked, startled. The airborne attacker settled on Marcus's head: it was an extra-large mosquito. Marcus swatted it away. A swarm of bugs surged through the air, roaring like a squadron.

Albert covered his ears. "Ow. Why is it so loud?" He lowered one hand and scratched his neck. "And I'm so itchy. This heat and humidity, man." He wriggled frantically, seeking some relief. "I feel like my body is on fire. Everything is—"

"Too much," Bones finished. He squinted against the unbearable sun. They were in Kyle's world now, a crush of sensory overload.

The boys stood on the edge of a thick swamp. Insects buzzed, frogs croaked, and birds cawed, every sound amplified and distorted as if screamed through a megaphone. The stagnant swamp belched noxious gases into the air. The heat was all-consuming, wilting their energy. Every sound, sight, and smell grated against their senses. Even the atmosphere felt like an attack, clawing at their skin. Bones desperately wanted to peel off his clothes and submerge himself, but he could tell the cloudy green waters would provide no relief.

"I can't take this," Albert panted. "Think about ice cream, Kyle, before you boil us alive."

"Don't give him ideas," Marcus objected.

Too late.

Beady antennae poked from the muck. The slime roiled as great green creatures rose from the swamp, water dripping from their exoskeletons. They crawled forward on thin legs, with tails fanning behind them as they reached for the boys with bulky, grasping claws.

"Lobsters," Albert gasped. "Run."

None of them had the energy to run. Bones managed only four steps before his lungs constricted and he doubled over, desperate for fresh air. In moments, the swamp lobsters captured the boys and jammed them inside a giant lobster trap. Tangled in the trap's mesh, Bones wound up pressed shoulder to shoulder with Kyle. He could feel the in-out, in-out of Kyle's shallow, erratic breaths.

"Easy," he said gently. "It's all right, Kyle. It's not real. You can pull through this."

Kyle pinched his eyes shut. "I'm sorry. I know I should know better, but I can't stop it."

The lobsters hoisted the trap until it hung suspended over an enormous steaming cauldron. The creatures formed a circle, clacking their claws. They didn't speak, but somehow, Bones understood what they were thinking: *For their pestilence and destruction, the humans must be exterminated.*

The trap lowered toward the boiling swamp water.

"Come on, Kyle!" Marcus pleaded. "Think of, uh, anything but this."

"Not seafood!" Albert shouted. "Think rainbows! Happy science thoughts!"

They sank lower. Foul steam rose from the pot, mingling with the sweat pouring from their faces.

"What happens if we die in here?" Albert hollered. "What if we have a heart attack and die in real life? What if our brains turn to mush and we're trapped in the sunken place forever?"

"Stop shouting, Al," Bones cautioned. "It's not helping."

"Nothing is helping! Evil swamp lobsters are about to boil us alive!"

They hovered inches above the water. Heat seared against Bones's face. He forced himself to stay calm and steady, the way he talked to Raury after a nightmare. He wriggled an arm free enough to find Kyle's hand and squeeze it.

"Everybody think about the same thing," he said. "We're at the Common. We're on the field. Think about baseball. Picture the field."

Albert scrunched his eyes shut. "Baseball. Baseball."

"Baseball," Kyle whispered. Marcus joined the chant.

The rope snapped. They were falling—

Bones's cheek tickled. He lay facedown in a patch of grass. As he rolled over, he recognized the familiar outfield wall at Langille Common. The others sat around him.

"It worked!" Marcus said. "We made it. We—" He did a double take. "Albert! Why are you dressed like that?"

Bones, Marcus, and Kyle all wore their Falcons uniforms. But Albert was sporting a black tuxedo.

He tugged at his bow tie. "I was concentrating. After my dream at Marcus's house . . . I didn't want to end up naked again."

"So you pictured yourself in a *tuxedo*?" Kyle fell back in the grass, giggling. The effect was contagious. Even Albert chuckled as the others rolled in hysterics.

Marcus let out a contented sigh and stretched in the grass, staring at the sky. The others settled around him. They lay spread like points in a compass, heads meeting in the middle.

Albert patted his belly. "Know what I could go for right now? A donair."

"I'm starving," Bones agreed. "How about a Woody's burger?"

"Mmm. Woody's donair burger."

The heavenly smell of grilled meat wafted in the air, making their stomachs gurgle.

"There you go," Marcus said. "This is our dream now. What else makes you happy?"

"A root beer float to wash down my burger," Albert said.

"Amen." Bones raised a fist and they bumped knuckles.

"A meteor shower," Kyle said. As he spoke, the sky darkened to a soft purple and points of light streaked in golden trails through the atmosphere.

"Whoa," Albert said. "Cool."

"It's beautiful," Marcus said. "We really did it, guys. Together."

Bones felt Marcus give him a pat on the arm. He did the same to Kyle on his left.

"You were great in there," he said. "And you," he told Albert, "you saved me from that dog. Way to be brave."

"Huh. I guess I was. I didn't really think about it in the moment."

Bones grinned. "See? Thinking is overrated."

Albert went *heh*. They lay still, watching meteors streak across the sky.

"Thank goodness you held out, Bones," Kyle said. "If there's anything out there awful enough to scare you, I'm glad we didn't have to face it."

Silence. Gradually they all had the same disquieting thought.

Of course, it was Albert who said it out loud. "Guys? If we made it, why are we still here?"

"Aha. The annoying one is the practical one."

They all knew that voice.

Slowly, they sat up. Ray Giraud leaned against the outfield fence.

"I'll admit, I'm impressed. You did well. Especially you, little Q. While Donny Downer's heart rate spiked"—he waved toward Albert—"yours only picked up like you were out for a light run."

Giraud strode across the field toward the boys. Bones rose and clenched his fists.

"That's not even the best part," the man continued. "Your blood work, hoo boy. Dopamine and serotonin off the charts." He turned to Kyle. "You know what I'm saying, Science Guy?"

Kyle blinked. "Um . . . those are things your body makes when it's feeling good."

"Something like that. You know, you're not so bad. I might find a use for you." Giraud turned to Bones. "But you, shortstop, you *love* danger. No wonder you get in so many fights. When other people are scared, you feel a rush."

Bones gritted his teeth and looked away. He never talked about this part, because how could he explain it? Sometimes, when his father was on edge, Bones used to push him on purpose. He did it to get it over with, he told himself. He'd rather face the man head-on than tiptoe around waiting for him to blow. But deep down, he knew that wasn't the only reason. He pushed his father and he pushed himself—curious to see how much he could endure. He took pride in the fact that his father couldn't make him plead or cry. He was unbreakable.

He felt the same rush diving in the river, scaling the Flux-Board, fighting three bigger kids on the soccer field. *Think I'm too small, I can't handle it? Try me. I dare you.*

He knew it was messed-up.

Marcus stepped in front of him. "Leave Bones alone. We tested your machine for you. Now let us out of here."

Giraud smiled. "Oh, but we're just getting to the good part. When we were testing, we could rarely go past fifth-level intensity. Wade blew a brain gasket at six." He jabbed a thumb toward Kyle. "But Captain Chemistry here set a new record. You didn't even wobble until level seven. Congratulations."

Kyle blinked. "I made it further than anyone?"

"Of course you did, Kyle," Bones said. "We told you, you're an action hero."

"Don't get too cocky. Your record may not last long." Giraud flashed his sharkish grin at Bones. "I might skip eight with you and go straight to level nine."

Heat surged through Bones's chest. "You think you can just mess with whoever you want. Before today is over, I swear—"

"There it is! Go with that anger, shortstop. Cut loose. Let the monster out to play."

Then Giraud vanished.

And beyond the outfield, the world crumbled away, swallowed in the wake of an enormous shadow.

30.
MONSTER

Bones stood his ground as the shadow took shape. It gathered strength, sweeping into an enormous tornado. A familiar resolve settled in his limbs. *Finally.* Whatever this thing was, he'd confront it head-on.

His friends pleaded with him to run, but he wouldn't. Suddenly, before he could object, he was airborne and moving as Marcus scooped him over his shoulder and ran. Bones wriggled and hollered, but it didn't do any good. Draped backward over Marcus's shoulder, he watched the tornado swallow the outfield fence. Marcus dashed into the dugout, which opened into an underground bunker. As soon as they were inside, Kyle and Albert pulled the heavy doors shut, plunging them into darkness. The tornado roared overhead, shaking the walls, consuming everything in its path. But the bunker held.

After a terrible cacophony, silence fell. A chain of dim light bulbs switched on one by one, illuminating a long concrete hallway stretching farther than the boys could see.

Bones stood apart from the others, facing the doors.

"You should have let me fight it," he said bitterly. "I don't run away."

Albert shook his head. "Come on. Even you can't fight a tornado."

Bones glowered at him.

"Let's take a minute to think," Marcus said. "Kyle, what do you—"

"If this is my dream, we're doing it my way," Bones interrupted. "I'm not scared. I don't run."

"Bones, get *real*," Albert said, exasperated. "You run all the time."

"*What?*"

"You run *at* danger. Even when you don't have to." Albert stood straighter. "Sorry, but Giraud's right. If we had two choices to cross a bottomless pit, you'd skip the bridge and take the tightrope."

Kyle stepped in before Bones could lose it. "Albert has a point. Giraud wants you to charge in blind. He expects it."

Bones lowered his eyes. "So what am I supposed to do?"

Marcus set a hand on his shoulder. "*You* don't have to do anything. We go as a team. We've got your back."

Bones started down the tunnel, a step ahead of the others. The path angled steadily downward. Water dripped from cracks in the ceiling, each *plink* reverberating on the cement floor. As Bones walked, graffiti scrawled itself along the walls.

dangerous
reckless
hoodlum
thug

He heard Albert whisper, but he didn't look back. He kept his eyes fixed ahead. Still, he saw the words. They appeared faster, thicker, darker, piling on one another.

Are you stupid, kid? *Freak loser troublemaker ungrateful no respect badinfluence* changethatattitudemister iwillBEATSOMESENSEintoyou little punk *YOUR FAULT ALWAYSYOURFAULT* youmakemedothis youdoittoYOURSELF

The lights flickered. Bones picked up speed. He hated that the others were seeing this. He hated that he'd brought them to this place.

The tunnel ended at a door. On the other side, he suspected, he would find his father.

Good. Time to finish this, here and now.

"Bones," Marcus called. "Wait."

He threw open the door. A glint of light struck him from across the room, and he shielded his eyes. When he uncovered them, he stood in the center of a circular chamber lined entirely with mirrors. The others stood behind him, staggering as they gathered their bearings. The door they'd entered through had disappeared. No matter where they turned, they met a legion of their own reflections, stretching into infinity.

"Where are you?" Bones shouted. "No more hiding."

There: Across the room, a shadow lurked in the mirror. Bones didn't even have to think before he had a baseball in hand and was in mid-windup, unleashing a fastball. The mirror shattered. Thick, dark smoke poured from the gap, clouding the room. The others coughed. A buzzing grew louder and louder until a swarm of gray hornets erupted from the hole. The boys hollered as the hornets attacked. Albert swatted frantically while Kyle cried out in pain and pulled his shirt collar over his face. Bones batted an insect from his neck and kept searching the mirrors through the smoke. The hornets dove over and over, each sting a hot coal on his skin, but he wouldn't be distracted. Pain was nothing new. Each sting only made him angrier.

"Come on!" he screamed. "I'm not afraid. Are you? Come on!"

There: to his left. Again, the ball was instantly in his hand, and again, he threw. The mirror exploded. A torrent of water surged through the broken pane. The boys struggled to hold their footing as water thundered against them, quickly rising to their knees. The sound was deafening, a waterfall inside a room. Kyle pressed flat against a mirror, eyes wide with panic. The water blackened as it mixed with smoke and soot, a grimy flood climbing above their waists. They were all shouting, but Bones couldn't hear over the rushing water. He searched the room wildly as he waded against the current. He had to stop this. He had to find the shadow—

It was behind him. He didn't fall for the trick this time. He saw it directly ahead, but he spun around to the far wall instead, letting the current press him against the glass. This pane was no longer a mirror but a window. He saw his family: his mom with her arms around his brothers, all three of them cowering.

The shadow had them. It was in the room.

He had a baseball bat in his hands. He raised it above his head and tried to swing, but it caught. Bones tugged. The bat wouldn't give.

He turned. Marcus held the barrel.

"Stop!" Marcus hollered over the roaring water. It was midway up Bones's chest now, climbing toward his throat. "You can't."

"Let go!" Bones screamed. "I have to save them! I have to stop him!"

Marcus tightened his grip on the bat. "You can't see it, can you?"

An unfamiliar feeling stirred in Bones's belly. "See what?"

He had a terrible feeling he didn't want to know the answer.

Marcus's eyes were heavy. "It's not your dad you're chasing. It's *you*."

The

        entire

               universe

                        stopped.

Bones stood in his own living room. A tornado had blown through, scattering sofa cushions, flipping the coffee table, tearing curtains from the wall. The TV lay smashed on the floor. An unsettling stench fouled the air, something sulfurous and unmistakably sinister.

Bones's mother braced in the doorway, stretching across the frame to shield Raury and Dillon, who huddled behind her. Her face was older, creased with despair. When she spoke, her voice shook.

"I put up with an awful lot, Quentin. I tried. But this is the last straw." Her lip trembled. "Raury? Your own brother? How could you?"

Raury peeked from behind their mother. He seemed barely there, like a ghost.

A ghost with a black eye.

No, Bones wanted to scream. *Not Raury. I would never.* But he stood frozen.

He had done this. All this chaos, this destruction. He caused trouble. He hurt people. Even the people he loved. He couldn't help himself. This was who he was.

Thick crimson ink oozed through the walls of his living room.

THUG
DANGEROUS *HOODLUM*
MONSTER

His mother's voice grew forceful. "I won't put your brothers in danger again. You have to leave! And you can't come back."

A roar filled the room. Bones realized it had begun in his own throat. But it was too big for him. It rattled the walls and shook the ground, the howl of an enormous beast unearthing all the rage and anguish in the world. He sensed it behind him, smelled its horrible stench, heard its ragged breaths wheezing in mirrored rhythm with his own.

The monster.

"Hooooly," Albert breathed.

Bones jumped. He'd forgotten the others were there. His stomach burned with shame that they were seeing what he'd done. Who he was.

Before Bones could turn to confront the creature, Marcus clamped a hand on his shoulder.

"Don't even look! It's not real."

Marcus didn't understand. He had to slay the beast. It was the only way.

"Let me go!" he shouted. He shoved at Marcus, but Marcus didn't budge.

"Leave me alone! I need to kill it!" He cocked his fist, but Kyle wrapped both arms around him.

"It's an illusion," Kyle said in his ear. "It's not real. It's not what I see."

Bones struggled.

"It's not who you are," Kyle said. "You're my best friend."

"You'd never hurt your brothers," Marcus said. "I know how much you love them. This is a lie, Bones. It's not real."

"I'm jealous of how brave you are," Albert admitted. "You always try to do the right thing, even when it's scary. You're kind of a hero."

"You *are* a hero," Kyle said. "You helped me be so much braver than I was on my own. You're so kind, and caring, and a great brother, and an excellent friend."

Bones shook his head. They didn't know all the things he'd done, all the ugliness bottled up inside, waiting to explode. His father hated him, and his mother could barely look at him, because they knew—

"It's not true." Marcus stared into his eyes with fierce determination. "You. Are Not. A. Monster."

Bones felt like his ribs were cracking, his entire chest heaving open, his insides being torn from his body. He screamed—

—And when he opened his eyes, he lay on his back in a blank room, staring at a white ceiling. Three faces hovered above him.

"Bones!" Marcus laughed in relief. "You did it! You beat it. We're out."

Bones shook his head. His voice trembled. "It wasn't me, it was . . ."

"It was us." Kyle's eyes clouded with tears. "Fear can't win if you don't face it alone."

One of his tears slipped free and splashed onto Bones's face. And Bones came undone.

His friends lifted him from the floor and swept him into a hug.

"No!" Giraud barked, bursting into the room. "How? That wasn't supposed to happen. That *can't* happen. The rest of you messed up the program somehow. I'll send Quentin back alone—"

He was so fixated on Bones that he didn't see Albert step up and swing with all his might.

Giraud fell with a thump and lay still. Albert shook out his fist. The others stared at him. Bones wiped his eyes on the front of his shirt and grinned.

"That was hard-core, Al. High-five."

Albert winced as their hands connected. "Ow! I think I broke something."

Bones took one last look around the blank room. Kyle's hand still rested on his back, his fingers spread along the ridge of Bones's scar. The feeling was a comfort, reminding Bones of Kyle's kind words in his dream. His friends had told him the truth, and the lie lost its grip. Now this was only an empty room, the way a spooky cellar was only a cellar as soon as the lights come on. Its monsters weren't real. He would walk out and leave them behind.

He stepped past Giraud's crumpled form. "Let's go before he wakes up. We've got to shut this place down."

Marcus leaned down and grabbed Giraud's phone, headset, and key card. Giraud stirred just in time to see Bones shoot him a look of supreme satisfaction as he locked the door and pulled it shut.

31.
REBEL ACTION HERO

With Giraud contained, the boys raced into the real control room down the hall. Albert watched the muted security monitors as Giraud yelled at the camera, shaking his fist and stomping like an angry toddler.

"It would be wrong to crank up his own room and scare him senseless, right?" Albert said.

"Yes," Kyle said. "It would."

"What if we just turned it on a little? You know, for science. See if *he* pees his pants."

"That's not an honorable experiment." Kyle paused. "Wait, when we . . . did you . . . ?"

Albert reddened. "No! I was just, you know, wondering if it's possible. I absolutely did *not* pee my pants in there. Not at all. Nope."

Kyle turned to the MindFlux system's main console. He smiled at his good fortune. In his rush to confront the boys, Giraud hadn't locked the system. Kyle had access to the entire network.

"Do you know what you're doing?" Bones asked.

"Maybe. We'll see." Kyle dug his modified FluxBox from his backpack and connected it. He uttered a silent plea before he searched the network map. There it was near the center, his lone green beacon shining in a sea of blue.

It couldn't be as simple as that, could it?

"Uh, Kyle?" Albert sat up in alarm. "Whatever you're doing, hurry. A *crap-ton* of cop cars just came through the main gate."

"Almost there," Kyle said. The others peered over his shoulder as he dragged his modified FluxBox into the master control position. A message popped up on the screen.

> Override Source Input? Yes / No

"Whoa," Albert said. "This is like the moment in a movie when the hero stops a nuclear war." He glanced at the security cameras again. "But the bad guys are closing in, so hurry up!"

Kyle clicked *Yes*. The display froze. A multicolored wheel spun on the screen.

"Come on!" the boys all shouted.

The wheel vanished.

> Override complete.

The blue lights switched to a tide of green.

Kyle leaped up and pumped his fist. "Yes! Congratulations, Langille. You've just been UnFluxed."

Bones laughed. "You even made up a catchphrase! You're definitely a rebel action hero!"

They slapped Kyle on the back and exchanged high fives.

Albert yelped in pain. "I have to stop doing that."

The control room door burst open, and a swarm of police officers entered, led by Chief Schofield.

"Back away from that computer, right now," the chief ordered. "You boys are in a heap of trouble."

The boys slowly stepped away from the console with their hands in the air.

"Wait!"

Two women rushed through the door behind the officers.

"Mom?" Kyle and Bones said at the same time.

Mrs. Specks and Ms. Malone stared down the chief. Kyle felt a swirl of emotions. He was thrilled to see his mom, but how furious would she be for all he'd done?

The chief frowned. "You're off duty, Constable Specks. You're trespassing, Ms. Malone. And you both have a conflict of interest here." He glared at the boys. "You need to stand down."

"In a moment," Kyle's mom said. "There's something you need to see first." She turned to the other officers. "You all need to see it." She handed Kyle a flash drive. "Can you—?"

"Of course." He booted it up.

"Hold on now," Chief Schofield said. "This isn't—"

As he was talking, Kyle opened the flash drive and launched a video: Chief Schofield, Giraud, and the boys in the holding cell.

"This video shows Raymond Giraud, a civilian, interrupting an officer during an interrogation and manipulating the outcome." His mom's jaw tightened. "Needless to say, it's a massive breach of procedure. That *is* you in the video, isn't it, Chief?"

Murmurs spread among the other officers. Chief Schofield reddened.

"I let the boys off with a warning! Clearly that was a mistake, given the stunts they pulled today. I won't make the same mistake twice."

Kyle's mom folded her arms. "There's something else you should know. That footage is from our camera, but I imagine the same scene is already on file in this very room." She turned to Kyle. "You were right. I read your note and went back to the station. Our FluxBoxes had hidden cameras in them."

"So do the units at the *Record*, and at Town Hall, and probably a few other places," Ms. Malone added. "Ray Giraud wasn't just manipulating us. He's been spying on us."

Kyle smiled in satisfaction. The idea had occurred to him that morning. He remembered Bones wondering how Giraud knew so much about everyone. Sure enough, his hunch was right. Kyle returned to the computer, where he found and called up video feeds from FluxBoxes all over town.

"Town leaders let this happen, because they had side deals with Fluxcor." Bones's mom dropped a folder on the desk in front of the control panel. "There's some fascinating information in this text thread between Mayor MacKenzie and Chief Schofield."

The chief turned almost purple. "How did you get that? And how dare you share our private . . ." He trailed off as he realized all his officers were staring at him.

"Perhaps," he said timidly, "I ought to excuse myself from this case."

Kyle's mom set her hands on her hips. "That's wise. It seems like you may have a conflict of interest here." She turned to another officer. "That leaves you in charge, Sergeant. I have to excuse myself as well, but I strongly recommend you find Ray Giraud and bring him in for questioning."

Bones grinned. "You don't have to look far. He's right there." He pointed at the security monitor, where Giraud was pacing in Room 2B.

"And we shut down his evil experiment," Marcus added.

Albert put a hand on Kyle's shoulder. "Thanks to Kyle Specks, *Rebel Action Hero*, the town of Langille is officially UnFluxed."

Kyle's mother looked at him. "You did it?"

He nodded. What was her expression? Pride, maybe. But there was more.

Wonder. That was it.

"I'm not sure you'll ever stop surprising me," she said. "But I hope I'll learn to stop underestimating you."

He smiled. Then he gave her a very public hug.

32.
BRING THE HEAT

The Sunday morning chatter at the Langille Tim Hortons reached its liveliest in weeks. Townsfolk who'd fallen into prickly silence with one another—for reasons none of them could quite recall—clustered in the crowded coffee shop, where the conversation invariably turned to how well they'd slept the night before.

"Haven't had a night so refreshing in years. Almost felt like waking out of hibernation, didn't it?"

"Must have been the storm on Saturday, finally broke the humidity."

"What was all this business about Ray Giraud being arrested?"

"He always was an odd duck, that Ray. Took things awful personal, even as a kid."

"Yep, a lot of strange business round here lately. Whatever possessed those children to strip down and run amok in the parade? Who's ever seen the likes?"

One thing was certain: The Centennial Jamboree would live on in Langille folklore forever.

Laughter spilled from the coffee shop and into the street, catching in the smiles of passersby as they strolled under a bright blue sky. On Maple Street, Kyle waved over the fence to Alice Vanderpol as she worked in her back garden. She smiled and waved back.

"Pancakes are ready!" Kyle's dad called out.

Kyle stepped inside and sat down at the table. "How's Dr. Elliott?" he asked as he dug into a stack of pancakes.

"The doctors think he'll make a full recovery, now that they know how to treat him with Serenity." Kyle's dad beamed. "I'm still so impressed you figured all that out yourself. Maybe you should go into neuroscience."

"Maybe," Kyle said. "Hey, could Bones spend the night tonight? And maybe we could go to the beach this afternoon."

"We'll see if the Malones feel up to that, honey," his mom said. "It's been quite a week for everyone. But you can certainly have Bones over soon."

"So you're not mad?" Kyle said. "And you don't think Bones and I should stop being friends?"

His mom set down her fork. "Kyle, I know I reacted strongly the other night, but that's because I was worried about you." She glanced at his father. "We've been talking, and maybe we've worried about you too much."

"Not that we can promise we'll stop worrying completely," his father added. "But you keep showing us that you know how to advocate for your own needs, and we'll try to trust you more and be better listeners."

"Thank you," Kyle said. "I'd like to advocate for more pancakes, please."

His parents laughed, and he helped himself to seconds.

Bones dreamed of the most beautiful music. But as he stirred, the melody dissolved and he could only recall the impression of its sweetness. He also had the vaguest memory of standing before a mirror. The face staring back surprised him: proud and strong, ancient and soft and new all at once. It was his face, he understood, yet he felt he was seeing it for the first time.

He woke with Raury burrowed against his side, still asleep. Dillon was wedged against the wall, snoring—they'd both shown up not long after he'd turned out his light.

His mother was sitting on his bed. She smiled at him.

They'd had little time to talk in the aftermath of everything at Fluxcor. Kyle's mom had insisted the boys should go to the hospital after their exposure to Room 2B. Once everyone was cleared by a doctor, the questions began. The boys realized with relief that they weren't going to be arrested, but they had to repeat details over and over as authorities struggled to make sense of the story. When they were finally released, Bones and his mom barely had the energy to retrieve Raury and Dillon from the Robesons' and rustle up some food before they fell into bed, exhausted. As he drifted off, Bones wondered if she was truly recovered.

Here she was, smiling. He wasn't used to her looking in his eyes so intently.

"What?" he said shyly.

"Just thinking about how you're the world's best big brother. And you're turning into an awfully handsome young man."

"That's weird, Mom."

She laughed, a sound like light. Raury twitched in his sleep.

"Moms can be weird and sappy sometimes," she said. "It's in the contract."

She gently brushed a few frizzy curls from his hairline. She was definitely extra sappy that morning. As she bent and kissed him above his eyebrow, he decided he didn't mind at all.

A week later, Bones stepped onto the baseball field, and Coach Robeson tossed him a ball.

"Loosen up, big guy." Coach gave him a warm grin. "You're king of the hill today."

Marcus beamed as he and Bones stretched near the fence. Coach was back to normal.

The bleachers filled while Bones tossed his last warmup pitches to Gavin, who started at catcher as Albert sat on the bench with a bandaged hand.

"I have a deep bone contusion from punching Ray Giraud in the face," Albert had informed his teammates, the umpires, the fans behind home plate, and the lady in the canteen who sold him a bag of sunflower seeds.

The crowd was younger and rowdier than usual: Many of the kids who'd joined the parade uprising showed up to cheer the Falcons. Even Tony Spezio stood near the outfield fence, silent but watching. Bones noticed with a grin that Jayden never took her eyes off Kyle.

Wade Elliott sat beside Kyle's parents in the bleachers. Three days of Serenity exposure had freed him from his fog, and his interview with Bones's mom in the *Record* had set off a flurry of turnover at Fluxcor. Meanwhile, Mayor MacKenzie and Chief Schofield took leaves of absence after the stories exposed their roles in giving Fluxcor free rein in Langille.

As the umpire called, "Play ball!" Bones took the mound brimming with energy—so much that his first pitch sailed inside and plunked the Arrows' leadoff batter in the ribs. The kid doubled over before trotting to first base with a glare. Bones started the next batter with three balls, high and outside. Frustrated, he kicked the mound. He had to find his control.

In the dugout, Albert whispered something to Coach. Coach called time, and Albert trotted to the mound. Marcus jogged in from first base to join them. Bones wrinkled his nose as they approached. Four pitches and he needed a pep talk already—and from Albert, of all people?

"Listen," Albert said. "You're the most hard-core kid in the history of Langille. But you're thinking too much. Thinking is not your strength."

"What Albert's trying to say," Marcus added, "is *relax*. Have fun."

Albert nodded. "Stop thinking. Just bring the heat."

Marcus swatted Bones on the butt with his glove, and they returned to their places. Bones took a breath. In the stands, his mom stood.

"You got this, Bones!" she hollered. "Bring the heat."

He threw two fastballs down the middle of the plate. The batter swung at the third and didn't come close. Strike three. Bones settled in and blistered a string of heaters past the next batter, and the next. As the innings passed, the scoreboard filled with Ks and 0s as Bones mowed through the Arrows' lineup. His teammates gave him all the support he needed when Kyle ripped a two-run double in the fourth inning, earning a piercing whistle from Jayden.

Kyle sat beside him as they returned to the dugout for their final turn at bat.

"You haven't even given up a hit," Kyle said. "You're three outs from a no-hitter."

"Quiet," Albert cautioned. "Don't mention it. It's bad luck."

"Why?"

Albert sighed. "I don't know, Specks. I didn't make it up. It's baseball tradition."

"Well, I'm not superstitious. I'm autistic." Kyle grinned. "You neurotypical people are ridiculous sometimes."

Bones and Marcus cracked up. "Dude, quit rubbing it in," Bones teased. "We're already throwing you a party tonight."

The party was Bones's idea. They'd been hanging out at

Marcus's house two days earlier when Kyle shared the outcome of his sessions with the autism specialist.

"*Congratulations,*" Bones had said. "*Now that you're officially autistic, you should celebrate. With cake.*"

Marcus's eyes lit up. "*Definitely! We can do it here, after Saturday's game.*"

Kyle mulled it over. "*I like that idea. But only if it's vanilla cake. I don't like chocolate.*"

Albert poked Kyle's shoulder. "*You don't like chocolate? That's weird, Kyle.*"

Kyle had just laughed.

Bones took the mound in the final inning knowing he was working on something special. Nothing had ever felt so right. His arm was strong, every pitch leaving his hand with as much fire as when he started. He could have kept throwing all day.

The first batter managed one weak foul before missing Bones's next two pitches by a foot. One out. The second batter chased a fastball and a curve before he gave up and watched a third strike land in Gavin's glove. Two down.

As the next batter strode to the plate, the crowd rose, cheering in anticipation. Raury and Dillon whooped beside the Robesons. Kyle's mom clapped and whistled. Bones's teammates shouted encouragement. His mom paced the fence by the dugout, too antsy to sit still.

"You got this," she mouthed.

His first two pitches missed wide. The third was a strike. The batter connected with the fourth and sent it arcing toward right field, but it hooked and landed in foul territory. Strike two.

Gavin would tell Bones later that he barely saw the final pitch. He only felt the whiff of the bat and the *oomph* of the ball slamming into his glove one last time. Strike three. Bones had a no-hitter. Marcus rushed him and lifted him off the ground. The rest of the team piled on, rubbing his head and slapping him on the back. Kyle gave him a chest bump.

As he pulled himself from the dog pile, laughing, a large hand settled on his shoulder.

"You're the stuff of legend, Bones Malone," Coach said. "And I have a feeling you're just getting started."

Bones smiled. "Thanks, Coach." He leaned in and let Coach Robeson wrap an arm around him.

After the excitement eased and as he was unlacing his cleats in the dugout, a hollowness settled in his chest, pleasant yet bittersweet. At first, he felt something was missing, but then he realized the absence was silence. The needling voice in the back of his mind had disappeared. In its place was something so unfamiliar he couldn't name it, until Marcus flashed him an easy smile and the word surfaced.

Peace. He felt at peace.

The dugout emptied. Coach rubbed his sweaty head affectionately as he passed. A moment later, his mom rounded the corner and found him sitting in his dusty socks.

"Hey, slowpoke. Savoring the moment, huh? You pitched an incredible game." She knocked the dirt from his cleats. "I'm going to run home for the boys' swimsuits before Kyle's party, but Carlos said you could ride with them. Do you need anything else at home?"

Bones shook his head. "I'm good."

She raised an eyebrow. "You're good?"

He grinned, slow and wide. "Yeah. Real good."

ACKNOWLEDGMENTS

This my second published novel, but its original draft was the first novel attempt where I reached the words "The End," and I soon learned that those words are only the beginning. Many people have helped shape this story along the way.

I feel lucky to be making another book with the great crew at Abrams Kids, starting with my fantastic editor, Emily Daluga. My thanks to copyeditor Richard Slovak and proofreaders Michael Clark and Shasta Clinch; managing editor Amy Vreeland and production manager Jenn Jimenez; Mary Marolla, Jenny Choy, and all the folks in publicity and marketing; and everyone who helped bring this book into the world.

Ashanti Fortson captured the spirit of this story on the deliciously spooky cover, and designers Deena Fleming and Chelsea Hunter made this book look great.

Huge thanks once again to the powerhouse team at McIntosh & Otis for their wisdom and support, especially Christa Heschke and Daniele Hunter. Special thanks to Jessica Corra, whose insights on this story were invaluable.

I was fortunate enough to work with two different mentors on this book. My thanks to Darcy Rhyno, the Writers Federation of Nova Scotia, and the Alistair MacLeod Mentorship Program.

It's a blessing to have such a great organization supporting Nova Scotian writers.

My gratitude as well to Rebecca Petruck, whom I first met through the Writing in the Margins mentorship program led by Justina Ireland, and who has helped so much on this and other projects. You're a gift to the middle grade community, Rebecca.

Thanks to Saba Sulaiman, who was incredibly generous with feedback, and to Autumn Reynolds and Trudy Goold for their valuable input.

Early readers Jesse Hayward, Michael Dempsey, and Dale Kehler encouraged me that I might be onto something, and plenty of others have given feedback on drafts along the way, including Cyndy d'Entremont, Janet Sketchley, Jeff Wooten, Rochelle Hassan, Jen Klug, Philip White, and Susan Vizurraga.

I'm grateful to the first-voice readers who offered their insights into Kyle's character. Any shortcomings are my own.

My thanks to the many writer friends who offer ongoing support, celebration, and occasional commiseration through the highs and lows of the publishing world, including Eric Bell, #The21ders, and the indomitable Slacker crew.

To all my extended family who have supported this dream, thank you. Special shout-out to my brother Josh, sister-in-law Heather (the queen of hugs), and my nephew Matteo for hyping my work with your teachers. Love it!

To Shawna and my four amazing kids, I'd never be here without you. I'm so glad we get to go on this adventure together.